A Cat in the Tulips

David Evans was born in Malvern, Worcestershire in 1947. He attended Hanley Castle Grammar School before being accepted as a founder-undergraduate at the new University of Kent at Canterbury in 1965. After graduating in 1968, he worked for the British Council for a year before landing a job on the film production of Joe Orton's *Loot* and then in 1970 joined Barry Krost's artists agency and management company in London which handled several careers including that of Cat Stevens. In 1975 he moved to John Reid's office which looked after Elton John and Queen amongst other artists. In 1976, after opening the Playhouse Theatre in Edinburgh for Reid, he left the music industry and worked in an antiques business.

Since 1979 when he opened a restaurant in Malvern, he has worked with his partner Nigel Quiney designing and publishing greetings cards and has written full-time since 1988. His first novel *Summer Set* was published in 1991. *This Is The Real Life . . . Freddie Mercury* was published in 1992 and he is currently working on a book centred on the life and times of Cat Stevens. His third novel will be published in 1994.

A Cat in the Tulips

David Evans

Millivres Books
Brighton

First published in 1993 by Millivres Books (Publishers)
33 Bristol Gardens, Brighton BN2 5JR, East Sussex, England

A CIP catalogue record for this book
is available from the British Library

ISBN 1 873741 10 3

Typeset by Hailsham Typesetting Services, 4-5 Wentworth House,
George Street, Hailsham, East Sussex BN27 1AD

Printed and bound in Great Britain

Distributed in the United Kingdom and Western Europe by Turnaround
Distribution Co-Op Ltd, 27 Horsell Road, London N5 1XL

Distributed in the United States of America by InBook, 140 Commerce
Street, East Haven, Connecticut 06512USA

This book is dedicated to the memory of

MARION ELISE QUINEY

1908 - 1990

And to the memories of Harry Chambers, Douglas Chalmers,Freddie Mercury, Gordon Heath and our other friends, sadly too numerous.

ONE

It was April, in England; late April.

Norman knocked gently at Ned's bedroom door. Hearing nothing, he entered the room, crossed to the windows and flung back the heavy, Liberty print curtains. This ritual of letting in the light was always a hairy moment in Norman's day. Although he had been the letter-in-of-light for fifteen years, he could never be sure as to the precise photosynthetic effect that early morning light on Ned was going to have and, therefore, of what kind of day he could expect. However, this morning, there was no low moan of complaint from the bed and so Norman luxuriated in the view across the square.

In the gardens, huge billows of pink cherry blossom cascaded over the railings and across the pavement. The sun was out, the sky was clear. What an absolutely lovely morning, he thought.

He caught sight of Ivy Williams, the sub-postmistress, rounding the corner of the square. Ivy trudged, grudgingly, to her daily duties on the GPO barricades as she had done for the last thirty-two years. She *is* a poor thing, Norman thought and indeed, Ivy's life was an un-ending daily routine. She constantly complained and talked relentlessly about her retirement, the only perspective she seemed to have to motivate her. Ivy envied everyone else's life but, sadly, no one envied her's.

However, Norman was more sympathetic to Ivy than most and this morning, as always, he waved gaily from the window. His cheerfulness went unacknowledged. Norman watched as Ivy continued on her way and then withdrew from the window, thinking that days like today should never be started with that particular joylessness of Ivy's and reminding himself of his own good fortune to lead a life which, though not perfect, was inestimably more fun than Ivy Williams'.

At that moment, Ned woke up as though he had sensed Norman's levels of sympathy rising to danger point. Unlike Norman, Ned felt absolutely no sympathy for Ivy and in general regarded sympathy as a perilously negative virtue, so much so that he would avoid Ivy even to the extent of posting letters unstamped rather than face her through the bars and grills which separated her world from his.

"I suppose that was her?" Ned said. "The woman's a disgrace to the race. Has she gone yet?"

"That rhymes, dear," Norman said. "How clever. And so early in the morning. You must be in for a really creative day."

Ned pulled himself up out of the tangled mass of bedclothes, flung another pillow behind his head and slumped back. He blinked and held his hand up to shade his eyes.

"Creativity has nothing to do with moons and Junes, Norman," he said and yawned widely. "It's awfully bright. Have we overslept?"

"Not at all. I think it's spring at last," said Norman and he began to sing in a high, thin tenor . . . "The sun has got its hat on, hip hip hip hooray, the sun has got its hat on and he's coming out to play . . ." Norman stopped singing and bit his lip, remembering how Ned hated noisy mornings.

"Oh, please, Norman! That kind of cheerfulness is enough to send me straight back to sleep. What time is it?"

"Five to," Norman replied and he returned to the window. He tied back the peacock patterned curtains, smoothing out the folds to his symmetrical satisfaction. "Ah, there he is. On time for once."

"Post?"

"Yes," said Norman in that spying voice he always used when looking out at people passing in the street. "And what a big bag he's got today. There must be something for us amongst all that."

"Junk, man. Nothing but rubbish about double glazing

and invitations from lunatics trying to sell you flats in Spain."

"Probably," Norman murmured, "but you never know."

"Always the optimist," said Ned as he banged the top of the TeasMaid. The switch had broken years ago but the machine always seemed to respond to a sharp tap as the immediate gurgling in its pipes proclaimed. "Where's my dressing gown, Norman?"

"I washed it yesterday. Don't you remember? It's not dry yet."

Ned's mouth set in a cross line.

"So," he said, irritated at this interruption of his routine, "I'm to walk naked across the windows, am I? For all the square to see?"

"Well, you will sleep in the buff," Norman retorted. "Ne'er cast a clout 'til May be out," he said with some quiet pleasure. Ned emerged from the bed.

"Norman, you're so quaint I sometimes think you should be in a museum. 'In the buff' indeed. Haven't heard that one for years. And, you silly old fart, as you can see, I'm not!"

Ned was indeed clothed. He was wearing one of his favourite garments, one of a pair of vastly out-sized T-shirts with which the couple had been presented by a young friend during a visit to California. In the privacy of their hotel room, Norman had given his to Ned, remarking that he didn't think it was "quite me". Ned had gleefully appropriated the garment which had emblazoned across the chest the legend HOLLYWOOD WOMEN'S REFORMATORY atop a rather brutish cartoon of a woman warder. Ned found the whole thing wickedly amusing and had threatened more than once to wear it to a bridge game with two of their more shockable friends.

"Must you wear that awful thing," said Norman with a pained, wincing expression. "Someone might see."

"Let them," said Ned defiantly and strode across the room to the window. He rapped on the glass and waved.

"Ned, no!" cried Norman. "How could you?"

"It's only the postman, Norman. He's no more than a

child."

"Children can be very grown up these days," Norman said primly. "Young men aren't necessarily young gentlemen anymore."

"Poppycock," said Ned dismissively, waving again to the young postman, who was by now chuckling on his way, relishing the anticipation of being able to recount yet another story about the dotty Mr Cresswell, however incredible it might have seemed to his workmates that Ned had ever been an inmate in an American women's penal institution.

The TeasMaid emitted a gargled hiss and a cracked bell clinked somewhere down in its electrical depths.

"Tea up, Norman. I'll pour if you bring up the post."

"I'm picking up clothes," said Norman. "Age may have made you a little wiser but it's made you no tidier, Ned."

"Do stop being so quibblesome and fetch the post," retorted Ned. Norman did his best to huff and flounce but he wasn't very convincing. Years of what sociologists now called peer pressure had inured him to a certain role and, in truth, Norman liked it that way. It certainly would never have suited him for that role to change. Norman felt uncomfortable in the face of any sort of change. Ned smiled to himself as he heard Norman stamping down the stairs. He poured out the tea, his in a mug and Norman's in a china cup *with* saucer. Norman was most particular about the way he took his tea. Ned sipped at his mug and moved over to the window, wrestling the challenge of even thinking about cigarettes. "Norman! Have you seen the state of that cherry tree?"

Norman returned with the post.

"Yes. Isn't it too glorious?"

"Damn vulgar suburban things," snorted Ned indignantly. "In our day I can remember being satisfied with good old-fashioned white."

"Well, times have changed, dear, along with the colours of cherry blossom. Just ask Ivy. She'll tell you." Ivy's cheerlessness was too strongly pervasive even for Norman to be able to forget quickly. "People don't go in to her for stamps anymore or any of the other things she used to sell like string and brown paper or even dog licences. It's all giros now and people paying their electricity bills."

"And pensions," added Ned. "Don't forget our pensions. I've worked too damn hard to forget those." Ned was devoted to his retirement pension and, being otherwise comfortably off, squandered it every week on superflous luxuries much to Norman's disapproval. "Anyway, the woman should be pleased to have a job. With her sour old face, nobody else would employ her!"

"Perhaps," Norman demurred, "but, honestly, Ned, she's not that bad. Sometimes." Norman began to warble again as he thumbed through the envelopes which had arrived through the letterbox. "In pink, in pink, my sister's dressed in pink, it is a rather unbecoming shade of pink, I think . . ."

"What on earth's that?"

"Noel Coward," said Norman. He finished sorting the post. He always looked at each envelope for ages, turning it this way and that, holding it up to the light before he finally opened it. It was a habit which Ned found particularly irksome.

"Anything for me?" asked Ned insistently.

"Two browns for us, a brown for me and a white for you," said Norman. They opened their respective letters, except the brown ones common to both. Ned had no interest whatsoever in brown envelopes, stubbornly believing that anything that came in a brown envelope wasn't worth knowing about. He sent them all, unopened, in an even bigger brown envelope to his accountant which usually meant that the long-suffering Mr Thrubb became the recipient of not only Ned's tax demands but also football pool coupons, free offers from the *Readers' Digest,* summonses for jury service and the chaps' polling cards.

"Good God," exclaimed Ned. "At last! It's from Ba." He unfolded the letter which he obviously found to his liking. "Oh, good old Ba!"

"Ba who?" asked Norman vaguely, engrossed in his own letter.

"Ba who? Ba Ba Blacksheep, you silly old coot! Ba WHO indeed! How many Ba's do we know. Ba Barthorpe of course."

"Oh, you mean Biddy," Norman corrected.

"If I'd meant Biddy, I'd have said Biddy. I said Ba. If I said Ba, I meant Ba. Who, pray, is Biddy?"

"Biddy Barthorpe," said Norman, putting aside his letter. Elizabeth Mary Barthorpe. No wonder I couldn't put a face to Ba."

"Well, I've always called her Ba," said Ned. "And," he added after a moment, "I met her first."

"You certainly did not," Norman countered. "You know jolly well we both met her at exactly the same time, heaving those enormous bags of clay up the backstairs to the sculpture studio." Ned grunted. "Anyway, what does she say?"

Ned knew Norman was right but he sulked all the same. Norman was invariably right about things that had happened fifty years ago but when asked what he'd done five minutes ago, Ned often found him lost for a sensible answer.

"She says we can have the house," Ned announced. "So, it's on, thank goodness."

"What's on?" asked Norman, puzzled at Ned's unusual exuberance so early in the morning.

"Our weekend," said Ned. "The weekend. The 30th."

"Oh, Ned!" said Norman, horrified with himself for forgetting. "It had completely slipped my mind." He paused, remembering something. "The 30th . . . ? That's today, dear."

"Can't be," said Ned. "That's ridiculous."

"It might be ridiculous," said Norman patiently, "but it's still April 30th today. What's the date on the letter? It might have been delayed in the post."

Ned looked at the postmark and then the date on the letter.

"Damn fool of a woman," he cried. "She wrote the blessed thing in February!" Ned tossed the letter on the bed and humphed. He always humphed when he didn't quite know what to do, although on this occasion a decision was quickly reached – the last weekend in April was sacrosanct, an immutable date in Ned's calender. "Well," Ned said turning to Norman, "better get your skates on, Norman. We've got to get moving or else we'll be driving to Sussex in the middle of the rush hour."

"But, Ned," pleaded Norman, "it's only ten past nine. Can't we finish our tea?"

Ned was already in the bathroom, preparing his shower. He poked his head round the door, his shower cap pulled firmly down over his eyes.

"I said moving, corporal." Norman jumped. Ned often re-lived the war, usually in moments of stress or apparent urgency. Ned and the war had got on awfully well despite his never having actively served. Ned had been in charge of a whole section of an Intelligence unit in Whitehall. Norman had volunteered to join it. Even now, so many years later, there were still some days Norman regretted his rash, though indubitably patriotic, gesture.

"Oh, must we, Ned?" Norman beseeched mournfully.

"Norman!" Ned warned, "Stand by your bunk!"

"I suppose we have to dress up?" said Norman with a resigned sigh.

Ned peered out from under the shower cap.

"You'd look a damn fool in your pyjamas if we had a breakdown in the middle of Tunbridge Wells, corporal. Now, move!" Ned disappeared into his bathroom and Norman heard the familiar gasp as the jet of cold water hit the warm flesh.

"Yes, sir!" he whispered to himself . . .

TWO

Eventually, after much debate about what to pack and the writing of hurried notes to Rimanda, their daily, for her to find on Monday morning, the friends passed through Tunbridge Wells without incident and headed out into deepest Sussex in the direction of Frant.

Norman, a front-seat back-seat driver, sat with the relevant map on his lap as he always did when they drove further out of London than their furthest bridge session in Bromley. On this occasion, Ned was entirely familiar with the route although he noticed that Norman, as usual, had placed the neatly folded map upside down, which meant that had Ned been forced to ask the way, right would have immediately become left and left, right. Ned had long since given up asking Norman the way. Navigating was a little too practical for Norman but, as Ned was wont to remark, they had still won the war.

Just after they had driven past a hillside plantation covered with pollard chestnut trees and had 'oohed' and 'aahed' at the carpet of bluebells on the woodland floor, Norman felt the rumblings of a little wind, which reminded him that in the rush to leave, he had forgotten to have breakfast.

"I think I'm a bit peckish, dear," he said to Ned hopefully. Whilst Ned functioned on only one good meal a day, Norman's constitution had confirmed him a breakfast, lunch and dinner person.

"No rations in the car?" barked Ned who, in his mind, was still winning the war, moving around little markers with flags on top of them over vast table maps of Southern England and feeling very military. Norman opened the glove compartment.

"Four mint imperials and a rather old toffee," he

announced.

"Bah!" said Ned, "not enough to feed a snake!"

"I don't think snakes like mint imperials,"observed Norman innocently. "But look," he exclaimed, "there's somewhere."

He pointed at a black and white painted cartwheel, several of whose spokes had rotted and above it a hand painted sign proclaiming 'Tyler's Cafe'. Ned peered ahead and decelerated although he hadn't much momentum to lose, never driving anywhere at a speed faster than thirty miles an hour. He steered the Mini into the car park in front of a single storey, brick-built edifice against the facade of which struggled a rather straggly rambling rose and the remains of a late-starting *clematis montana*. Despite the early date in the season, tables and chairs had been hopefully placed on a grassy patch, which passed for a lawn, waiting for such a day as this when the sun had decided to show its face.

"It amazes me how easily you can spot something when you want to," said Ned, turning off the ignition and withdrawing the key. "Ask you to read a bus number in Oxford Street and you plead myopia."

"I don't particularly like buses," said Norman, justifying his aversion to being squashed by humanity in all its worst guises. He collected his bag and pulled his jacket onto his shoulders. "I don't mind the underground, but I draw the line at buses when I don't have to go in them." He looked out of the window at the prospect of lunch. "Oh," he said, now uncertain, "do you think we should? It doesn't look much of a place."

"Food is food, corporal," said Ned. "And," he added rather unkindly, "we usually have sandwiches."

"Usually," Norman said tartly, "we are given rather more notice of a holiday than ten minutes. Rimanda had to go to the chiropodist today so I had to do everything in the house." He paused. "Oh!" he said. "I do hope I remembered to turn off the gas.

"They got out of the car and Ned locked all the doors.

"Norman, really!" said Ned in a tone of utter despair,

"we don't have gas anymore!"

"Oh," said Norman, "so we don't. But that's exactly why I find it so confusing. I told you I would at the time."

"Let's not start that one again," said Ned, marching ahead to the door of the cafe. "We only changed from gas because you always thought you'd forgotten to turn it off." Ned pushed the door open.

"Yes, alright, Ned. I remember when you remind me but today's been such a rush."

Ned always entered rooms as though he owned them, whereas Norman was more timid. The cafe was empty save for a mildewed old soul of about ninety, puffing on a Craven A, accompanied by a man of somewhat lesser years whom Norman surmised was probably the old lady's son. There seemed to be a family likeness but, Norman thought, age does have a habit of blurring the edges. Ned and Norman nodded to the elderly couple, who had turned to appraise the new arrivals. Each party smiled politely to the other, a proper acknowledgement but no more.

A woman, nicely coiffed and on the right side of sixty, emerged from the kitchen, wiping her hands on one of those wrap-around pinnies that come from church sales, hand-made from a pair of old kitchen curtains.

"Good morning," said the woman brightly and in perfect English, a rather clipped, county English. "Lunch, is it?" She indicated a table and the boys sat down, for Ned had indeed become very boyish. He was, after all, on holiday.

"Capital," said Ned accepting the proffered menu folder. "Absolutely capital!" The woman left them, offering them time to peruse both the menu and the specials, which, today, she announced, were steak and kidney pie and mushroom quiche.

"I think capital's a bit gushing, you know," whispered Norman across the table as he put on his glasses. Ned ignored the reprimand as his eyes alighted on an item charismatically described as an All Day Breakfast.

"Capital," said Ned again in a gleeful tone not a million miles away from that favoured by Billy Bunter. "Just like school again."

"If you'd had food like this at school, Ned, you wouldn't have been so beastly to all those people you bullied into surrendering their tuck!" Norman observed smartly and his observation was correct for although Ned survived on one meal a day, that meal had to be gargantuan. "Anyway," Norman continued, "that apart, just think of all the 'Es' in this menu to say nothing of the cholesterol."

"Stuff and nonsense, Corporal," scoffed Ned. "Good English food. Solid, dependable and . . ."

"Awfully fattening," interrupted Norman.

"Better than that frightful rabbit food you churn out these days."

"But it's good for you, Ned. Doctor says," Norman said, scouring the menu trying to find something approaching a salad.

"And a damn fool he is too," said Ned, although he rather liked Doctor Peter. "What does he know anyway?"

"He has had *two* heart attacks, Ned. He should know if anyone knows."

"Not everyone gets heart attacks," said Ned defensively, "or else England would become a cemetery overnight! Anyway, we're on holiday and as far as I'm concerned, I'm having the All Day Breakfast, with chips and baked beans. So there!" He snapped the plastic menu folder shut with evident relish.

"Well, just don't forget I can't drive," Norman said despairingly.

"What in heaven's name has that got to do with cholesterol?"

"I meant if you have a heart attack," said Norman. Ned sighed.

"If I'm going to have a heart attack, it's not going to happen immediately after an All Day Breakfast, is it?" said Ned with some logic.

"Please yourself," said Norman. "You usually do. But don't say you haven't been warned. I'm having the mushroom omelette." Norman too closed his menu but with more gentility. The woman returned and Ned gave their order, adding one tea and one coffee as prandial libation. Their attention now became diverted into looking around the room.

"Rather nice, don't you think," said Norman, allowing himself some congratulation. Norman was usually famous for suggestions of places to eat which ended up as being disasters of fabulous magnitude. Pubs which advertised 'Home Cooked Food' often turned out to be seedy public bars with a microwave oven and a pile of inedible pies from the Far Famed City Pie Company; cat food with cardboard crusts as Ned called them.

"Well," said Ned as he formed his opinion of the place, looking around at the crude and wretchedly-framed paintings of floral mysteries on the walls, each priced, for some unknown reason, on a small red sticker at eighteen pounds, "If you really want to know," he went on, taking in to his assessment the left-over tureens of at least three Ironstone dinner services and the variegated and unvariegated varieties of two profuse spider plants, "I can honestly say," he continued, eying the unadmirable pine dresser laden with home-made jams and bags of tempting home-made toffee, "without hesitation," he concluded, running his fingers over the fading oilcloth on the tables and appraising the ill-assorted, un-matched pairs of chairs culled from a long history of local monthly auctions, "you wouldn't find this place anywhere else but England!" He sounded England with a fair note of triumphant pride.

"Then you do like it?" Norman asked and waited, hesitant, poised to bask in even the tiniest ray of praise. Ned beamed.

"I'd like to wrap it up in good old brown paper and hide it away in a secret cupboard so I would always know where it was and I could take it out on those days when I think everything is crumbling round me and feel that at least somewhere there's still something worth remembering." Ned paused and became slightly conspiratorial. "Norman, promise me . . ."

"Anything. Absolutely anything. I'm just so thrilled that I haven't made one of my usual bloomers." Ned shushed him with a gesture. Norman was all ears

."Don't tell a soul about it. Got it? Not a single soul!" The woman brought their tea and coffee at that moment which temporarily interrupted Ned.

"There you are," said the county lady. "Nice and hot and I won't be a tick with the rest."

Norman smiled and said "Thank you" while Ned remained hunched over the table, elbows wide, still deep in his torrent of concentrated secrecy.

"Did you hear me, Norman?"

"Yes, I heard you. But . . . why?"

"Can't have it advertised, y'see. Tell one person and then they'll tell another and before you can blink, everyone will be here and it'll be ruined, turned into another one of those fast food dumps. All burgers and kesp."

Norman nodded his assent, looking round over his shoulder to make sure that no one was listening and wondering whether it was the right moment to confess his ignorance as to what kesp might be. He pulled his jacket lapels closer together.

"Promise, promise honest injun," he said. "Cross my heart and hope to die!"

"Good," said Ned, satisfied. "It'll be our secret." Norman nodded and then, after a moment, a frown creased his brow. A question mark.

"Ned, do you mean by a soul, no-one? Not even Anthony?" Ned pondered the exception. Anthony was Ned's favourite nephew who monitored the friends' affairs as best as either of them would allow him.

"OK," Ned allowed, "Anthony. But no-one else." Norman was greatly relieved as he was very awkward with secrets and found it very difficult coping with information he had to remember and that which he was sworn to forget.

"Oh good." The question mark bell rang again. "But not Heather and Mongo, that's for sure."

"Certainly not!" spat Ned. "They'd be here like a shot. Mongo'd go anywhere we've been just to say he's been there and then he'd spend hours picking holes. I loathe

Mongo."

"But not Heather," Norman said hopefully. "You couldn't loathe poor Heather, surely."

"Pity, then. Pure pity. Snivelling woman and always was," said Ned of one of his best friends. Ned was often irrationally intolerant and one of his pet irritations was anyone of the opposite sex who had allowed themselves to become subordinate to their husband.

The meals arrived. A vast platter of sausage, bacon, eggs, tomatoes, baked beans and fried bread was placed in front of Ned. The fried bread, an unadvertised addition to the meal, really caught Ned's fancy. Two browned and crisped triangles of fried bread were propped on either edge of the oval platter, like the front and back covers of a wonderful book, enclosing a feast within. Ned fairly pounced on his cutlery after covering the pile of chips with great showers of salt. Norman winced at the unhealthy excess but Ned did so love to taste his food. Norman attended to his own choice of the mushroom omelette which looked almost lonely on its huge plate, unadorned by even a sprig of parsley, unable to emulate the cornucopia of Ned's selection. Norman took up his fork and tasted, gingerly. It was good; simple, perhaps, and certainly plain but, on the whole, not bad. He had no need to enquire whether Ned was enjoying his meal. Ned was lost in a paradise of taste sensations and reflecting on the inequities of heredity whereby he had been consigned to the fate of being endomorphic.

The waitress returned and turned the dial of a radio away from a pop music channel to one broadcasting classical music. Suddenly there was Elgar, very loud Elgar, throughout the cafe.

"Have we everything we want?" asked the waitress brightly. Norman nodded through a mouthful of omelette and noticed the green eye shadow for the first time. There was, he decided, a touch too much and concluded reluctantly that perhaps the woman was not a duchess in reduced circumstances after all. He managed to swallow in time to reply.

"We have, thank you. The omelette is quite delicious."

"Thank you, dear," said the woman, instantly betraying herself with the familiar. "I'll tell chef."

Ned almost choked on a mouthful of sausage and tomato as the woman, humming the theme of 'Nimrod' in duet with the radio, withdrew to the kitchen.

"That's rich! Cook, perhaps, but chef? Bit posh don't you think?"

"Perhaps they're on hard times, Ned," Norman said, forking off another section of the omelette. Perhaps he is a real chef. You never know. I first thought that maybe she ... once upon a time . . . in the old days. . . " Ned stopped eating.

"You're incorrigible, Norman." Ned laughed. "From society to skivvy, the story of the Hon. Daphne Dandelion, the darling of the season of thirty nine, feted by Court and thwarted by fate, now working in a transport cafe in Frant!"

"Oh, Ned, you're awful, but . . ."

"But bilge," said Ned loudly as the mildewed matron and her son rose from their table, perhaps in an effort to escape before they too became the object of Norman's excitable speculation. "Woman's wearing green eyeshadow."

"And she called me dear," Norman added. "Hons. wouldn't call you dear, would they?" He chuckled. "Other people are so fascinating."

"Wrong," said Ned vehemently. "Some other people are fascinating. Most are definitely not. To be fascinating, you have to have depth, something to keep you afloat after the first toe-in-the-water introductions, the 'Hello, I'm Mr so-and-so and this is my wife'. All that stuff."

"But that's just being polite," observed Norman. "You wouldn't get far without politeness."

"Well I don't want to get very far with just anybody," said Ned stubbornly. He indicated with his fork, through the window, the couple endeavouring to seat themselves in a car that seemed even smaller than the Mini. The mother seemed to find the exercise easier than her supposed son, who put in one leg, then the other and finding both impossible, tried it bottom first, only to succeed with what appeared to be utmost discomfort. "Like them," Ned said. "Hate to say it but neither of them would hold my attention for a second. Good morning, nice day, lovely place, goodbye. Finis."

More foreign cars, thought Ned as the elderly couple in their Fiat left and a family in a rusty Honda pulled in."You've eaten that awfully quickly," said Norman, eyeing the fragments of bacon rind draped over the edge of Ned's plate, the only evidence of the mountain of breakfast. "You'll suffer and I know it's not going to be in silence. Anyway," Norman said, unable to finish the remainder of his omelette, "you're just being beastly about people. They were probably very nice."

"Almost certainly nice but we were talking about fascinating, Norman."

"It's only a word, Ned. You know what I meant," Norman said sniffily. Ned was always accusing him about being lazy with his vocabulary whilst Norman countered with the charge that Ned once must have swallowed a dictionary. Where Ned could and would choose between three words, Norman, with his inate sense of economy and moderation, was quite content with one and would often use that word to mean whatever he was thinking, not necessarily what he was saying.

"I've always known what you've meant, Norman which is jolly useful as otherwise we'd never communicate. Most inconvenient." Ned opened his purse. "How much was yours?"

"One pound and sixty pee plus the tea," said Norman. "And don't forget her tip."

"Probably included," said Ned." Usually is these days and the VAT whatever that might be. Whatever was wrong with good old fashioned Purchase Tax, I'll never know. I'm going to ask her." Norman winced.

"Oh, don't, Ned. Not at these prices. It's hardly the National Debt." But Norman was ignored and Ned turned to catch the eye of the waitress.

"Excuse me," Ned called, seeing no one immediately apparent. "Damn staff," he said to Norman, "never there when you want them." He waited two seconds. "I say!" he said loudly. As Ned summoned the waitress, the gaggle of people from the Honda came into the cafe; a family. Mother, care-worn; father, regretful and resigned and three assorted children, ill-mannered and over-jocular. The waitress appeared at the kitchen door and caught Ned's eye. She had obviously been interrupted in the act of snatching a mouthful of her lunch.

"Bill is it, dear?" said the waitress with difficulty. "Be with you in a minute."

"And a question too," Ned added. "If you don't mind." The waitress valiantly downed the remainder of her lunch and came over to the table and Ned asked her as to the precise configuration of their bill. Meanwhile, the children, bored with sitting down at the table only half a minute, had clustered around the coin-in-the-slot game machine which Tyler's Cafe sported. Blips, bleeps and electronically sourced noises began to be emitted by the unfortunate machine and the children jostled between themselves noisily as to which amongst them was to play first.

The coin they had been given by their mother had obviously jammed in the works and the dysfunction was causing a near riot. The Elgar was drowned. In petulence, the eldest, a boy, first kicked the machine, then his younger brother shook it violently whilst the third child, a girl, obviously the youngest and not to be outdone by either of her brothers, aided and abetted with another well-aimed kick. This last infraction prompted gales of raucous laughter and by this time, all eyes at Ned and Norman's table were glued to the scene of prospective vandalism.

"I say, Norman said to the waitress, "ought they to be doing that?" The waitress shrugged and Norman saw Ned's expression becoming more and more militant by the moment. Bad behaviour was one of the current bees in Ned's bonnet. Mindless violence and vandalism on television left him enraged at his own impotence but this firsthand experience of loutishness presented him with a toehold on what he viewed as an escalating national avalanche of ill manners. Whilst Ned bristled, the mother of this rude tribe was taking no notice of the antics of her brood. Out had come the powder compact with attendant lipstick and mama was attempting to repair the more obvious ravages of time as her husband obliviously perused the menu.

"Young people," shrugged the waitress. "You know what they're like these days." She spoke in a low voice. Norman began to make a sympathetic rejoinder but Ned launched into a more immediate line of action.

"You there!" he bellowed. "You children! What the heck d'you think you're up to?"

The children turned, as one, to face their assailant; pale faces, acres of acne and three sullen glares peered out from beneath ill-cut thatches of streaked hair.

"Playin' the bleedin' game," the eldest boy spat. "Why?"

"Then play it quietly," Ned ordered in decibels which shattered the quiet tranquillity of the cafe. Reactions were swift. 'Chef' appeared at the kitchen door. Mama, stung by the imperious quality in Ned's command and now immediately mindful of the welfare of her chicks, snapped her powder compact shut. Her lips twisted into a snarl which, had she had fangs, would have bared them.

"Don'choo talk to my kids like that!" she hissed at Ned. "'Oo d'yer think you are?"

This was quite the wrong thing to say to Ned who, of all people, knew exactly who he was. Norman cringed as he could see Ned mentally donning armour and tilting his lance. As Norman expected, the gauntlet was taken up but, would vengeance be Ned's, he wondered?

"I, madam, am a paying customer at this establishment and I do not intend to have what remains of my luncheon spoiled by your badly behaved children kicking that wretched machine. I suggest you control them!"

"Oh, Lord," said the waitress under her breath.

"I'm so terribly sorry," whispered Norman apologetically and remembered at that point to take off his glasses.

Outrage ensued, spreading over the incensed mother's face like a red rash. Norman realised how allergic mothers are to any disparaging remarks aimed at their own children and he thought of how much Ned's own dear mother had been put through when Ned's childhood and student escapades had provoked the wrath of shopkeepers and neighbours alike.

The poor waitress hovered like an referee at a potentially violent football match and for some reason which Norman could not fathom out, chef picked up a fire extinguisher.

"'Ere, Phil," the mother spluttered. She lunged at her benighted husband, who, like Norman, wished that at that moment he was anywhere except hiding behind the menu holder in Tyler's Cafe, "Tell 'im! Just you tell 'im! 'E can't speak to me like that!"

Husband was now forced into looking up at sputtering wife who was exploding like a roman candle stuck inside a bucket.

"He just 'as, Doris. Wotcha want me to do about it? Go over an' 'it 'im?"

Chef aimed his fire extinguisher more ominously as Ned and the mother rocked back and forth on their seats, tilting at each other. The children had by now totally abandoned their game of Masters of the Cosmos and clustered around their mother, seeking both to be protected and to protect.

"Go on, mum," goaded the eldest, the boy of about fifteen. "You tell 'im!"

"Don'choo worry, Shane, love. I shall tell 'im! Tell 'im where 'e can stuff 'is luncheon." Doris, for that was her name, laid heavy sarcastic emphasis on luncheon. "Very 'igh an' mighty, if you ask me is Lord Muck 'ere! All la-di-da and a lotta plums in the mouth, aren't we milord?" Ned boiled over at this final, stinging riposte which insulted the stainless middle-class perceptions he so unshakeably held of himself. He stood up, sending his chair squeaking across the floor like a cat with its tail trodden on.

"I really think we should be off now," Norman said as valiantly and brightly as he could muster. "How much do we owe you?" he asked the waitress.

"Eight pounds and ten, if you please dear," said Miss, her reply squeezed out of vocal chords as taut as overwound harp strings and her attitude desperately neutral.

"And what about the service charge?" said Ned with more threat than concern, his eyes pinning Doris to her seat, daring the woman to make even the smallest move in any direction. Norman paid a ten pound note, waving away the offer of change and the waitress' affections were instantly purchased. The transaction seemed also to defuse the intensity of the atmosphere of animosity. Even chef, sensing detente, lowered, although did not abandon, his portable water cannon.

"Thank you very much, sir," said the waitress, mentally separating out her ninety pence tip and gone was any mention of the familiar dear. "Have a pleasant day."

Norman nudged Ned somewhere in the region of the lower back and muttered words of exit as he positioned himself between the feinting Ned and the simmering Doris.

"Thank you," Norman said to the waitress. "Quite delicious. I'm sure we shall be seeing you again. Quite soon I expect. Probably Monday, in fact. I know my friend will insist."

The waitress reacted to this bit of news with an expression of abject horror.

Oh," she gulped, "that wouldn't be next Monday?"

"Yes, Monday," Norman confirmed. "On our way back from the coast. You're quite convenient here, you see."

"Ah!" said the waitress, relief flooding her face,"What a pity. I'm off next Monday!"

Ned had remained stock still, ramrod stiff, his back as straight as a sentry's. Norman pushed him again.

"Ned. Gee up. Starters orders, old chap," said Norman and one of the children sniggered, the youngest, the girl.

"D'y'ear that, mum? Ned. 'E's called Ned!"

"I'll call 'im more than Ned," Doris ventriloquised through clenched teeth," and while I'm about it, I could call yer dad a few names, an' all!"

Before Ned was given a chance to bite the bullet, Norman gave him an enormous shove and, thankfully, at the end of this momentum, the friends found themselves at the door. Ned reached out and jabbed the red play button on the machine, banging it quite as hard as he had earlier hit the TeasMaid, causing a great battery of bells and bleeps and whirring noises to sound, covering up Doris's parting retort.

"I think you're probably right," Norman said as he steered Ned firmly down the paved path to the car park. "I think only some people are fascinating these days."

Ned suddenly stopped in his tracks. A slow, satisfied smile played on his lips as he realised how he could usefully turn apparent defeat into at least a pyhrric victory.

"Here, Norman, take the keys. Dammit all, I'm going back!"

Norman was horrified. The very thought of violence upset him and now the prospect of the reality of it was too much.

"You can't Ned. You mustn't!"

But Ned wasn't fighting; in fact fight had turned to plegm.

"It's alright, Norman, don't fuss. I'm not out for fourteen rounds with those people. I've made my point."

"Then why?" asked Norman incredulously.

"I want some of that homemade toffee! Now, where's my purse?"

THREE

The little Mini pottered through the Sussex countryside, past converted oasthouses with smart gravel drives, past ancient farms and assorted ages of barn set fast in the green and pleasant landscape. Well, thought Norman to himself, that was all a silly storm in a teacup, wasn't it? He spotted a windmill and pointed it out to Ned who was secretively gloating to himself over what had now been established in his own mind at least as one of his more important battles.

And so they drove, not as ancient old codgers but as Knights Errant, one with dragons yet to slay but the other with the problem of how to dispose of the poor dragons once they had met their appointed end.

The status quo between and surrounding Norman and Ned had always been quickly re-established because they were each so obviously different and absolutely non-competitive.

Neither had the slightest desire to ever attempt to emulate the character or doings of the other. The parameters of their youthful personalities had, it seemed, been well drawn and had remained intact, encompassing both the griefs and joys of their subsequent lives with equanimity and affection.

Although each seemed to take the other for granted, neither rarely overstepped certain unspoken boundaries.

"Do you remember," asked Norman, turning to appreciate a particlarly effusive rockery, spilling over with aubretia and daffodils, "that thing we used to do with sweets. When they were rationed?"

"God, yes!" said Ned relishing, but wrestling at the same time, an overlarge and very gooey lump of toffee which had adhered itself to his top plate. "Quarter of a pound a week, wasn't it? That was worst part of the war for me. No sweets. Ugh!"

"How long was the longest you ever kept a mint lump going, Ned?" said Norman. "Tell the truth, now."

However much Ned used his tongue to wriggle and worm the congealed sweet from his plate, referred to more politely by Mr Sutaria, their dentist, as an engineered prosthetic device, he couldn't budge it.

"I remember exactly," he managed to say, "It was on the way back from Aldershot. Forty-six minutes precisely." Speech then became an impossibility as, briefly, top and bottom plates became bonded together, immovable and inseparable. Oh, thought Ned, not unreasonably alarmed as others who have been similarly compromised will understand . . . Bloody hell!

So you always said," Norman challenged, "though I can't honestly say I ever believed you. Best I ever managed was half-an-hour and I've got twice your patience."

At that moment, Norman's attention was gripped by the umpteenth forsythia that afternoon, a sighting which would usually have prompted yet another rhapsodic observation of the rites of spring. However, Norman could not help but notice that Ned seemed to be in mortal difficulty; his jaws were wandering about his face as if in torment as he contorted lips, tongue and every facial muscle in a vain attempt to dislodge the toffee.

"Ned, are you alright?" Briefly, the saccharine weld sheared.

"Damn thing," Ned mumbled. "It's stuck. Started off on the plate and now its underneath. I'll have to stop, Norman. The teeth have got to come out or we'll have an accident."

Ned slowed the car immediately, quite oblivious of the need to look in the mirror. The twenty-three cars and two lorries backed up behind them, the foremost of which queue was all but riding on Ned's back bumper, honked and hooted, scattering a herd of cows being marshalled by the cowman in readiness to cross the road for milking.

"Oh Ned!," said Norman who had been as startled as

the cows, "everyone seems awfully cross." No car had been able to pass them since Mayfield and that village had been traversed some miles back. "Don't you think you could hold out for another few miles. We're almost there, you know."

"What?" Ned blurted out, now almost completely incapacitated, "and risk the *Telegraph* saying in my obituary that I'd choked to death on my own teeth? Don't take any notice of 'em, Norman. Just damnable rudeness. That's all you get these days. Impatience and plain bad manners. Give 'em cars and they all think they're in a Grand Prix. Roads aren't race tracks!" he snorted. "Let them wait. It's that sort of folk that drive over toads!" Most of this tirade Norman was unable to catch as Ned's words came out as a spray of spit, so preventing any real comprehension.

One by one, the queue of traffic behind pulled out to overtake the Mini, each complement of passengers turning as they passed to glare at Ned and Norman and uttering foul yet mercifully unheard oaths and recriminations as they were at last able to acccelerate their vehicles at a reasonable speed.

There seemed nowhere for Ned to stop and so, in desperation, he turned the car into the driveway of a house called London Beeches and pulled on the handbrake. Though Norman was concerned for Ned, he couldn't help, at the same time, being nervous about parking in someone else's driveway. Norman hated being anywhere he wasn't supposed to be; walking across a field which was not clearly marked with a public footpath sign was anathema to him and he would only ever resort to such trespass because of Ned's insinuations about being a cowardy-custard.

"Norman, this is an emergency," was all that Ned said on this occasion, as he sensed Norman's neurosis. "Now, let's get at 'em." Ned licked his fingers for hygiene's sake and stuck them in his mouth. He still retained two of his own teeth from his upper set and Mr Sutaria had cleverly worked the plate to be fitted around these hoary old fangs. Devilish clever chap, Ned had remarked when he had ultimately been presented with his new, perfectly fitting teeth but he had never thought then that one day he might have to reckon with a renegade gobbit of toffee. "Hab a 'ook," gummed Ned, his fingers in his mouth, which Norman translated as 'Have a look'. Norman was completely baffled, unable to understand.

"Are you stuck, Ned?" he asked in that helpless yet sympathetic way that those not discomforted ask of the suffering. Ned removed his fingers from his mouth.

"'Course I'm bloody stuck!" he thundered. "Look inside and just tell me what's stuck where!" Ned lay back and opened his mouth as wide as he could. Norman removed his seat belt and manoeuvred himself into a position from which he could look into the oral cavern.

"Well," he began to opine, "your tongue is very brown; at least, what I can see of it is very brown but then that's probably the toffee and," he paused, craning his neck for a closer analysis, "there's more toffee than tongue 'cos your tongue's sort of trapped under one of your plates."

Ned closed his mouth as he needed to swallow but then when he opened it again, the bottom plate came away completely, un-anchored, unlike its upper partner, to anything of substance other than naked gum. Now, both plates were stuck together

."I think, Ned," said Norman who licked his fingers with clinical precision, "if I just pulled the whole lot out, that would be our best bet. Open wide." Norman reached in.

Just at that moment, very silently, a rather beautiful Jaguar purred down the drive of London Beeches bearing Major Mace away to the golf club. The links were always less crowded on a Friday afternoon than on a Saturday morning with less of the common element which, or rather who, although necessary for its money was, to Major Mace a grisly reminder of the times in which he lived.

The Major just managed to brake in time to avoid a head-on collision as he had not prepared himself for the possibility of the presence of the intrusive common element picknicking at the bottom of his drive. Norman had successfully established a grip on the tangled mass of teeth, plastic and toffee and triumphantly extracted this as the Major, apoplectic with righteous rage, jabbed his thumbs onto the horn of his Jaguar, wishing he could rather have been operating the firing button of a bren gun as the sworn enemy were inescapably in his sights.

The klaxon made Norman jump a mile in his seat and Ned's jaws snapped shut like a crocodile's around empty air. He sprang upright in an instant so giving himself the beginnings of what Doctor Peter would later diagnose as a nasty case of whiplash neck. Norman was terrified and immediately dropped the sticky teeth onto the floor beneath Ned's feet, which was never the cleanest of places as Ned never hoovered the inside of the car as he was asked.

Major Mace operated his electrical window and stuck out his head, his face red with the usual over-generous tot of afternoon brandy. In doing so, he also knocked off his hat, which enraged him even more and he let rip with a fair yardage of invective. For the sake of decency and honour, Norman's rather than the Major's, the jist of Mace's barrack-room communique was:

"What the hell d'y'think you're doing here? This isn't a public park, damn you!" He parped his horn again, at least three times, to underline his indignation. "Shift that bloody car or I'll call the police!"

Norman, who had some miles ago wound down his window for a little air and also because there was a fly in the car, hurriedly raised his window and locked his door, remembering the time that he had been caught in a field with a friend when a bull had appeared in the rear view mirror of the friend's Standard Ten.

Ned, toothless and still in the sort of fighting dudgeon he had mustered at what was to become known in their mythology as The Tyler's Incident, opened his door and sprang out. Norman watched his chum march around the front of the Mini to confront the second major adversary of the day, discounting but not forgetting the skirmish with Ivy Williams as that was a running battle. Ned, now on his feet, wasn't as small as Major Mace had first thought and with his motor in overdrive as it was, Ned bowled along, a cross between a First World War tank and a Renaissance galleon. In response, Major Mace pressed another button, the one that electrically raised the Jaguar's window. Ned may have been without his teeth but there was bite in his bark.

"You, sir, are extremely rude!" Ned began as an opening salvo. "Have you always behaved towards persons in distress in such a foul manner?" Major Mace opened his mouth to reply but found himself wordless, void of an answer. In truth, he'd never been confronted by a person in distress in such a brutally direct manner in his life.

A barrage of bluster and bluff had been both his attack and defence since an early deduction that strangers, unless ignored or restrained, could very easily dominate his world as unacceptably as the common element now dominated his golf club. He thought of his wife, comfortless little Enid up at the house and he reflected briefly how lucky he was that she was not cursed with such an agressive nature as this person standing on his drive confronting him. Little did Major Mace imagine that at that very moment, Enid was herself downing a very large tipple of gin, celebrating her relief that the house and she were to be free of the Major for a few hours at least. But then, little did Enid Mace imagine that her arrant husband had at last been reduced to shivering in his beautiful Jaguar, open-mouthed like so much dead cod on the fishmonger's slab. The Major's bluster wilted.

"And, sir," Ned continued, "I must tell you that I suspect you're as drunk as a skunk. That's brandy on your breath if I'm not much mistaken and so I heartily second your motion to call the police. I'm sure they'd take a very dim view of you! May I remind you that you are in command of a lethal weapon and you shouldn't even be on the road!"

With that, Ned marched back to his car where Norman waited, holding Ned's teeth in cupped hands as though they were the relics of St George himself. Ned got in, closed the door and buckled in. With a final wave of his fist at the amazed Major Mace, he started the engine and drove away.

And so Ned and Norman began the final stage of the eventful journey to Ba's house overlooking the Greensward at East Dean rather later and certainly more harrassed than they would have preferred.

FOUR

East Dean had been but a tiny rural hamlet, nestling in a gentle fold of the South Downs when Ba, now Mrs Croker-Symes had bought her brand-new house, facing the newly created Greensward, in 1938.

The Second World War completed the job that the First World War had started by warping a great number of originally good ideas which, by 1945, began to be considered either impractical or unteneble in the face of a new democracy.

The Greensward, a protected area of some acres of mown grass, was so named because it referred to an era when all residents of English villages enjoyed the uses of a green regardless of social position. The green was a laudable institution and the Greensward at East Dean had been the brainchild of a certain Mr Arnatt who, by all accounts, was an aesthetic philanthropist as well as being a doughty property developer. Mr Arnatt realised that good money could be made out of the burgeoning demand of the economically stable middle classes for country estates, not the vast manors and mansions of the tottering aristocracy nor the follies and fantasies of the barons of industry, but small, well-designed homes, surrounded by manageable gardens for use as sanctuaries either in retirement or just at weekends, away from the hurly burly of commerce and trade.

In those days, Mrs Croker-Symes had indeed been Elizabeth Mary Barthorpe and indeed answered both to Ba and to Biddy.

Unfortunately, she had warped her own very good idea of maintaining an aesthetic, philantropic and very well-heeled spinsterhood by an experience directly brought about by the Second World War, namely that of marrying

Eustace Croker-Symes in a silly, elated moment of sentimentality in 1942, hence denying her Barthorpe label forever, except, of course, in the minds of such trusted companions as Ned Cresswell and Norman Rhodes.

When they had left art school, Ba had harboured no ambition to paint for a living but rather hankered after being an architect, having been much impressed by the new Memorial Theatre at Stratford-upon-Avon of which the architect had been a woman. Having been also much impressed by the aforesaid Mr Arnatt at a cocktail party in Hampstead one evening, Ba had become his most devoted disciple and became the third buyer to purchase one of the plots on his new development at East Dean. The Barthorpes were Yorkshire brewers, famous for their bitter and their money, although the bitter, as far as Ba was concerned, referred to her relationship with her father. All her efforts at creating a paternal entente proved futile and for this reason she decided to remove herself as far as possible from Yorkshire and live in the south, where all her friends were to be found. As soon as the Sussex style house was completed at East Dean, she moved in, commuting between her bucolic refuge and various London parties until 1940.

Returning to East Dean intending to take up residence again with her recently repatriated Eustie, who had fallen foul of a faulty Spitfire whilst flying a mission over Holland three weeks after they were married, Ba had found that Mr Arnatt's idea was turning sour in direct proportion to the extra numbers of houses which were appearing on what had been a pleasant, uncluttered skyline. Eustace hated the place on sight and immediately dubbed it Dorking on the Downs. He was a terrific, though groundless snob and, as Ned had so correctly prophesied, had only married Ba for the beer money as her inheritance had become known. Ba and Eustie took off for the divorce court via Yorkshire and hardly ever set foot in East Dean again. By the mid-sixties, Mr Arnatt's initial vision had become adulterated by tributaries of non-Sussex style bungaloids, as Ned called them and now Ba only used the place once a year. For the remainder of the time, she organised a sort of matriarchal time-share scheme, packing off all her good causes for a week by the sea. The good causes were mostly Yorkshire widows or single parents from Dewsbury, but they could be anyone who had had the recent good fortune to qualify for Ba's conditional philanthropy.

Ned retained an inordinate fondness for East Dean and especially for Ba's house. It was in Ba's house that Ned had agreed to marry Dulcie and it was to Ba's house that the former Miss Dulcie Hogge came, however briefly, as Mrs Ned Cresswell. These, as many other memories of past poignancy, were water under the bridge although, as Norman often remarked, there seemed to have been been an awful lot more water in their lives than in most. There were very few people left, other than Norman and Ba, to even remember that the bellicose and, now, rotund Ned was once a blissfully romantic swain.

As Ned and Norman drove along the Jevington road, they approached the gentle slope which lay between Friston Manor at the bottom of the hill and Friston church, by the pond, at the top. Suddenly, Norman became very animated and clapped his hands in excited anticipation as though a veil of forty years had been pulled aside.

"Faster, Ned, faster!" he squeaked and Ned, smiling, changed gear and laughed as the needle on the speedometer hiccoughed and lurched towards forty.

"Faster!" Norman urged."Here it comes . . . now!" There was an undulation in the road almost at the top of the hill which, if taken at speed, induced a bucking motion, which in a pre-war Morris represented a thrilling experience.

"Wheeee-up!" chirruped two excited pensioners as the little Mini bounced alarmingly over the hump. Norman was in a delirium of happiness.

"How wonderful, Ned. Just think, it's still there after all these years."

Ned, after that moment's indulgence in such high spirited jocularity quickly re-assumed his more matter-of-fact brand of levity.

"Probably the only thing that is," said Ned although he said the same thing every year he came down. His glum philosophy hid his real emotion which was one of inextinguishable hope that everything would still be the same, not as last year or the one before but as they had first known things, driving down in Ba's old Morris so many years before."

Do you ever think . . ." Norman began to say.

"No," Ned said quickly. "You know I don't . . . Well, not often," he added a little more plausibly.

As close as they were, Norman knew when not to pursue a line of conversation that Ned found uncomfortable and so, instead of saying what he was going to say, he shut away his thoughts and began tidying up the car as Ned turned off the Brighton road and onto Mr Arnatt's estate.

Norman was an invererate tidier-upper. Messes, muddles and memories alike were all the less bothersome for a spell of tidying up and so the maps were neatly re-folded and stowed in the glove compartment, sweet papers collected, robbled into the tiniest balls and neatly tucked into a little bag which he kept for the purpose. Since Ned had given up smoking, there were usually rather a lot of sweet papers. At the end of a particularly good radio play or television documentary at home, such as Mastermind which always caused special tension, Ned would be found sitting heavily in his armchair surrounded by a ring of sweet papers, tumbled around him on the floor like the fallen petals from an over-large old peony.

"Don't forget my teeth," Ned reminded Norman as they drove down the road known as Hillside. White cherry blossom graced the Greensward, much to Ned's satisfaction and the breeze had blown the fallen flowers into heaps against the stone edging. Inside the car there came also the smell of freshly-mown grass, strong and completely distinct on the afternoon air. The man from Hailsham council had just finished mowing and was driving away on his tractor, the rotor blades of the mowing attachments streaming bits of grass and petals of blossom in his wake. As he edged the machine off the sward, the Mini reached the junction and Norman waved to the man in his cab. It turned out to be not the man whom he remembered from last year, with whom he had had a very intense conversation about retirement. Last year's man must have reached his retirement for in the cab this year there was a young man, once dark haired but now sporting a fashionably peroxided topknot, piled underneath the headband of a pair of Walkman earphones. He looked down at Norman, rather astonished and then winked at him, a little suggestively, Norman thought to himself. His hand hung in the air as he was caught between cancelling his acknowledgement of the young man and pretending instead to swat at an imaginary fly.

Ba's house was almost at the apex of the oval, slightly sloping Greensward. She hadn't ultimately, despite her devotion to Mr Arnatt, been able to secure either of the plots with a direct seaview but Ned had once climbed the tall oak behind the house and had irrevocably established that the property had a seaview even if the house did not. For a long time, the house had remained un-named. A letter posted in London in the morning to Miss Barthorpe, East Dean, Sussex before the war had usually arrived by the afternoon and Ba had never seen any point in giving her house a name. However, after her marriage, Ba had christened the house *Barthorpe* to perpetuate her maiden moniker as she felt that the name Barthorpe was not a suitable middle name for any prospective offspring of her marriage to Eustace.

The Mini pulled up outside *Barthorpe* just as the milometer notched up the hundred and twenty thousandth mile of its running history. Ned had been watching for this moment for the past ten miles and had driven twice around the Greensward to create this motoring achievement. He had only ever had two cars in his life and he was fiercely proud of the longevity of his much-vaunted British car, one of the first Minis to have been made.

"Oh, isn't this lovely," cried Norman. "I'll open the gates." He got out and opened first one and then the other of the double gates. "OK, Come on in!" he called out, standing aside as Ned revved and manoeuvred the little car until it came to rest at the top of the drive outside the house. Ned turned off the ignition and the Mini gave a shudder and coughed a couple of times, almost as though it did not want to be stopped. "Ahh," said Norman, patting the bonnet of the car as he always did at the end of a journey, "Bit tired are we?" It was obfuscatory at times, Norman's habit of anthromorphising everything mechanical as he would never have dreamed that the ascription of the Mini's wheezing condition could be to such a mundane factor as retarded ignition. Ned got out of the car and stretched.

"I'll fetch the key," he announced and stumped off, listing slightly to port, to retrieve the key which Ba always kept in the hollow of an old sycamore tree outside the kitchen door.

Norman began to wander around the clumps of daffodils, tulips and narcissi, examining the smells and scents of the flowers, admiring the size of the various blooms and looking forward to being able to do a good bit of weeding the following day. He always did his bit in the garden for that was as much as Ba would ever accept for their weekend tenancy.

As Norman experienced each spring scent, he uttered a little purr of satisfaction. Their garden in London was very small and, although Norman kept it as perfectly as any municipal gardener, there was something about the garden at *Barthorpe* with its wilderness areas burgeoning with bluebells and cowslips, that could not be improved on. He was just bending to catch the full glory of an early *viburnum fragrans* when the afternoon calm was shattered by Ned, shouting from behind the house.

"Oh, hell!" Suddenly the *viburnum* lost its *fragrans*. "You stupid senile old fool, Barthorpe!" thundered Ned. Norman ran round the corner of the house to where Ned stood, arms akimbo, surveying a neat pile of cleanly-sawn logs and a patch of sawdust where the old sycamore once had been.

"Good heavens, Ned. You're making enough noise to wake the dead. What is the matter?" said Norman in alarm. "That," said Ned, pointing at the stack of wood. "That's what's wrong, Norman. The key was always kept in the sycamore. Surely even you remember that?"

"Of course I remember, Ned," said Norman, upsetting himself because it was unclear why Ned was so overwrought. "I'm not a complete fool. I'm sure Ba would have remembered to take the key out of the tree before she chopped it down. Don't take on so."

"Norman, Ba didn't chop the tree down," Ned said at the pinnacle of a spiral of exasperation. "She's damn well near her seventy second birthday! Can you honestly see Barthorpe wielding a chain saw half way up a forty foot ladder?" Norman looked up at the sky where the tree had been and tried to imagine how high forty feet was.

"No, Norman," Ned elaborated. "Men did this! Workmen, tree butchers. How would they know that the key was in the tree?" Light dawned in Norman's comprehension.

"Oh," he said slowly. "I think I'm with you. We can't get in, can we?"

"Pre-cisely," said Ned. "Pre-bloody-cisely." There was a short silence and Norman saw that Ned was beginning to go through a series of well-known motions. His elbows were slightly raised, the left leg held bent and the right leg starting to shake. Ned, when really furious, was prone to kicking things, the last recipient of his physically manifested rage having been an indestructible wheel clamp, padlocked onto the front wheel of the Mini which they had discovered when they emerged from the summer sale at Peter Jones.

"No!" Norman exclaimed, clamping his hands to his mouth, "No, Ned, You're not to. I forbid it!" Visions of the unharmed wheel clamp and Ned's subsequently cracked toe sprang vividly to mind. "Just stamp your foot and count to ten instead," instructed Norman. Reluctantly, Ned willed himself not to vent his rage on the pile of logs and, after a moment's uncertainty, he calmed, rather amazingly, as the practical aspect of their predicament thwarted the tantrum. He humphed.

"You're right. Won't make a scene. Promise." Norman let himself down from the precipice of anticipating how he would have got Ned to the casualty department at Easbourne General Hospital. He went and stood next to Ned and together they surveyed the sawdust wondering what they were to do next. They both began to speak at once.

"What are we going to . . ." and simultaneously they both burst out laughing.

"Well," said Norman, "After all, it is funny, Ned, I mean, when you think about it!" Norman giggled helplessly.

"And we've got nothing to eat," he said, "except that wretched toffee!" Peals of laughter followed this. "But then, as you've got no teeth, that's about the only thing you can eat!" Ned howled with mirth and they clung to each other and danced around, jumping up and down as far as age would allow on the back lawn.

"Gosh! What a scrape," laughed Ned, gasping for air for he now had a stitch because he'd laughed so much. "Who'd believe it?" he said trying to pull himself together. "No wonder Anthony says that we should be committed!" He wiped his eyes.

"Alright? asked Norman and Ned nodded.

"Fine. Now, you just wait a mo' and I'll break a window and climb in. That sitting room one's been cracked for years. We'll ring the man in Eastbourne first thing in the morning and he can come round and put in some new glass. Nobody'll ever know."

"Should you? Don't you think I should ring Biddy and ask if she hasn't found another place for the key?"

"We can't get in the house to use the telephone, Norman, can we? And there's no point. Ba might not be in and this way she gets a new window. Amazing how mean the very rich are," he said as an afterthought, or perhaps a justification. Ned started to look around and his eyes fell on the pile of logs. "Ah, there we are. Just the ticket." He picked up a manageably sized lump of the wood and weighed it thoughtfully in his right hand, making sure he could keep a grip while it did its work. "That's my boy," he said and strode off to the sitting room window, wading through a badly tangled bed of purple periwinkle. "You go and start to unpack the boot, Norman. We'll be inside in a jiffy."

Just as Norman was about to obey orders but before he could add a warning to Ned to be as careful as possible, they were aware of a dark figure standing at the corner of the house. The man quite startled them as they were not expecting intruders.

"You can say that again, sir," said the man. "And for quite some time, I'll be bound." The voice was quite soft but strong and authoritative and belonged to Trevor Hopper, Police Constable Trevor Hopper who had arrived, summoned by the newly installed next door neighbour, just in time to make his first live arrest of the year, there being little crime in East Dean that he didn't know about.

"Oh," said Norman.

"Cripes," said Ned.

"Yes," said PC Hopper, taking out his notebook.

Norman now imagined that he would shortly hear their statutory rights being intoned and he prepared to do one of his faints before the policeman got to the bit about " . . . and may be used in evidence against you" because he didn't want to hear that at all, ever again . . . However, there was no immediate charge and instead Norman remained conscious to hear Ned bluster: "But constable, I can explain!"

"I'm sure you can, sir," said PC Hopper, "but before you do, I would suggest that you put down the offensive weapon."

"What offensive weapon?" Ned began belligerently. Norman caught his eye and put his finger to his lips. "I mean," Ned continued more amenably, "to which offensive weapon are you referring, constable?"

"That 'un, he said, "in yer 'and, sir."

"Oh, the log," said Ned.

"Careful, mind," instructed PC Hopper. "Might be evidence, that."

"But we aren't doing anything wrong, officer," Norman chipped in. "We're just breaking the window so that we can get in. We haven't a key, you see, because when the tree was . . ." Ned interrupted him.

"Leave this to me, Norman. We'll start from the beginning and when the constable hears our story, we can all get in the house and have a cup of tea." Without his teeth, Ned told the story and by the end, PC Hopper put away his notebook, tipped his cap back on his head and put his hands on his hips.

"We're still left with one small problem, sir," he concluded, shaking his head doubtfully. "How are you going to get into the house? I really can't let you go around breaking folks' windows willy nilly now, can I?"

Ned and Norman looked at each other, crestfallen. Ned was specially cross as he'd been so much looking forward to the weekend. Ultimately, it was PC Hopper who solved the problem by employing a time-honoured technique of basic police work. He used his eyes.

"I s'pose, sir," he droned, "we wouldn't 'ave read that note wot's pinned to the back door, would we?" For the first time, they noticed the manila envelope attached by a drawing pin underneath the knocker. The envelope was of a similar brown as the kitchen door and, their eyes not being what they were . . PC Hopper removed the note and looked at it.

"You are Mr Cresswell and Mr Rhodes, I presume?" he said, holding the envelope up to the light, though why he was looking must surely have been his own affair, thought Norman although he reminded himself that it was probably more basic police work, checking for letter bombs or illicit heroin. Norman was so relieved to be off the hook, as he saw it, that PC Hopper had undergone a heroic transformation in his estimation.

"I am," said Ned righteously.

"And which might that be, sir?" enquired the policeman.

"Whom," Ned corrected and then thought better of it.

"I'm Mr Cresswell. And this," he said, graciously indicating Norman, "is my colleague, Mr Rhodes. You are . . .?"

"Police Constable Hopper, sir." Formal introductions having now been made, each party nodded their acquaintance.

"Of course, you can identify yourself, can't you, Mr Cresswell?"

"I just have," Ned replied stiffly. At least I know how to make formal introductions, he thought to himself.

"I meant, sir, do you possess any documentation about your person?"

"Such as?" said Ned to whom documentation meant sheaves of dusty files corroborating evidence.

"Such as, sir," said PC Hopper, his temper now well-tested, "a driving licence or passport." Ned pulled himself erect.

"As a matter of fact, Constable Hopper, I possess both. However, I don't usually bring my passport with me to Sussex. As far as I am aware, Sussex is still a county of the United Kingdom and has not yet declared unilateral independence!" Ned was beginning to sound a little too haughty for his own good but one glance of the now-don't-take-that-tone-with-me variety from the policeman was sufficient discipline. Norman rummaged in his bag.

"Would our pension books do?" he asked, handing the envelope to PC Hopper. He examined the books, looking at each one in turn and then alternately at Ned and Norman before returning the envelope to Norman.

"Thank you, sir," he said to Norman. "Seems to be in order."

"Then shouldn't we open the envelope?" suggested Norman.

"All in good time, sir," said PC Hopper, continuing in his line of duty. "I am already aware of the contents of the envelope," he elaborated and then paused. "Would that be your car in the drive, sir?" he asked Norman in a tone which immediately regressed him into a complete dither.

"The car?" he whispered. "No . . . No. It's not actually my car . . ."

Ned raised his eyebrows to the afternoon sky and, looking up, caught sight of a row of pigeons perched on the ridge of the roof, arranged like a jury, he thought, staring cynically down onto the scene of crime below. Remind me to deal with them tomorrow, thought Ned as he took a deep breath. "The car belongs to me, constable," he said, "and, yes, I do have my driving licence and my insurance in my wallet in the car." He sighed, as though such a question was really too boring to answer. "I suppose you would like to see them?"

"I would indeed be very interested in verifying your statement, sir, but I would be specially interested in seeing the MOT certificate relevant to that old . . . to that vehicle!" Although he had had to avoid the use of the term banger regarding Ned's car, PC Hopper still ended his final request on a note of triumph. Though it seemed that he'd been done out of a breaking and entering with intent, he was determined that he was going to book Ned for something. Norman thought that this time he really was going to faint.

"Certainly, constable," Ned announced confidently, whereas Norman cringed. Norman knew exactly what an MOT certificate was; moreover, he knew exactly where it was. He could see it, lying in the top drawer of the bureau in the sitting room at home in London, along with Ned's driving licence and the insurance certificate where Ned had left them after buying the new road fund licence the previous Wednesday.

"Ned," Norman said hoarsely. "Ned, old chap."

"What?" said Ned, crossly, on his way to the car.

"They're in the bureau drawer. Don't you remember . . ." Norman's revelation brought Ned to a dead stop.

"Oh," he said quietly. "Bloody hell."

"And which bureau drawer might that be?" PC Hopper said glibly. At last, he thought, I've got the old goat at last. He took out a different pad this time as Ned turned slowly to face the music. The arrival of a giant magpie on the roof scattered the pigeons and there was a great beating of wings as the jury fled to the safety of a nearby scots pine.

The magpie sat warily by the chimney stack, its long tail slowly waving up and down, balancing itself. And now the judge, thought Ned as his attention reverted to that other harbinger of bad news, PC Trevor Hopper.

"May I ask what happens now?" asked Ned lamely.

"You have five days, sir," said PC Hopper, relishing every word he spoke and every word he wrote down on the form he was filling out on his pad. He spoke without looking at Ned and the sentence he pronounced was word perfect. "Five days, that is, to produce these documents at any police station."

"Any police station?" asked Ned. "Anywhere?"

"Anywhere in the United Kingdom, that is. I must further advise you that failure to do so could result in prosecution." He fairly drove the tip of his ballpoint into the pad as he finished off his signature with a flourishing full stop and handed the ticket to Ned. He took it, looked at it blankly and exhaled deeply.

"How will you know?" said Norman to the policeman.

"How will I know what, sir?"

"That he's done it. Produced his documents," Norman said, thinking that all this paperwork made Ned look like a much sought-after pedigree dog.

"We have our methods, sir. Don't you worry." Norman shook his head in bewilderment.

"Computers, Norman. That's what he means. Vast computers logging our every step," said Ned knowingly."

I wouldn't go as far as that, sir," said the satisfied policeman. "At least, not regarding most people, that is." Ned ignored him.

"And now, young man," he said. He felt crazily valiant as he was sure that short of a strip search there was no further humiliation he could possibly suffer. "May we have our envelope."

"You may, sir," said PC Hopper. "And," he said, raising his cap to Norman, "may I wish you a very pleasant stay in East Dean. Here for long are we, sir?"

"Er, no," said Norman. "Not long actually. 'Til Monday, Officer."

"Then please, sir, do your colleague a good turn and make sure he gets himself to a police station before Tuesday. Yes?"

"Oh I will, " said Norman. "Scouts' honour." He laughed nervously and the policeman took his leave. The magpie screamed from the roof and Ned looked up.

"And good afternoon to you too," he said, scowling. Norman urged him to open their envelope and, inside it they found the key."

And there's a note," Norman said. "Read it. Who's it from?" Ned removed the note, rather a nice note on rather nice notepaper.

"Mrs Croker-Symes asked me to leave you the key," Ned read. "Perhaps you would be free for sherry after Church on Sunday. Heard tons about you both."

"But who's it from?" insisted Norman."Someone called Withers," Ned said. "Genevieve Withers." Ned folded the note and stuffed it into his pocket. "At last," he said, putting the key into the latch, "perhaps we can now have our tea!"

FIVE

Ba's house had never been a place in which the cares of the real world were able to survive. In fact, cares seemed to evaporate on entry. Ned opened the front door and helped Norman in with their luggage. Before distributing the bags and boxes to either bedroom or kitchen, Norman filled the kettle for tea, even though they had no milk as yet. However, he had brought a lemon with him, not so much for tea but with an eye to cocktails. It might, he thought, just be warm enough to have drinks in the garden. The clocks had gone forward just the previous weekend and the lighter evenings were back.

Both Norman and Ned loved the summer as neither could remember anything particularly happy ever having occurred during the winters. Ned called the English climate the off and on variety, six months off and six months on, and truly believed that he could tell the day when Mother Nature flicked the switch.

"Now what are we going to do about my teeth?" Ned asked.

"First things first," said Norman. "Tea or teeth?"

"Teeth," said Ned. "Where are they?" Norman opened his bag and removed the teeth which he had wrapped in a paper napkin he had saved from one of their favourite watering places, a tea shop in Richmond. He had been saving the napkin for an emergency. "I know," Ned said, "there was always a bottle of tar remover in that cupboard. That'll do it." Norman was not so sure.

"I rather think it might melt the teeth as well," he said. "Now let me think, what would be best?"

"How about turps?" suggested Ned. "Or paint stripper?"

Norman shook his head.

"No, I honestly think boiling water." Ned looked

horrified.

"D'you mean to tell me you intend to cook my teeth? In a saucepan, on the stove?" Now it was Norman's turn to exercise a little authority.

"Ned! Would I?" He paused, rather enjoying Ned's anxiety and his temporary dependence, for it was a rare moment. "We put the teeth in a Pyrex bowl and pour boiling water over them. Like making a jelly. We stir them round and round and the toffee will melt away. Magic!" Ned was not thoroughly convinced by Norman's magic but then as Norman always referred to anything scientific as magic, Ned was prepared to be persuaded as Norman's argument seemed to contain an basis, although unintended, of science. As the kettle boiled at that point in the experiment, Ned conceded.

"Alright, but be careful, Norman. I don't want to live for the next three days on mashed banana and soup." Norman found a Pyrex mixing bowl large enough to contain the teeth and a reasonable amount of boiling water.

"Perhaps if I could get most of it off," he said,"You could just put one plate in your mouth at a time and keep it there until the really sticky bits dissolved."

"We'll see," said Ned grudgingly, regretting bitterly all the tons of sweets he must have consumed in his life which, and only which, had been the cause of his current dental state. Norman set the bowl on the edge of the dresser and put the teeth in the bottom. He filled the bowl with boiling water, took a wooden spoon out of the cracked Clarice Cliff jug on the window sill and began to stir. Ned got down on his knees and peered at the swirling teeth. The water began to turn pink and bits of toffee and grit floated away from their sugary mooring.

"How are we doing," asked Norman. "Perhaps I ought to change the water?"

"Not much happening down here," said Ned from the floor. "I think perhaps you should." So Norman poured off the water and refilled the bowl. "Right," said Ned, "start stirring." More brown water and more toffee circled around the bowl but it was not half a minute before the two plates came apart. Norman poured off the water and after sluicing the plates under the cold tap handed them back to Ned.

"Marvellous," said Ned and gratefully inserted his gnashers. "Ummm," he said, rolling his tongue around his mouth. "Tastes good too. Perhaps we should patent it."

Norman laughed and refilled the kettle whilst Ned wandered off to do his usual bit of exploring. Ned was one of the nosiest people ever created. To whomsoever's house they went, it would not be long before Norman would realise Ned was missing and it would never be for the obvious reason as Ned had a bladder of infinite flexibility. No, Ned would be peering into cupboards, under beds and in drawers, incapable of controlling his snoopiness and quite guiltless if ever discovered by their host or hostess. Most of their friends were quite used to Ned's idiosyncrasy by now and would merely call out something like: "Ned, don't bother. I haven't opened that cupboard since you were here last time", although there had been occasions when events had taken a more embarrassing turn.

"I say, Norman," Ned said from the sitting room. "Just come in here . . . so kind of her." Norman finished setting the tea tray with the green Berylware cups and saucers. He remembered buying them with Biddy in Gamages on the day Chamberlain returned from Munich. He joined Ned in the sitting room. On the dining room table, for the rooms were as one, there was a posy of primroses in an egg cup and another note which Ned was reading.

"Hope you find everything as you'd like it," he read. "I've put some milk in the fridge for you and turned on the hot water at lunchtime. Do try and come on Sunday."

"Adorable," said Norman. "Genevieve Withers I suppose?"

"Yes," Ned said nodding. "Seems as though Ba has found a new friend. Good to have someone keeping an eye on the place. Isn't that tea ready yet?"

"Coming up, said Norman, "and now it'll be with milk. I hadn't even thought to look in the fridge. You'll have to go down to the village afterwards or it's going to be fish and chips in Eastbourne tonight. I only brought some gin with me," he said, disappearing back to the kitchen.

"What? No sherry?" Ned said. Norman threw open the hatch from the kitchen.

"Of course sherry," he said. "You look after your department and I'll look after mine. When have I ever forgotten anything really important! I think that after that run-in with the officer you should be more careful what you say to people."

"Well today was such a rush," Ned said defensively.

"That's my excuse," replied Norman as the kettle finally boiled. He used the last of the Earl Grey and made a mental note to get more tomorrow. "No biscuits either, I'm afraid."

"Inside or out," Ned called to Norman.

"In, I think. Just have your tea and then do the shopping. It's ten to five already." Norman poured milk into the jug and took the tea tray through to the sitting room.

"No rush," said Ned. "The grocer's always open 'til six and we only need food for tonight." He rubbed his hands as Norman poured the tea. "At last," he said. "Mouth's as dry as a vulture's eye."

"Haven't heard that one before," Norman said, sinking into an armchair with his tea. "Quite good. And clean for once." Ned sipped at his tea.

"One of Dulcie's," he said. Norman looked at him. For once, Ned's face did not betray the annoyance which was usually immediately apparent after mentioning Dulcie. Poor Ned, Norman thought. It always irritated Ned when his memories struggled to the surface. It was hard for him to keep them at bay, a conscious struggle he only occasionally lost. Not that he wanted to forget, but he couldn't bear the pain of remembering. Pain was a nuisance and Ned had no room in his life for nuisance. It must be the house, Norman thought, working its old spell.

"What a nice old house you are," said Norman aloud. Ned nodded and finished his tea. He had, as he always boasted, an asbestos mouth and seemed impervious to even the hottest tea and coffee, in fact the hotter, the better which worried Norman since lately reading that tea, if drunk too hot causes cancer. But then, as Ned always said, what doesn't nowadays? Ned remained in his chair for a moment, lost in his own, private thoughts and apparently oblivious that he had even mentioned Dulcie's name. Norman's words broke the daydream.

"Yes, it is," Ned said. "A very nice old house." But he got up quickly, so terminating further reminiscence. "Right. I'm off," he announced and went through the check list. "Wallet, money, keys . . ."

"And shopping bag," Norman added. "They might not have carrier bags here. Oh," he added, also getting up from his chair, "and can you take these egg boxes to the butcher? I know he appreciates them."

"So that's what's in that huge box," Ned said. "Hardly left room in the boot for the cases."

"I always save eggboxes, said Norman who saved everything, stamps, silver tops from milk bottles; he had enough plastic flowerpots to open a nursery and when asked as to why, always gave the same answer: "You never know". What it was he thought he was never going to know remained unspecified. Somehow, Norman managed to insert the cardboard box containing the egg cartons under Ned's arm and Ned left. Norman stood at the French windows and watched Ned sauntering down the drive and then turned his attention to the room. Though Genevieve Withers, or the previous visitors, had left it in an apparently immaculate state, Norman couldn't resist a bit of tidying up.

SIX

As Ned came down the drive, whistling as he walked, a pair of net curtains twitched at the front windows of the house next door. Ned thought he saw something but couldn't be sure. He hated net curtains, especially the new variety, popular in bedrooms for some reason, which arched in the middle. Ned and never been able to understand this fashion. Surely, he thought, if anyone was going to look into a bedroom window, the bit of the glass that wasn't covered by the curtain would be the exact spot that would reveal the very bit of a person that was supposed to be hidden. He shook his head, adjusted the egg box and strode off purposefully to do his shopping.

He passed one house called *Foxhole* and stopped for a moment. The house stood exactly on a piece of the Downs where he had once lost something and the memory of it made him laugh. Oh, he thought, if only the current owners knew what they were sitting on! They, the current owners, were either gardeners of the got-to variety or else they had little imagination. The lonicera hedge was trimmed to a meticulous, short-back-and-sides alignment and the lawn was shorn with a similar lack of detail. And there were no flowers.

Ned marched on, remembering the little copse of trees that had stood there during the war and the aconites and wild anenomes covering the ground on which they had lain. There had been no lights then as there were hardly any houses and overhead they had heard the drone of wave after wave of bombers. Somehow, for those few hours and those few days, the war hadn't mattered and for once he and Dulcie had forgotten the realities and indulged merely in the dreams of life, making wild plans and looking only and always to the tomorrows. That had been Ned's promise to her, that he would always look forward, never back. But in making that promise, he had never imagined how hard it would be at times to keep it.

His thoughts were disturbed when he stepped out of the road and onto the grass to allow a rather beautiful Rolls Royce motor car to pass. In fact there was plenty of room for both Ned and the car but Ned had always felt rather deferential about Rolls Royces. The man behind the wheel smiled and waved, prompting even Ned to return the acknowledgement. Gosh, he thought, perhaps there's hope for the old place yet and chuckled. Even Ba, with all that beer money, had never splashed out that far.

Mr Arnatt's East Dean had been built on the north side of the Brighton-Eastbourne road. To the south, on the sea side, there was an altogether different East Dean, which had its own village green. Ned approached the shops. There were six, all of them newly built except the grocers which had been established in the conversion of what had been once a barn, hence its name, *The Barn*. In addition, there was a hairdresser, an odds and sods shop where everything from a parsley seed to a bridge napkin was displayed and a tea shop which also purveyed a fresh daily range of home-baked cakes. Then there was *The Barn*, separating the first three shops from the butchers, which Ned recalled was rather expensive but had frightfully good meat. Finally, there was the newsagent and tobacconist. Shan't be in there much, Ned reminded himself having renounced the deadly weed. His renouncement, however spiritually strong, was a bit weak in the flesh department and this presented a daily temptation. He was after all, he told himself, on holiday and why not? He thought better of it as he remembered last winter, the bronchitis and poor Norman running up and downstairs every five minutes but he knew it would not be long before the devil would again be at his elbow. Cocktail time was always the worst. Gin seemed to taste too polite without a cigarette to keep it company as it washed down the little red lane.

In front of the shops, on either side of *The Barn*, there were parking spaces and the whole area at any time of day was usually bustling with people hello-ing and how-are-you-ing in what was a very pleasant social arena.

What's up, thought Ned, as he spied the empty car park? The place was like a graveyard. He checked his watch and it was as he thought, twenty-past-five. Of course, everything was shut. He went up to the butcher's and peered in. The slabs were as clean as a whistle. The grocer's too was locked and barred. Ned saw the cover on the till. Oh well, he thought, fish and chips it is and began to walk back to the house, abandoning Norman's egg cartons on the pavement outside the butcher's door. He passed a woman who was wearing rubber gloves and one of the nylon housecoats which seemed to have become de rigeur. The woman was planting out some petunias into a planter which looked to Ned to have been made out of a car tyre.

"Good afternoon," said Ned. "Early closing?" It was a car tyre, after all. Very odd, thought Ned. The woman looked at him suspiciously, not at all friendly.

"Yes," she said, returning her attention to the work in hand. "Five o'clock."

"Good Lord," said Ned determined to make a bit of conversation. "Whatever next. Wasn't like that in the old days."

"Wouldn't know," the woman said. "We've only just moved in." The dibbing continued; rather desultory dibbing, thought Ned.

"Didn't a Mrs Janes live here before?" Ned tried again.

"Wouldn't know," the woman repeated. "They died, whoever it was."

"Hmmm," said Ned, realising that there wasn't much headway to be made here. "Comes to us all, I suppose," Ned concluded cheerfully. Instead of replying, the woman dropped her dibber and burst into tears, rushing into the house and slamming the door. Whoops, thought Ned, who had obviously put his foot in it again. He looked around him, feeling somewhat responsible but as the woman did not re-appear there was little he could do. Must remember to tell Norman about that, thought Ned as he walked back up the hill and reminded himself that he had not done too well that day as far as the making of new acquaintances.

Norman too had seen the beautiful Rolls Royce and so had the nextdoor neighbour who, safe behind the purdah created by the net curtains, watched Norman watching the Rolls Royce. The car stopped and reversed into the drive of the house across the road so that it, and Ned's Mini, were ranged on opposite sides of the road facing each other. Ah, thought Norman, that's nice for Min; she's got someone to play with and jolly good company too. A man got out the Rolls carrying a briefcase and a cardboard box and went into his house. Norman stood for a moment at the French windows. He was just going to turn away and return to his unpacking when he saw it. He froze. Very slowly, down from the pelmet above the window, on an ever-lengthening thread, descended the biggest and most active spider that Norman had ever seen. There must be a word for people who had spiderphobia although Norman couldn't in his wildest imaginings even bring himself to even *look* at the word spider. Ever onwards came the beast, its hairy legs waving in the air. Norman's panic had paralysed him. He knew he'd stopped breathing and could hear his heart pounding in his chest. The spider stopped just as it reached a point in space directly in Norman's eyeline and he screamed. The scream released him from the paralysis and he ran out of the room and through the front door, still screaming. In the garden, he burst into tears but only after his initial screams and brought the man with the Rolls Royce running from his house. He ran across the road and into *Barthorpe*. Poor Norman was shaking and helpless with tears.

"What's wrong?" said the neighbour. "Are you alright?" He looked with alarm at Norman's tear-stained face and his ashen complexion. "What's happened?" Norman was speechless and, worse, he felt so foolish and yet it was a real fear. Mice, frogs, snakes, wasps – all of these presented no problems to him but spiders were his private hell. The man was very comforting and managed to calm Norman sufficiently for him to catch his breath and speak.

"Oh," he said, "I'm so sorry . . . Really I am. You're going to think me quite ridiculous."

"No I won't," he said, " but just tell me, what happened?"

"And you won't laugh?" Norman said. "You'll think me quite pathetic."

"No I won't," said the stranger gently. "We can't have you being so upset."

"Well," Norman began, still not absolutely sure whether he should not just wait for Ned to come back. "It's a . . ." He tried to say spider but the word stuck somewhere. He shivered. "Can I whisper it?" The man bent his ear and Norman whispered the word.

"Oh," he said, with all seriousness, "I'm just the same about maggots. Can't abide them; I'd run a mile from a maggot."

"Really?" said Norman, much encouraged by the revelation. "They don't bother me a bit. My father was a great fisherman and I was always fascinated by his tin of maggots. I used to tip the tin out onto a newspaper and have races with them." It was the man's turn to shudder and Norman smiled, coyly. "Oh, sorry!"

"Well, I suppose a phobia shared is a phobia halved," his new friend said. "But, come on. You can't stay out here all night, so I think I'd better go and do battle with the monster. Where was it?"

"In the sitting room. Above the French window," Norman said. "What will you do?"

"Find it first," he said.

"But you won't kill it, will you?" Norman said earnestly. "I mean it's not its fault, is it?"

"Let me find it first, Mr . . .?" Norman realised that neither he nor his rescuer knew each others names.

"I'm so sorry, how impolite. I'm Norman Rhodes." He held out his hand.

"Tom Maxwell," said the new acquaintance. "Pleased to meet you, Mr Rhodes."

"You must have driven past Mr Cresswell, my friend. We're just here for the weekend. He's just gone down to the shops. He'd know what to do in an instant. Nothing scares him. Do you know Mrs Croker-Symes?"

"Indeed, I do." Tom Maxwell paused. "Look, before we go on, let me get rid of the unmentionable for you." And he went into the house. Norman had to walk to the bottom of the garden before being able to force herself to look round. Mr Maxwell appeared in the window, bending and craning, for he was rather tall, hunting the . . . thing. Then he went away. Then he came back with a stool and something else in his hand but Norman couldn't see what it was.

"Norman! Who's that in the house!" It was Ned. Norman turned to see him appear at the gate. "Are you hurt? Who is it?" Norman quickly re-assured him.

"No, I'm perfectly alright. Now. Thanks to Mr Maxwell. He heard me scream."

"Scream?" Ned said in alarm. "Whatever for? Oh! Don't tell me you found a . . . a . . ."

"Yes," Norman said quickly, interrupting him. "I did. It was horrible, Ned."

"Wait here," Ned ordered and marched off into the house, where he found Mr Maxwell standing on a stool in front of the French windows with a feather duster and a jam jar.

"Not yet, Mr Rhodes!" Tom warned.

"It's alright," said Ned, "It's Mr Cresswell, carry on." Mr Maxwell looked briefly over his shoulder and smiled at Ned.

"Nearly got him," he said, tickling somewhere under the pelmet with the duster. "Bit cat and mouse at the moment. He knows, you see and he's dug his heels in."

"Probably a she," commented Ned. "They're always the bigger. Usually eat their husbands, you know."

"I know the feeling," said Mr Maxwell deep in a concentrated battle of wits with the spider. "Ah! Got you!"

"Well done, sir!" cried Ned, as Mr Maxwell stepped off the stool with the spider in the jam jar. "Ugly brute, aren't you?" he said, peering at the monster. "Into the garden with you and you can chew up a few greenfly and earn your keep."

"Or her next husband," remarked Mr Maxwell with some feeling. He proffered the jam jar to Ned. "Do you want to take over?" said Mr Maxwell. "I've already been told that you're completely fearless and I understand that mercy is to be the order of the court."

"Absolutely," said Ned. "I was once a buddhist, for a while, and that's one of the things that rubbed off. Can't abide unecessary cruelty."

"And your friend?" asked Mr Maxwell.

"He's just squeamish," said Ned and marched off with the spider. At the front door, he called to Norman.

"Coast's clear. You can come back now." Ned exited by the back door as Norman came in to the front hall.

"Oh, thank you, Mr Maxwell. I don't know what I would have done without you. You will stay for a drink, won't you?" gushed Norman gratefully.

"Well, I . . ."

"Oh, please. It's the least we can do." Norman realised he was flirting, just a little. Now that he came to think about it, Mr Maxwell was very attractive.

"How could I possibly refuse," he said graciously. "But I must go and close my front door first. Shan't be long."

"I'll leave the door on the latch," said Norman, as Ned returned, having disposed of the spider as far away from the house as possible.

"Seems a reasonable sort of chap," he said as Norman went for ice. "Honestly, Norman. They're always more afraid of you than you realise."

"Nonsense, Ned. How could Mr Maxwell possibly be afraid of me?"

"I meant the bloody spider," said Ned. Norman ignored him.

"Now," wondered Norman aloud. "I wonder if he drinks gin? Did you buy any nuts, Ned?"

"Didn't buy anything," Ned replied. "Everything shuts at five." Mr Maxwell returned and overheard him. "Since when did all that start? When we first came here, shop hours didn't exist."

"Mind you," Norman pointed out, "there was only one shop . . . and the post office in those days."

"And the bakery," added Ned. He shook his head. "A

pretty pass, Mr Maxwell? Wouldn't you say?" They were standing in the hall.

"Manners, manners," said Norman. "Please come in, Mr Maxwell. I'm so sorry. We've only just arrived, you see and it's been a rather hectic day, all in all." He ushered them in to the sitting room. "We've only gin, I'm afraid. Or sherry?"

"What? No tonic either?" Ned asked.

"Yes, tonic we have," said Norman.

"Gin and tonic's fine by me," said Mr Maxwell, seating himself on the sofa. "I've only been here six months and so I really can't tell you much about the place as far as the shops are concerned. I only get down at weekends and I bring everything with me." Norman handed round the drinks.

"Odd sort of place for a chap like you to move into," said Ned bluntly.

"Ned!" Norman said, horrified. Mr Maxwell laughed.

"And what sort of a chap would that be?" he asked, toasting the gentlemen with his glass.

"Cheers," Ned said.

"And thank you," Norman added.

"Sort of chap with a Royce," continued Ned. "Sorry, couldn't help but notice it. Lovely motors. And British through and through."

"Thank you, Mr Cresswell," he said with a humility which was instantly attractive.

"Oh," Ned said, being no less immune to masculine charm than Norman, "Please. Call me Ned. Everyone does." Mr Maxwell looked slightly uncomfortable for it was an unusual name and not one of the names he was expecting.

"Ned," Norman repeated. "It's a . . . a you know . . . a thingummy. An abbreviation?"

"No. Acronym," Ned said. "N-E-D," he said, spelling the letters.

"Oh," said Mr Maxwell intelligently. He knew the meaning of acronym but, as to why, he was completely in the dark.

"Nathan Evelyn Dermot," Norman said.
"Ugh!" said Ned. "Hated it. I mean, can you imagine going through life with a name like Nathan? Desperate. Parents never realise what they're lumbering their children with."
"So he's always been Ned," said Norman. "I've always been Norman so, please call me Norman, won't you?"
"That can't be an acronym," said Mr Maxwell, "surely?" Norman giggled. "And I'm Tom. All right?" They raised their glasses to their new selves.
"So," said Norman to Ned. "No dinner for us tonight? Jolly good job you had that enormous lunch."
"Starvation rations," Ned said. "Or," he added impishly, "Fish and chips?"
"You'll have to go to Eastbourne," Tom said. "Or, alternatively, you could come across and have a bite with me."
"Oh, we couldn't," said Norman demurely. "We couldn't impose."
"We could," said Ned.
"But . . .," said Norman.
"But nothing. Thank you Tom. Accepted. What's on the menu?" he asked eagerly, visualising a juicy steak. "And by the way, do you play Scrabble?"
"It has been known," Tom replied. "But something tells me I'm going to lose."
"Then we'll both be on the same side," said Norman. "I always lose. Especially on holiday."
"Not that I'd mind losing," Tom said. "After all, in a game of words. I'm hardly a match for Celia Enderby, am I?" Ned looked at Norman and Norman looked at Ned. "Or Catherine Whitehead?" he said. "Or even Kate Jackson?" He paused.
"Shall I go on?"
"Well, blow me down," said Ned in astonishment. "How on earth did you know?"
"Mrs Croker-Symes," said Tom.
"Big mouth Ba," said Ned. "Wait 'til I next see her!"
"Really, Ned. Why shouldn't people know? It's not a

state secret or anything."

"Come on, Tom," Ned said, "out with it. How did you know?"

"Found out when I inherited the house," Tom said. "Piles of 'em. I couldn't understand why someone like Annie would have had such an inordinate fondness for paperback fiction. So, I took over the place the weekend that Mrs Croker-Symes happened to be here and . . . I asked."

"And she blabbed," humphed Ned. "Who else knows?"

"You must have been invited to the party of the year, surely?" said Tom. "Genevieve's a vicious organiser."

"The Withers woman," Ned said.

"Oh please don't take Um, Ned," Norman begged. "After all, she did leave us with some milk."

"Hell's teeth," said Ned, "I need another drink." He got up from his chair. "Anyone join me?"

"I don't think I'm quite understanding all this," said Tom Maxwell, who was indeed at a loss to fathom out why such a prolific, if elusive, author should be so put out over the unmasking of his various literary selves. Norman enlightened Tom as to the less complicated reasons for Ned wanting as few people as possible to know that not only was he Celia Enderby, Catherine Whitehead and Kate Jackson but had also been, at one time or another, Baron von Herzig, Robert E. Lee and Bob Martin. Ned filled their glasses with a second round.

"It's just a job, you see," said Ned, butting in. "Who the hell wants to go round the place yapping about their work. It pays the builder and Rimanda and the ludicrous tax bills and gets us about the place." He omitted to say that getting about the place included expeditions to anywhere from Tasmania to Macchu Pichu to Disneyland. "I mean, what do you do?" Ned felt oddly comfortable with their new friend, not at all inhibited as he usually did in the company of strangers.

"Not a lot," replied Tom. "At the moment."

"See," Ned said, quite his bombastic self again. "You're pretty cagey too."

"If Tom doesn't want to say, I'm sure he has very good reasons," Norman interrupted, doing his best to defend Tom from an onslaught. But, he wondered to himself, what does he do? Tom smiled mysteriously.

"Go on," he challenged. "what would the famous Celia Enderby make of the mystery?"

"She wouldn't make anything," Ned said. "She's the one that writes about slop."

"Romance," said Norman, interpreting. "Try Kate Jackson."

"Too easy," said Ned. "Too many clues."

"Go on," said Tom who could see that Ned was now in top gear. He sat with his drink, the glass to his lips with a faraway look which was focused somewhere through the French windows.

"Yes," he said slowly. "It's coming . . ." He paused and then snapped his fingers. "Got it. When you said 'Annie' that was Ann Wingfield. You remember her, Norman. Used to live over there, where Tom is now. Ann Wingfield had a sister who married a chap called Maxwell, something to do with . . . what was it, Norman?"

"Typewriters," Norman said. "You got your first typewriter in 1946 and that was a Maxwell."

"That must have been the Elite," said Tom.

"Ned called his the Blunderer," said Norman. "No offence."

"None taken," replied Tom, smiling widely as he listened to Ned's denouement.

"And," continued Ned, "I seem to remember reading that Maxwell was sold last year to some American outfit and as you are Tom Maxwell, I believe you are one of those Maxwells. I can also remember that Ba told me that your aunt died at about that time and so, hey presto, here you are." Tom applauded.

"Well done," he said.

"And here's something else, young man," Ned said, flushed with success and not a little gin for his drinks were never small, "you won't remember, but I taught you to swim. I remember you very well, all four skinny limbs of you, flailing away down on the beach with your Aunt and your Mother convinced that either I was going to drown you or that you were going to drown me!"

"Of course," said Norman and looked at Tom more closely wondering how it was that forty years could have gone by so quickly. "You told me all about him."

"Now I am embarrassed," said Tom, putting down his glass on the hearth. He looked at his watch. "And, I must be going or you'll get nothing to eat." He got up.

"Are you sure we can't help?" Norman said. "I feel terribly guilty." He rose from his chair to show Tom to the door.

"Don't," said Ned, "he still owes me for the swimming lessons. And," he added, "what's more, from the City page in the *Telegraph*, I seem to remember that he can afford it."

"Ned!" said Norman. "You really are awful!" They showed Tom Maxwell to the door. "And thank you once again," Norman said. The sun had come out and the sky was clear with only a whisper of high cloud showing far out over the sea. They walked with Tom Maxwell to the gate and waved as he crossed the road and into his own house.

"Nice chap," said Ned. "Glad he didn't drown. Of course," he added, "what else could have happened with me as his swimming teacher?"

Norman laughed. "Lovely evening, Ned."

"Marvellous . . . just perfect."

Somewhere, not too many gardens away, someone was having a bonfire and the smoke wreathed through the hedges and shrubs, not in clouds but in wisps on the calm evening air.

"Takes me back," said Ned. "Odd smells like a bonfire or that grass this afternoon. Somehow tells you that everything's still alright. D'you remember Frank Howard?"

"Your old gardener when your family was still at *Fairlea*. Yes," Norman said, the reminiscences flooding back. *Fairlea* had been Ned's family home.

"I remember sitting round the fires he used to make at the back of the greenhouse? After he'd gone home, I'd sit for hours and pretend that I was an Indian chief at my camp fire or . . . or an explorer in Africa," murmured Ned.

"The world was our's," said Norman. "Then." He sighed. "It's all such a long time ago, Ned. So much to miss, so many people to miss. I wonder what Mumfie would have thought of it all now."

"You haven't talked about Mumfie in years; what made you think about her?" said Ned, remembering Norman's old nanny.

"Those." Norman pointed to the corner of the garden.

"That clump of white bluebells. Cyril and I brought her down here with us one year. We picked her up from the station at Eastbourne and she gave us some bulbs from the garden of my parents' home, just before it was demolished."

"You mean she stole them?" Ned laughed.

"Not exactly steal," Norman said. "She said she'd 'come by 'em'. Anyway, there they are . . . Mumfie's whitebells. She said it was the nicest holiday she'd ever had." Norman paused. "She only ever had two holidays in her life."

Ned shivered. Suddenly it was chilly. The warmth of the day had created a mist over the sea and a faintly salty breeze was urging little patches of it up the valley from the coast. "Come on, Norman. We'd better make ourselves ship-shape."

They were just about to go back into the house when Norman saw something moving in one of the flowerbeds. "Oh, Ned, look. There's a cat in the tulips." Two sleepy yellow eyes peered out from a hiding place in the tulip bed. As Norman approached, making pussy noises, the eyes blinked and the cat yawned. It was a tortoise shell, mainly black but with tan and white blotches.

"There, kitty-poo . . . hello, kit-kit," said Norman as he bent down at the edge of the tulips and held out his hand. At first the cat looked at Norman's fingers rather disdainfully and then decided that the fingers might provide a welcome scratch and so succumbed, nuzzling Norman's hand with its whiskers and arching its back in friendship. "There's a pussy poodle . . . there's a girl . . ." Norman wittered on in what he fondly imagined was a language comprehensible to all cats the world over and, in truth, it had never failed him. From over-fed literary cats in London to the rapaciously hungry street cats of Morocco, Norman always got his message across.

"Norman," Ned said sternly. "That is someone else's pet." Ned knew Norman's propensity for collecting things and cats were high on the list of potential acquisitions. However, after many years of successive generations of feline friends, he and Norman had pledged that there were to be no more. Their last bereavement had left Norman exhausted as Orlando, tenacious to the last, had spent the last three months of his life wrapped in an old gardening jacket with a hot water bottle on top of the boiler and required re-hydration every three hours with milk and water from a teaspoon. Three weekend trips to old friends had had to be cancelled and Ned had been forced to resort to invention, which he loathed, in order to complete a pre-revolutionary Russian romance he was writing as their visit to St Petersburg had also to be cancelled. Even Norman agreed with him, after the emotional interment at the bottom of their tiny garden, that Orlando would have to be the last.

"I know, Ned. I know. It's just that it's so adorable." Norman could not resist the irresistible and picked up the cat, who seemed to have no objection. In fact, the adoration appeared to be entirely mutual.

"She," corrected Ned. "She is so adorable. I mean, not adorable exactly but female. All tortoiseshells are. Come on, Norman, put the cat down and come in and finish your drink." Reluctantly, Norman deposited his new friend, who made no attempt to move but watched, tail twitching, waving gently from side to side, as Norman walked away across the grass. Ned saw the net curtains moving in their neighbours' bungalow as he had suspected he had seen them earlier. He made a note, for he now had confirmation that the newly arrived occupants of Ba's house were under observation by the natives. Moreover, he further suspected, after the unannounced arrival of PC Hopper earlier in the afternoon, that this particular native was not particularly friendly. With one last look behind him, Norman joined Ned on the step and they went into the house. Pussy cat remained where she was, looking rather disappointed, Norman fancied, as the front door closed.

When Ned went to his room to change what he called his driving clothes before going across to Tom Maxwell's, Norman remained downstairs on the pretext of tidying up, knowing that he was physically unable to leave the cat alone. He opened the front door, just a crack, and peeped out into the garden. Pussy immediately got up and sidled up to the porch. Norman stretched his arm through the crack and tickled the cat's ears.

"Hello, kitty . . . Now what are you after? Little drop of milky, isn't it . . . That's what you need." But Ned had heard the door open.

"Norman," he shouted down the stairs. "Are you playing with that cat?"

"No."

"Then what are you doing at the front door?"

"Putting the milk bottle out."

"Why?" called Ned, who was only prolonging the conversation out of curiousity to see what sort of excuse Norman would come up with, for he knew very well what Norman was up to.

"For the milkman," said Norman, now embarrassed and trying to shut the door as quietly as possible without decapitating the cat who had now quite made up its mind that a little drop of milky was indeed what nice pussies should get for their suppers.

"Norman, if you don't leave that cat alone, I shan't be responsible for the consequences!"

Right, thought Norman, if I can't go to the cat, then the cat can come to me and he decided that he would leave the kitchen window open, with just a tiny saucer of milk on the sill, just to see what would happen. It was very naughty of him but a little wilfulness was not entirely alien to Norman's character. "Alright, Ned," he called. "The cat's gone now." And he opened the kitchen window before going upstairs to change.

SEVEN

The evening at Tom's proved to be a great success and was, upon his own admission, entirely catered by Marks and Spencer. Even Norman, a staunch advocate of the fresh over the fast, became a convert. Before they played Scrabble and before he got totally pickled, Ned did a little investigating. One of the reasons for his uninhibited snooping did in fact lie with his own strange humility. Although he could never bring himself to ask anyone what they thought of his books, he did love it when he found the titles produced by his pseudonyms on people's bookshelves. He was also never averse to totting up the royalties which had devolved from the purchase of the books.

It seemed that Ann Wingfield's house had changed little since Tom had assumed occupancy. Apart from a large new refrigerator in the kitchen and the installation of central heating, Tom had made few alterations. Annie had been an odd fish, extraordinarily parsimonious as many older folk can be. Ba dined out on her stories of Annie's economy, her favourite being the tale of Annie making her own scouring powder out of ground up cakes of the ends of soap and similarly pulverised chalk from the beach. Her clothes too, although of the very best, were a veritable patchwork of precision darning. It was as though she hadn't bought anything new since the thirties when she had moved into the house opposite Ba's. Ned felt very moved as he came upon the shelf in Annie's bedroom upon which the paperback volumes were arranged. The books must have been the only extravagances Annie had ever allowed herself and Ned felt all the more complimented by the fact that Annie had never raised the subject of the authorship when Ned had been visiting in the past.

Downstairs, feeling that he could confide in Tom,

Norman explained the reason for Ned's abscence. He laughed.

He won't find much in this house, I'm afraid," he said. "If my wife's private eye couldn't turn anything up, I rather think Ned will be just as disappointed." Norman's ears pricked up.

"Oh," he said, instantly fascinated. Should he, he wondered? Bother it, he thought, why not . . . "Do you mean your wife had you followed?" Tom nodded. "Is she . . . I mean, was she . . . Are you still married?" He sat more upright in the armchair and after Tom had poured yet another glass of the excellent Marks and Spencer '91, Norman heard all about Tom's pending divorce, remembering every detail for a cocoa session later, which he rather fancied would not end until the small hours. Upstairs, Ned was on the point of tearing himself away from an examination of Annie's wardrobe which confirmed that Annie's clothes had indeed been couture house originals, when he happened to look out of the window. From the house next door crept a mysterious figure wearing a woolly hat. After preliminary scrutiny of the otherwise empty road, the woman, for it was indeed a woman, walked to the gate of *Barthorpe,* peered into the garden and, apparently satisfied that there was no one there, opened the gate and went into the garden. She seemed to be searching for something. Under bushes and shrubs, beneath the hedge, peering into trees and parting the clumps of spring flowers. Ned was intrigued and completely baffled until he saw that the woman was carrying a pet's collar and lead.

Well, thought Ned, she'll be the cat's mother and then realised that the woman was also the native who had been lurking behind the net curtains all day. Ned went into the bathroom and pulled the chain, as he always did, thinking that the sound of the flush covered his tracks. Norman called from downstairs.

"Don't bother to flush the loo, Ned. I've told Tom all about you." Ned came down the stairs. Tom had by now exhausted his tale of woe, although Norman thought he displayed more regret rather than relief and had produced the Scrabble board. Norman cleared what remained of the plates and the Scabble board was installed on the dining table. This was obviously to be a proper game.

"Who's the bimbo in that bungaloid next door," Ned asked Tom as he took his place and, without being asked, took his letter out of the bag. Manners, thought Norman but said nothing, although he did think he might ask what a bimbo was.

"Tell you the truth, I've no idea," said Tom. They had by now each taken a letter. Ned, with his usual assumption of pre-ordained victory, showed his C whilst Norman displayed an N. Tom, very casually, capped the lot with an A. A look of irritation rather than concern flashed across Ned's face.

"Oh," he said, "you start, I suppose." Norman smirked. Perhaps once, he thought, just this once . . .

"Why?" Tom said to Ned.

"No reason," Ned said, arranging his letters in their wooden rack. "Has she been here long?"

"She came after me," said Tom. "Maybe three months. She only ever appears when she's looking for her cat. She knocked on my door at seven-thirty one morning." He looked at his Q and his U and then at the other letters and smiled.

"Bit early," observed Ned, deep in concentration and infuriated at the seven vowels which stared back at him, three of which were E's. "Seems somewhat obsessive." Norman began to feel a little guilty about the milk on the kitchen window sill but decided that it was too late to redress the situation. He was also rather pleased with his two blanks which, like everything else that might come in useful, he always kept until the end of the game.

"Yes," Tom went on, "does a bit. She got off on the wrong foot with your friend Mrs Croker-Symes about the sycamore tree. Claimed it was dangerous." He put out QUIETLY and sat back in his seat. "Who's scoring?"

"Me," Norman said. "I always score. Ned hates sums." For once, Ned was speechless and stared open-mouthed in the face of what could prove to be grim defeat. His aversion to sums did not, in this case, impair his mental arithmetic as he quickly calculated that Tom had totted up a nifty eighty eight with QUIETLY.

"Is that eighty eight?" Norman asked, somehow managing to repress a hoot of delight. "Jolly good score, Tom. Good, isn't it, Ned?" Ned coughed and cleared his throat.

"Not bad," he said. "Not as good as the hundred and ten I got in Australia but, not bad." He wondered what on earth he could do with three E's, an I, two O's and a U.

"Ned! When was that?" said Norman disbelievingly.

"I wasn't playing with you at the time," Ned said. "Had a bit of competition that night."

"Like tonight?" Norman murmured.

"Sorry, didn't catch that," said Ned who used Tom's Y and two of his E's to make EYE and crossed his fingers in the hope of better things to come. "That's six, Norman. God, what a rotten hand." Tom passed Ned the bottle of red as he fumbled in the bag for two more letters. Norman frowned as he tried to make sense of his hand.

"So," Ned said, "that's what happened to the sycamore. Not like Ba, though, throwing in the towel without a fight."

"She didn't have much choice," Tom said, "local power politics being what they are. I try and stay out of them as far as possible."

"What on earth do you mean, politics?" said Ned. He was somewhat encouraged by the appearance of a P and an M in his last selection from the bag. "Since when has a sycamore tree got anything to do with politics?"

"Is eyeline hypenated or is it all one word?" asked Norman."

Hyphenated," said Ned quickly, sensing an advantage.

"I'll get the dictionary," said Tom. "Won't be a tick." He returned to the table with the biggest and most up-to-date Oxford available. So, thought Ned, that's the way it's going to be, is it? He immediately changed his attitude to the game, adapting his strategy to this no-holds-barred arrangement which Tom had implicitly introduced by his production of the dictionary and wondering if he could get away with his own version of the spelling of the notes in the tonic scale, a measure to which he always resorted when his back was against the wall.

"No," Tom announced. "It's not, Norman. You can have it." Norman put down.

"Your go," Ned said, "and you haven't finished about the politics."

"Oh, yes," said Tom, still not sure about opening up the board for Ned, "the bimbo as you call her is the local policeman's mother."

"And a snotty little beast he is too," said Ned and told the story of their encounter with PC Hopper as Tom put down QUILT for twenty eight.

"Do you think that the ticket he gave Ned will make him a statistic," he said as he wrote down Tom's score. "In the police computer?"

"God, what a frightful thought, Norman," said Ned. "Thanks Tom, just what the doctor ordered," and he added an S to his QUILT and used his U and the M to make SUM for twenty seven which cheered him up.

"I should think we're all statistics now," said Tom, "all safely filed away on some little microchip somewhere in the bowels of high technology."

"I hardly think PC Hopper's memory could be referred to as high technology even with the greatest leap of the imagination," said Ned bitterly. "Something tells me we haven't heard the last of him. Your go, Norman."

In the end, Norman lost, as usual and Tom, as expected, had to look up doh in the dictionary as Ned, at least three sheets blotto, sang his way in a garrulous baritone through the scale to explain to Tom that his doh was D-O-H and not the bread variety. He still won and Ned vowed to live to fight another day. They said goodnight just after eleven o'clock. Norman was dropping but longing to get back to *Barthorpe* to tell Ned all about Tom's divorce.

Tom saw them to the door and smiled as he watched the friends totter across the road and back to their own front door. He waited until he saw lights being turned on before shutting his own door. He had so enjoyed the evening, perhaps, he reflected, the most enjoyable evening he had spent in a long time and with two dotty old chaps at least a generation removed from his own. But then, as Norman had observed when Tom had related the history of his own recent past, when one door closes, another will surely open as long as you use your eyes. Tom felt very fondly towards the couple, even a litle responsible and yet, as he reminded himself, he knew absolutely nothing about them at all. Were they, he wondered as he cleared away the glasses? Surely, Norman *must* be, he concluded . . . But what about Ned? Didn't *seem* to be in the least bit camp . . . Still, he averred, who cares?

When they returned to *Barthorpe,* Ned announced that he was completely exhausted and was going to go immediately to his bed.

"Not even a cup of tea?" asked Norman, remembering that there wasn't enough milk for cocoa. "Don't you want to hear about poor Tom?"

"Divorces have never interested me," said Ned, stumping up the stairs. "Always messy. One side gets what they want and the other gets what they don't want."

"Exactly. And I think it's poor Tom who's got what he didn't want," said Norman. "So don't you feel sorry for him?"

"Of course I do," said Ned, turning at the top of the stairs and yawning. "But there's nothing we can do about it, Norman and he's a big boy now. Goodnight."

"Yes," said Norman rather plaintively," I suppose you're right."

"I am," said Ned, going into his room. "Are you coming?" Norman said he was going to fetch a glass of water. He didn't want a glass of water at all but he did want to check the state of the saucer on the window sill. It was empty although there was no sign of the cat. Regretfully, he decided to close the kitchen window, knowing what he now knew and went himself to bed. At the top of the stairs, he met Ned coming out of the bathroom and was relieved to see that Ned was wearing proper pyjamas.

"Goodnight," he said. "Sleep tight." He sounded sad and Ned noticed.

"Don't fret, Norman. Honestly. It's for the best. The cat already has a home," he assured, although he felt he had to add, "however odd."

"Actually, I was thinking about Tom"

"He's got a home as well. Two in fact," said Ned.

"Yes. I know." Norman sighed. "'Night." Norman too went to his room. From the time when there had been just the three of them, Ba, Ned and Norman, they had each had their favourite room. Ned had always slept in the room at the back with the view of what used to be open country and where he was now, lying on his tummy on his bed, writing his journal. Norman had never read any of Ned's journals but, having once seen one of them open on Ned's desk, he knew very well how each day's entry began ... 'My Darling Dulcie'. Dulcie Hogge had been the object of Ned's life ever since his tousled head had appeared over the wall of her garden, behind the greenhouse, so many years before and even in death, she still ruled his latter years.

Norman had always taken the smallest room, overlooking the garden at the side of the house. All the bedrooms had cottage ceilings and little dormer windows set into the angle of the roof. Norman opened his window and sat next to it for quite a while before getting undressed. The wistaria was beginning to bud and curls of virginia creeper framed the window. The night air was fresh but chilly and Norman, in his head, heard Mumfie's voice calling from the nursery warning him not to catch cold. Nursery health was always such a delicate balance in the old days. Windows had to be open at night but cold had not to be caught. Dear Mumfie, thought Norman fondly. He heard first an owl, calling from the ridge of a nearby roof and then a pair of foxes barking on the Downs which, since he had first come to East Dean, had been pushed further and further back into the hinterland. It was so quiet, much quieter than the Islington square in London and quieter still than the house on Holland Park in which he had lived when Cyril was alive. Dear Cyril, he thought, for he missed him still so much. Norman closed the window, leaving it sufficiently ajar to prevent staleness. He began to undress, folding his clothes neatly or hanging them up. He turned down the counterpane on the double bed. He had abandoned his own double bed when he had moved in with Ned and now he slept in a standard three footer. Ned on the other hand loved his big Victorian four poster but then Ned had only been married for such a tragically short time. Come on, Norman said to himself, rallying against the memories, pull yourself together. He put on his pyjamas, got into bed and turned off the light. He closed his eyes but he knew somehow he wasn't going to be able to sleep. The moon was bright in the clear night sky. There were few clouds but millions of stars. Funny, he thought, it never occurred to him to think of stars in London. He turned once or twice, trying to find a comfortable position on the edge of the big bed. Then, suddenly, he was wide awake. He listened and sat up. He was certain he had heard a rustle. He had the clear feeling that he was not alone in the room. Yes. There it was again! In the dark, he fumbled for the light pull above the bed and switched it on.

There, sitting on the chair by the window, was the cat, quite content, her eyes fixed intently on Norman. The cat yawned then jumped off the chair, padded across the floor and jumped onto the bed. Norman felt himself beginning to cry and held out his arms.

"Oh, Kit," he said as the silly tears coursed down his cheeks. "Come to Norman. Come-a, come-a, come-a Kitty." For a few moments, the cat kept a respectful distance. Norman lay back onto the pillows and switched off the light. The cat's silhouette was strong against the rectangle of the window with its diamond-shaped panes. Although he was aware of his own heartbeat as he breathed as little as possible, louder still was a very happy purring and the cat nuzzled against Norman's hand, asking, as cats do, for their throats to be tickled. "Ned will be furious with us," Norman whispered in the dark. He sniffed and wiped his eyes with the hand that wasn't stroking the cat. "Absolutely furious and," he said as a very proper afterthought, "he's probably right."

And, indeed, Ned had been right, for at that very moment in a house on the other side of the village, a very important television broadcast was being interrupted. PC Hopper had been eagarly looking forward to the televised Test match from Australia. Penny, his wife, had already gone to bed and her Trev, for that was his name in off-duty hours, had just settled himself down with four tins of a popular lager in front of the screen. He was well into the fourth over, Gooch having just sent a magnificent six soaring into the crowd, when the telephone rang. Should he, could he ignore it?

"Pen," he shouted. "Pen, get that will you?"

"No," came the answering call. "I'm puttin' me rollers in!" Trevor swore a very unpolicemanly oath. The afternoon's brush with Mr Cresswell had left him prickly to say the least and the prospect of being called out in, what was for East Dean, the middle of the night did not appeal to him. Downing the remaining drops of the first tin of lager, he went to the telephone, thinking, at that moment, as is said in the song, that a policeman's lot is not a happy one. As soon as he picked up the receiver, his ear was blasted with a storm of maternal static.

"Now don't fret, mum," he said calmly. "The cat's quite capable of looking after itself." There followed yet more vocal objection from his mother about foxes and how a poor little defenceless pussycat is no match for a hungry vixen.

"Mum, I'm telling you, it'll be alright." As for the cat being defenceless, Trevor knew full well from years of having to retrieve it from under beds, beneath floorboards and, especially, from its basket from which it had refused to move after being unceremoniously transported in the furniture van from Highbury the previous year, that the cat was far from defenceless. Vicious little . . ., he thought to himself.

"Mum, I'm sure he'll come back." The ugly spectre of kidnapping then reared itself in Mrs Hopper's imagination. "But," he said, "who would want to kidnap a cat in East Dean?" He was soon told. "What strangers, mother?" And so it went on, and on and on and in the background, Trevor heard the roars of the crowd twenty thousand miles away and wished above all that he could be instantly transported there, if necessary in chains. He held the telephone away from his ear as he caught the ghastly news that Botham was out! Upstairs, Penny picked up the telephone by the bed and replaced it immediately when she heard the rantings of her mother-in-law. Downstairs, Trevor managed to bring the conversation to a close.

"Alright, mother. In the morning. I'll make some enquiries in the morning . . . Yes, I know, mum . . . I am the police!"

EIGHT

The following morning, Ned woke early. It was a quite usual out-of-London reaction. At home, he wouldn't even be seen dead at seven o'clock in the morning. Before Norman had moved in after Cyril died, his agent and publisher had both been under strict orders never to telephone before eleven but then, in the forty years of their joint relationship, they had become used to even more strange instructions.

Snugly curled up in his favourite room in the world, Ned was now far away from his life in London, free of the responsibilities and burdens which 'she' carried. Here, Ned was Ned and 'she', the woman who had materialised from necessity, from the sheer need to survive, could be banished for a while. Ned was quite objective about this apparent schizophrenia. He had placed it many years ago when he had reached thirty. He had made the same assessment of himself again at forty and he had repeated and consolidated the process every decade. It was the woman who was growing older, the woman whose body was ailing, whose hair was now grey, whose joints were beginning to seize up with rheumatism. (Ned could never bear the word arthritis.) It was the woman who had bills to pay, books to write and deadlines to meet. Here, in Ba's house, the woman was not welcome. Here Ned was as he had always seen himself, the fourteen year old who had swapped a jar of worms, a one-legged toad and three white mice for Dulcie Hogge's father's penknife and who had rescued the fair Dulcie from an inexhaustible series of fates worse than death at the hands of Indians (or cowboys depending on the day), pirates, Germans or, when Frank Howard the gardener could be persuaded to enact the role, the unspeakable force of evil which lurked in the greenhouse. Only Genevieve Withers' sherry party remained to cloud Ned's otherwise perfect horizon of nostalgia.

Outside in the garden, on which the promise of a perfect, sunny day had dawned and from which Ned could hear the birds singing as they went about their breakfasts, came another sound which broke in to Ned's waking dreams.

"Albert . . . Albert!"

The calls for Albert seemed to be coming from below Ned's open window. Again, Ned heard a woman's voice.

"Albert, come on out now. I know you're here, Albert." For Ned, there was no drifting back to sleep until Norman appeared with the tea. He pushed back the bedclothes and padded stiffly over to the window.

In the garden, wearing the same woolly hat as the previous evening, was the woman from the bungaloid, still hawking the collar and lead. Ned breathed a silent thank you to himself that he had put his foot down about the cat as the prospect of being drummed out of East Dean by the forces of law and order was not pleasant, although, Ned reminded himself, it would be the perfect excuse for missing the sherry party.

As the woman looked up, Ned was not quite quick enough to conceal himself behind the curtains. Eye contact had been made.

"Have you seem him?" the woman squawked from the garden. "My Albert?" Ned was not prepared for such an early morning call, the least of his unpreparedness being his teeth which were still in their glass of water by the bed.

"Just a moment," he mumbled, knowing that he really ought to be polite. "I'm coming down." Damn, thought Ned, as he armed his mouth, found his slippers and put on his dressing gown.

Norman's door was still closed as he went downstairs. Ned went to the back door, assuming that the woman would still be outside in that part of the garden, unlocked the door and came face to face with Mrs Hopper. Both were pretty sights for sore Saturday eyes, Ned being Ned and Mrs Hopper being in her woolly hat and nylon cover-all.

"Good morning," said Ned. "Can we help you?" Ned

stood in the doorway, blocking it and made no gesture that could possibly be interpreted by Mrs Hopper as an invitation to come in.

"Morning," said the woman, whom Ned judged to be of an age similar to his own. "It's Albert, see." Mrs Hopper's accent immediately ascribed to her the origins of one who had been born nearer to the Thames than to the English Channel. A Londoner.

"So I rather gathered," said Ned coldly. The woman was dipping and bobbing like a moorhen, or a chicken in a farmyard, her head seeming to move in directions opposite to those indicated by the position of her neck. She didn't look Ned in the eye but instead seemed to be focusing into the kitchen behind. Ned looked round, thinking that perhaps that Norman may have come downstairs. But Norman was still in bed, wide awake and listening with straining ears for any sign that Mrs Hopper might have invaded the house. The cat too was wide awake and was standing on the bed, tail straight and looking around, it seemed to Norman, for a quick exit should the need arise."

He's forever slippin' his collar," continued the bobbing Mrs Hopper and Ned remarked rather cruelly to himself that the cat obviously slipped his collar as many times as Mrs Hopper let slip her aspirates. "Gotta to watch 'em all the time, 'aven't you?" opined Mrs Hopper. "Especially in a strange place."

"We are talking about a cat, I presume," said Ned rather grandly for he could see how poor Mr Hopper could have been treated, happen that there was a Mr Hopper still alive.

"I saw 'im in 'ere last evening. Saw you playin' with 'im as a matter of fact," said Mrs Hopper.

"Yes," said Ned, "I rather thought you did. By the way, it's a her not a him." He sounded his aspirates rather consciously as Ned had a terrible habit of immediately picking up the inflexions of other people's speech to the point where he was often thought to be taking the mickey.

"Don't know about that," said Mrs Hopper snippily as though the very mention of gender offended her. "'E'll always be Albert to me. Same as my dear father, you see. My Trevor says I ought to have 'im done; you know. Put a stop to 'is filthy habits, wandering and that, you know."

If she says you know once more, thought Ned, I think I might cosh her. Ned was already much put out by the slur on the poor feline's gender as it indicated an utter lack of sensitivity. Ned hated the inaccurate, especially when it concerned dumb animals. As far as he was concerned, it would have better to curb the filthy habits of Mrs Hopper with a quick surgical snip than inflict such a veterinary calamity on the cat.

"Inherited 'im, I did. From my poor mother. Last year, when she passed on. Put 'im in 'er will, she did, along with . . ." and here Mrs Hopper looked round conspiratorially to check she wasn't being overheard, ". . . along with the money!"

"How interesting," said Ned, thinking how much better Norman would have coped with this confrontation than he. In fact, he was thinking about calling to Norman to come and take over when he saw the saucer on the window sill and the few tell-tale hairs stuck to its rim. Oh no! Ned thought.

"Norman!" he bellowed.

Ned turned to Mrs Hopper.

"I was just attracting my friend's attention," he said crisply. "I'm sure he will verify that we haven't seen your cat since last night." He called once again, although raging elephants have been known to trumpet less loudly.

"Norman!" There was a moment's delay, but only a moment's for Norman had heard Ned quite well the first time as, indeed, had almost the whole of East Dean north of the Brighton road.

"Did you call, Ned?" said Norman from the top of the stairs.

"Yes, Norman," Ned said meaningfully. "We haven't seen Mrs Hopper's cat since yesterday, have we?"

"Er," Norman said trying desperately to gather his wits, "would that be the cat in the tulips, or the one by the gate? Or there was a cat, I believe, in the fig tree."

"Norman, Mrs Hopper is waiting here," said Ned pointedly, "outside the back door. She's a little concerned . . . As," added Ned sinisterly, "am I." He paused. "But we can discuss that later, can't we?"

"Yes," said Norman. "I mean, No. I haven't actually seen a cat called Albert . . . ever."

Ned returned his attention to Mrs Hopper, hoping that Big Chief I-Spy hadn't spotted the empty saucer.

"I'm so sorry, I'm afraid we can't help you. Good morning." Ned began to shut the door, although Mrs Hopper, now that she had an audience, was not to be given the hook so easily.

"You know," she said, "you read about it all the time, these people who go around just stealin' cats off the street, all over the place. They sell 'em, you know, to them villysecters."

Oh Lord, thought Ned, and a Malaprop to boot.

"Absolutely frightful, I quite agree," he said. "But I don't think you'll find much of that round here. Now, if you'll excuse me, I'm afraid I have to go and see to my friend's wooden leg. Lost without it, you know!"

And with that, Ned shut the door, leaving Mrs Hopper to worry her way back to her house and rouse her daughter-in-law with the awful news that one of the strangers next door had a wooden leg, although the source of that perplexing rumour, much to Norman's later consternation, was always to be Ned's secret.

And now, thought Ned as he climbed the stairs, what have we up here? Norman met him at the top of the stairs. Norman had just closed his door, firmly. But even as he did it, he felt inside a sinking feeling which was the certain knowledge that he had been found out.

"But," pleaded Norman as Ned pushed past him on the landing, "there was nothing I could do, Ned. It was the middle of the night and honestly, honestly, Ned, I really didn't know she'd come in!"

By now Ned had opened the door to Norman's bedroom and was looking at Albert, who was poised for instant flight. However, seeing that Ned was Ned and not his dreaded step-mother, he, rather she, abruptly erased flight from the list of options and settled back into the warm patch he had created in the middle of Norman's bed.

"That cat goes," pronounced Ned, slowly and deliberately. "Either you put her out, Norman, or I do." Norman took in a deep breath, about to protest. "And no buts. It's a lovely day, I am determined it's going to be a lovely day and nothing, I repeat nothing is going to spoil it, especially a state of open warfare between our house and her house!"

Norman saw that it was useless to resist and, worst of all, he knew Ned was right. Forlorn and feeling very small and helpless, Norman picked up the cat and, cradling her in his arms, began the slow descent to the back door. Ned followed and opened the door.

"Now, Norman. The sooner the better."

Norman relinquished the cat and gently pushed her away. The cat made no move but merely sat down outside the door and began to wash herself. Ned shut the door and Norman, as tearful at the parting as he had been last night at the meeting, fled upstairs, howling.

Ned shook his head and put the kettle on. All this fuss and it was still only a quarter to eight.

While the kettle was boiling and while Norman was composing himself upstairs, sustained melencholy having never been a persistent trait in his character, Ned padded around the house.

Ba had only one rule about the use of her house and that was that people should treat it as their own. Although on the surface this could be interpreted as a rather guileless assumption, Ba had found that she had been let down only infrequently. Successive guests over the years had added to the original decor which, although still comfortable, had long since lost its contemporary relevance. Cushions of every shape, size and colour were now scattered over the armchairs and sofa. Inumerable pebbles, rocks and stones from the beach were arranged on top of the wooden pelmets over the windows, interspersed with a very varied assortment of beach-combed bric-a-brac amongst the nooks and crannies of which Norman's spider had made several its home. There was the head of a plastic doll, its once lustrous, nylon hair caked with oil, a starfish with one of its points missing, pieces of cuttlefish culled from the tideline, a whole history of the occupation of the house. Inherent in Ba's only regulation was, of course, the implication that the place should be left as it had been found, ready for the next occupant. Ned had only ever missed one year and only then because he had been in hospital. The unfortunate nursing staff had had to hide his clothes when Ned announced that he was discharging himself only three days after an appendectomy.

The kettle boiled and the whistle called Ned to the kitchen. He made the tea and set a tray.

"Norman," he called, "are you coming down or do you want it up there?"

"I'm coming," a weak voice was heard to reply.

Ned took the tray and set it on the dining table and poured, as usual a mug for him and a cup and saucer for Norman, who soon appeared downstairs.

"Sorry about that, old thing," Ned said as both apology and comfort.

"Oh that's alright," said Norman, sniffing and making a brave attempt to sound bright. "Take no notice, Ned. You know me. What a weed I am."

"Nonsense," said Ned, savouring his tea. "I do know how much you miss having one."

Norman sugared his tea and stirred it thoughtfully.

"Yes," he said, "we are at a funny old stage, aren't we? I've never minded getting old at all except for just occasionally." He sipped his tea. "And not having a cat is one of those occasions."

"That Hopper woman, you see," Ned said, "that's not her cat. It belonged to her mother. The mother died and the poor animal was landed with the dotty daughter."

"Really?" said Norman who had not been party to the information Ned had gleaned from the conversation with Mrs Hopper.

"And another thing," Ned imparted, "I know how she

comes to be here."

"That's easy," said Norman, "to be near her son."

"I said how not why," said Ned. "Her mother obviously left some money but also stipulated that the daughter was to look after the cat."

"Well, I think that's rather nice," said Norman.

"All very well, Norman. Except that poor woman can't handle it."

"It's only a cat, Ned."

"I mean" said Ned, "she can't handle the conditions. The money and the cat. She's somehow equated them."

"Ah, I see," said Norman. "You mean she thinks that she's only allowed to keep the money as long as she keeps the cat."

"Exactly," said Ned. "That's why she's so obsessed with finding it, why she keeps the poor thing on a collar and lead."

"She doesn't!" said Norman.

"She does," said Ned. "She'll end up in a loony bin, mark my words."

"Poor thing," said Norman. "Some people just aren't cat people, are they? But," he sighed and sipped again at his tea, "it's so hard knowing that you *are* one and not being able to be one."

"Norman," Ned said," if someone could give me a copper-bottomed guarantee that we'd still be around in twenty years and that Mrs Hopper wouldn't end up ga-ga, I'd have that cat packed into the car like a shot. But," he added, "there isn't enough copper in the universe to cover the bottom of that one."

"You're right," Norman agreed, feeling slightly guilty that his initial sympathies lay not with Mrs Hopper but with the cat. "I mean, who would we leave a cat to?" He paused, trying hard to come up with a copper mine. "Rimanda? No. She lives in a flat. Anthony?"

"No, no, no," Ned said. "Can't land folk with things like that. We drive poor Tony crazy from this side of the grave, we don't want to haunt him from the other. I'm even beginning to feel sorry for that numbskull policeman."

"And not even Rimanda?" said Norman as a last ditch suggestion.

"We have to face facts, old thing," Ned reiterated. "Rimanda's as old as we are. You know that you do more cleaning than she does. I've tried to pension her off twice but she won't hear of it."

"She'd hate not seeing you anymore," said Norman, "and she'd never come to see you just as your friend, would she? She's too proud."

Ned finished his tea and put down his mug. He patted the table quietly, but emphatically.

"Now enough of all this. We, Norman, are on holiday and I'm going to do some shopping for a beach picnic."

"Shall I come?"

"No. I'm perfectly OK. I'm not helpless yet," said Ned, getting up from the table. Norman poured himself another cup, rather pleased that for once Ned was assuming the mantle of chores.

"Can you remember Earl Grey and digestives," he said. "Chocolate ones."

"Milk or plain?"

"Both," said Norman knowing that each of them liked the other sort. "Why not!"

"Wish we could get out of that bloody party tomorrow," said Ned as he went out of the room. He stopped at the foot of the stairs. "We can't, can we?"

"No," said Norman definitely, "we can't. That would be rude."

"But all those wittery old women," said Ned sulkily, "with their endless inane questions and their helpful hints for plots with so many holes that you could water the garden with them."

"Ned, we're going and that's that," Norman argued. "We owe it to Ba, in a way. And Tom'll be there. He can monopolise you and keep the others at a safe distance."

"Hum," Ned said as he climbed the stairs. "that's as maybe," and went up to dress.

Dear Ned, Norman thought. After all, he reminded himself, what are we but two wittery old men?

As Ned dressed, Norman had even a third cup of tea, sitting at the dining table Ba had bought from Heals in the Tottenham Court Road. It was oak, of course, and rather severe in its fashion as was the sideboard, occasional table and accompanying chairs. Over the sideboard hung her last school photograph, a wide-angle study of three hundred virgins ranked either seated or standing outside schoolhouse at Malvern, fifty years ago. Barthorpes, Musselwhites, Steels, de Romeras, Newmans as well as all their nicknames. Many of them had stayed in this house, single or married, some having brought both their children and grandchildren, some dead but certainly, without question, all of them surviving now wittery old people like themselves.

Ned poked his head round the door.

"I'm off," he said. "Earl Grey and what was it?"

"Digestives."

"Right," said Ned, "see you in a tick. I'm taking Min. Don't fancy lugging stuff back up the hill. 'Bye."

NINE

Norman cleared away the tea tray. He heard Ned starting the car. It whined rather more than usual, Norman fancied. He had never learned to drive, even during the war, never having anticipated the need. There were many things he had not anticipated. Cyril's death had been the most profound. Norman had grieved, of course, but there had been few tears. His reaction had been more one of bewilderment, a kind of shock, Ned had said at the time for Norman had been very quiet. Ned still was used to finding him staring out of the kitchen window in London, a quivering, delicate little frown creasing his brow as though he were trying to work out a particularly intricate problem and was simply unable to find the key.

Norman washed up the tea things and, ruefully, took Albert's saucer off the kitchen window sill and washed that as well. There was a ring at the front door bell.

He pulled his dressing gown closer together, patted his hair down in the hall mirror and opened the door.

"Morning, sir," said PC Hopper.

"Why, good morning, Officer," said Norman gaily. Now he had nothing to hide, he felt that he could be quite open.

"Perhaps you could be of assistance in my enquiries," PC Hopper said rather pompously.

"Of course," Norman said. "Always dirty work afoot, eh?"

"You could say that, sir."

Over the constable's shoulder Norman thought he saw a piece of the hedge waving about by the gate and assumed that there must be a bird's nest in the thick lonicera for there was no wind to shake the leaves.

"My enquiries concern a missing animal. A cat, in fact," said PC Hopper as Norman realised that it was not the hedge that was moving but Mrs Hopper's woolly hat.

"Ah," he said, now thoroughly primed, "that would be your mother's cat, would it not? Albert, I believe."

The constable coughed for he was embarassed, fulfilling his line of duty while being scrutinised by his mother.

"Er, yes," he said. "I believe the animal is called Albert."

"Dreadfully wrong, you know," Norman said. "The poor thing's a she not a he. Could be the start of a severe personality disorder. I once had a cat called . . ."

He was interrupted before he could tell the strange tale of a fluffy chinchilla they had once had whom Cyril had called Rita.

"I'm sure you did, sir. But back to the animal in question. Mrs Hopper, who lives next door . . ."

"Your mother, we understand," said Norman. "I think she's waiting for you at the gate. Did you know?"

PC Hopper glanced over his shoulder and the woolly hat dipped quickly out of sight, but not quickly enough to escape the eagle eye of the law.

"Would you excuse me a moment, sir," said the policeman. Norman saw him lean at the gate and tried to hear what he was saying.

"Mother!" hissed the policeman. "Will you go back in the house! I am thirty four years old and believe it or not I'm quite capable of conducting my own enquiries without you interfering. Now, get off home with you!"

Through the hedge, Norman saw Mrs Hopper shuffle away but as Mrs Hopper walked in one direction, Norman saw Albert slinking in the other, belly almost touching the ground, stepping very carefully but with great determination amongst the purple honesty which grew at the bottom of the hedge. PC Hopper returned to his interview with Norman on the doorstep.

"Sorry about that, sir."

"Officer, we haven't seen Albert. Your mother has already been round to ask the same question. At seven-fifteen this morning, precisely."

"I see," said the exasperated man. Over his shoulder, Norman saw Albert framed in a patch of bare hedge and, at the same time, saw the undeterred woolly hat creeping back on the other side. The two co-incided and each let out of shriek.

"Trevor!"

"Miaoooouw!"

"Get 'im, Trevor . . . After 'im!"

Mrs Hopper appeared in the gateway as Albert shot across the garden, straight through the bed of tulips with the constable in full hue and cry. Mrs Hooper screeched instructions to her son as Albert bolted under a laurel bush. PC Hopper slid on a patch of dew and was brought to his knees, his cap went flying, his walkie talkie radio sprang from its housing on his lapel, sailed through the air and landed a little too heavily on the concrete path surrounding the house. It broke, lying in various hapless pieces.

"You've gone and lost 'im," shouted his mother in despair. "Trevor! You stupid boy!"

Something snapped in the policeman's brain and as he picked himself up, there came an outpouring of thirty four years' frustration as he railed against the fate which had consigned him to be his mother's son. He was a sorry sight. He limped back across the garden, shaking his fist in the direction of Mrs Hopper, the knees of his smart blue uniform stained green with grass. As his mother visibly withered before him, Norman went and retrieved the cap and picked up the pieces of the radio from the path. Albert was nowhere to be seen. Golly, thought Norman, what Ned would have given to have seen all this.

By this time, PC Hopper was out in the road. He took his mother by the arm and led her back to her own house. Norman waited for him to come back. Three or four children on bicycles clustered around the police car, intrigued. Poor PC Hopper, his dignity in as many pieces as his radio, returned for his hat. Norman handed it to him at the gate.

"Well, at least you found the cat," he said cheerfully.

"If I never see that cat as long as I live," replied the policeman with great feeling, "it won't be long enough. Thank you, sir," he said emptying the contents of his hat into his hand and then into his pocket. "Sorry to have inconvenienced you." He turned to get into his car. "Now buzz off, you kids," he ordered and four terrified bicyclists bolted like rabbits. Norman watched him drive away around the greensward as Ned's Mini returned in the opposite direction.

"Norman, what are doing wandering around the garden in your dressing gown?" asked Ned who was truly astonished at Norman's boldness. "It must be something in the air down here." He got out of the car with two bags of shopping. "Into the house with you at once." Norman took one of the bags from him.

"Ned," he said as they went into the house, "you'll honestly never believe this. What a to-do!" Ned shut the front door.

"Must have been something to do with the policeman," he said as he dumped his bag on the dresser. "Butcher says thank you, by the way."

"What for?"

"The egg boxes," said Ned hawking out a giant leg of lamb and a pound of herb sausages.

"Ned, that's an awful lot of meat."

"Shush, Norman. Can't have Sunday lunch without meat, can we? Now, what's been happening since I've been out. This place is getting to be like Piccadilly!"

And so Norman told Ned all about the Hoppers, mother and son and Albert's flight to freedom and in the end found himself feeling very sorry for everyone.

"What a shame Mrs Hopper couldn't live with Trevor," Norman concluded.

"Ah," said Ned, wisely, "but what about the other Mrs Hopper." Norman looked confused. "Mrs Hopper junior."

"Oh, of course." He paused. "I wouldn't imagine they get on, would you?"

"Not for a moment," said Ned. "Now," he said, changing the subject, "lovely croissants for breakfast. And," he said, emptying his other bag, "cucumber and sandwich spread sandwiches for lunch."

"With apples," said Norman discovering the bag, "I adore sandwich spread. Cyril hated it. He said it reminded him of sick."

"Dear old Cyril," said Ned. He put the croissants in the oven, switched the kettle on for coffee and Norman set about making the sandwiches.

"Did you see anyone in the village?" asked Norman.

"Such as whom?" said Ned as he stuck his finger into the pot of sandwich spread.

"Such as anyone who might have looked like Genevieve Withers," amplified Norman.

"They all look like Genevieve Withers to me," said Ned. "All those frightful trugs on their arms for a quarter a pound of mince and two slices of ham."

"But that's what shopping's all about, Ned. It's not as though anyone's actually desperate for the butcher, it's just nice to get out of the house and have a chat."

"Oh, spare me," said Ned who hated shopping more than anything else in the world.

"Did you remember the tea?" asked Norman.

"Yes, I did." Ned held out a box. "Fifty bags."

"Bags!" said Norman, horrified. "Earl Grey in bags! Whatever next?"

After breakfast, Norman packed up their lunch basket. Ned had bought ginger beer too and although Norman didn't hold out much hope for the canned variety, he knew full well that the days of it coming in bottles with ingenious wire and porcelain tops were long gone. They went to their rooms to change.

Norman glanced out of the window. The sun was now quite high in the sky and it certainly promised to be a glorious day. Although they had packed in record time, Norman had managed to include sufficient clothes in his luggage for the beach including plimsolls. There was little sand at Birling Gap and walking over the smooth flint pebbles had become something of a problem. He finished dressing and put two large towels into a canvas bag. He went downstairs and sorted out two reclining sunchairs from the pile in the hall cupboard.

"Ned, did you pack our windbreak?" he called out.

"In the boot," was the reply.

Ned came down the stairs. Ned's grip on convention of any sort was at best tenuous but today, his dress sense had exceeded even Norman's worst fears. On his head was an old straw hat of Ba's which Ned had had his eye on for decades. Around its crown was wound a handkerchief which Ned had bought years before in a bazaar in Lucknow. Ned had used his bathing costume as an undergarment as he hated struggling to maintain decency on beaches by changing underneath a shroud of towels which Norman invariably failed to hold sufficiently securely. He was wearing an old dress shirt, knotted at the waist. Norman thought it had once belonged to Ba'a father. The khaki shorts he had put on were the ones he had bought in a surplus store in Sydney the previous year before their trip to Ayers Rock. Ned had failed to scale the rock much to his chagrin and Norman's relief. Norman had stayed in the hotel that day as he had heard that there were spiders, much more terrifying to him than the much-advertised sharks which, if they had believed what they were always being told, were present even in hotel swimming pools. Ned's legs were mostly covered in tartan knee socks, bought at great expense during a holiday in Pitlochry and from the same shop where originated the hiking boots which, with his leather school satchel, completed the outfit.

Norman burst out laughing.

"Ned, you can't possibly go out like that," he managed to say eventually.

"Watch me," said Ned and carried out his threat, picking up the beach chairs and marching defiantly out of the front door.

"I shall walk behind you," said Norman. "People might think I'm on my own."

"Damn people," swore Ned. "They're the bane of humanity. Come on, Norman or we'll miss the best of the day."

As they loaded the car, Tom Maxwell pulled the curtains back in his bedroom, having managed to sleep through the cat hunt. As he privately admitted to Norman later, even he was taken aback by the vision of Ned, dressed for adventure, which greeted his bleary eyes.

As soon as they had driven away, Albert re-emerged from beneath the laurel bush, looked at the open ventilator in the kitchen window and made a beeline for certain sanctuary. Somehow, as Norman would remark later when he was putting two and two together, the cat must have known that Highbury was next to Islington and, to a cat, it was obviously the next best thing.

TEN

The Mini rounded the bend by Birling Manor on the way to the sea. The Downs sheep, heavily pregnant, had been gathered into a large pen in readiness. Several lambs had already been born and were gambolling about in a field next to the barn, alternately playing hide-and-seek or king-of-the-castle before rushing back to their mothers and burying their heads into the shaggy wool for more milk, their little tails shaking like catkins in a March wind. Norman was delighted. Lambs provoked the same reaction in him as cats.

"Aren't they so sweet?" he said, turning in his seat to catch another glimpse.

"Poor things," said Ned, "Gather ye rosebuds while ye may." He giggled. "Yum, yum," he said wickedly.

"Ned, that's awful! You are the most peculiar person. You'd move heaven and earth to avoid killing a . . . a, you know . . . and yet you cheerfully go out and buy a leg of lamb!"

"True," said Ned. "Sad, but true."

They drove into the car park on the cliff above Birling Gap. There were few cars and Ned nosed in as close to the edge of the cliff steps as he could.

Little had changed since their last visit. In fact, little had changed since they had first come to know the area. The row of coastguard cottages were still intact although few showed sign of occupation. The Birling Gap hotel still looked as rundown as ever, doomed as it was one day, to fall into the sea given the march of time, tide and the constant erosion of the chalk cliffs by the winter storms. At one time, walkers must have overnighted there although now, at forty-odd pounds a room, just as good a living was being earned from hotelling as from the bar at the back, from the large carvery and from the endless pots of tea dispensed during the summer months.

"Just look at that," said Ned, standing at the edge of the cliff and breathing in the panorama presented by the Seven Sisters, "you could go to hell and back and not find a view like that."

The section of the Sussex coast between Seaford Head and the Meads at Eastbourne which included the cliff formations known as the Seven Sisters and the infamous Beachy Head had always inspired the best efforts of good and bad painters alike. Mother Nature in her white, towering glory had engendered many a likeness of the cliffs in storm and calm. The walls of Ba's house were littered with oils and watercolours, gouaches and acrylics of this one subject purchased dutifully from the local art show. Though Ned had never continued painting after art school and scorned the waste of canvas which Ba subsidised, equally, he had never tried to describe his feelings about the place in words. But he kept the picture of it in his mind's eye always.

Access to the beach which lay some thirty feet below the car park had always been by steps. Although it was the lowest point on the cliffs, even the local smugglers in the bad old days would have had to have used some sort of ladder to hike their contraband from the boats below to a safe hiding place above. The winter storms and the high spring tides pounded at the foundation of the steps now erected for the public to descend to the beach. New structures sequentially replaced older, unsafe ones.

Norman was unpacking the car as quickly as he could to get Ned onto the beach as fast as possible. There, Norman thought, Ned might be less conspicuous, dressed only in his bathing costume.

"Look, Norman," Ned called from the cliff edge. "New steps."

Norman looked at the most recent in the series of steps, which seemed very solid and permanent, with white painted steel handrails, strong support struts and heavy mahogony treads.

"Looks like something off the damn QE2," said Ned disdainfully. Ned had never forgiven Cunard for abandoning the older Queens. The fact that the previous steps had been fashioned from builders' scaffolding and chicken wire, the descent of which had always made Norman feel vertiginous, went unremarked. Anything new to Ned was always an abomination until he became forced through necessity to get used to it.

"Ned, don't stand too close to the edge. There's even a sign there that tells you," Norman said, having never been fond of heights and brinks. "Danger. Cliff falls."

"I can read," Ned said distantly. He was looking out to sea to where the morning ferry from Newhaven had just emerged from the shadow of Seaford head, sailing for Dieppe. A thin wisp of smoke streamed from its funnel into a sky as clear and blue as the sea was calm. It's the only bother about England, he thought as he shaded his eyes with his hand and drank in the atmosphere. If there was weather like this five days out of seven, he thought, England would be paradise. As it was, Ned thought it pretty unimpeachable.

"Ned!" Called Norman. "I can't carry two chairs, the windbreak and the beach bag all by myself."

"I'm coming," said Ned, completing his reconnoitre of the beach which he was pleased to see was all but empty. He returned to the car and locked both doors and the boot and helped Norman with the equipment.

At the bottom of the steps, they stopped. The tide was about halfway out. Norman was always amazed how Ned could tell whether it was coming in or going out; today, apparently, it was going out.

"Left or right," asked Norman.

"I think we'll go to the right, today," said Ned. "Lot of cliff falls since we were here last."

"I told you," said Norman. "That's why they put that sign up. I don't fancy ending up under an avalanche of chalk. I'd feel like a fossil."

"You are a fossil," said Ned. "We both are. *Homo Sapiens Britannicus* . . . or something." Ned began to trudge over the pebbles, his hiking boots making better ground than Norman's plimsolls.

"What is that supposed to mean," said Norman.

"Wise men of England. They'd dig us up in two hundred thousand million years and re-erect us in the Natural History Museum."

"How awful," said Norman, "being gawped at by all those people without any clothes on."

"Private parts will be a thing of the past by then," Ned pronounced. "Evolution will have taken care of all all that. No more bottoms, front or back."

"No, I meant us without any clothes on, silly," said Norman, tottering in his friend's wake. "And please slow down. You're rushing again."

"Sorry," said Ned and waited for Norman to catch up.

"How far do you want to go," said Norman, slightly breathlessly. "I'm about pooped."

"As far as possible from the hordes," said Ned.

"Actually, I suppose here's as good a place as any. Yes," he said, looking up at the clifftop above and then out to sea as though judging his position to the most precise degree of both latitude and longitude, "not a bad spot. I'll make camp and you see to the provisions." Norman knew by this remark that Ned was back in the garden at *Fairlea* with Dulcie, making wigwams out of Frank Howard's beansticks whilst waiting to beg butter biscuits from mama or cook. "What's the time," he said looking up at the sun, gauging the hour from its position in the sky.

"Ten-past-eleven," said Norman looking at his watch. "It's certainly not lunchtime yet, if that's what you're after. It's amazing you haven't had indigestion from those croissants."

"Rot," said Ned. "I could eat a horse." He sighed. "Well, I suppose it is a bit early still." Ned set out the chairs, aligning them in the direction of the sun and unrolled the windbreak, a length of deck chair canvas set with poles but designed rather for sandy beaches than for pebbles.

"What do you want that up for," asked Norman.

"Privacy," said Ned, struggling to embed the first of the upright poles between the pebbles."But why?" said Norman. "You can only be private one way. People might come and sit on the other side of the windbreak."

"Then that's another problem," said Ned. "At least I'll feel private."

"But I like to see," objected Norman. "That's the whole point of coming to the beach. You can watch people."

"Then you can go for a walk," said Ned.

"Then I think I just will," said Norman. Ned could be very bossy at times and today was obviously going to be a bossier day than usual.

Ned had managed to create a version of the vertical with his poles although the windbreak swayed rather at one end for want of sufficiently firm anchorage. He seemed satisfied, nevertheless and began to take off his clothes, although he kept his socks and boots on. He lay down on one of the reclining chairs, his crimson bathing costume only just managing to contain him. Norman shook his head in utter disbelief but thought it better not to nag.

"Thought you were going for a walk," said Ned with his eyes closed, basking in the warm sun. "God, this is heaven on earth."

"Aren't you going to take your socks off?" said Norman. "If you lie like that all day you'll have burnt knees and a line just where your shorts come. It'll look very odd."

"You don't like my boots, do you?" said Ned suspiciously."

Not specially," Norman replied, "but it's not me wearing them. I'm just thinking that if the weather's like this again tomorrow, you're going to end up the weekend with all the bits of you in different colours." Norman too lay back on his chair and from his canvas bag he took a little tube of sun block cream and applied it to the bridge of his nose. "D'you want some?"

"Some what?"

"SafeSun Screener," said Norman, reading from the label on the tube. "I saved it from Australia."

"There's no heat in this sun, Norman."

"Ha," said Norman, remembering, "you said that in Australia. After half-an-hour on the hotel roof, you looked like a cooked prawn. And we have ozone to contend with now too."

Ned raised himself up on his elbows and bent forward to untie his laces, but did not go as far as taking off the boots.

"Australia is Australia, Norman. We are at the present moment on an English beach, it's April and still mid-winter as far as I'm concerned." He lay back again and closed his eyes. "And bugger the ozone," he murmured.

Norman ignored him, replaced the cap of the tube and put it back in the bag. He too lay back and relaxed into the warmth of the sun.

"Did you bring anything to read, Ned?"

"In my satchel," Ned murmured, the thought crossing his mind that perhaps the sun was a little hotter than he had thought.

"Like what?"

"Like the *Telegraph*."

"Papers blow about on the beach. They're like sails, The wind catches them everytime you turn a page. Anything else?"

"Bryan Forbes' latest."

"What is it?"

"Autobiography. Very good. You'd like it."

"Perhaps. But I feel I'd have to concentrate."

Again, Ned raised himself up and, squinting, looked out to sea. A small flotilla of sailing dinghies were making heavy going for the lack of wind.

"Norman, are you trying to tell me you're bored already?" Ned looked over the top of the windbreak. "There's quite a few people down at the other side of the steps. Why don't you wander along. Knowing you, you'll have made friends of them all by lunchtime.

"Norman opened his eyes and swung his legs off the chair. He too looked over the windbreak.

"Perhaps I will," he said. "And look, there's quite a bit of sand showing. I might even have a paddle." He got up, balancing unsteadily on the uneven stones.

Good, thought Ned, a bit of peace at last. He leaned forward to roll down his socks. At the same time, the canvas covering the reclining chair, having spent a rather damp winter under the stairs at Barthorpe, rent with a sound not unlike that of someone breaking wind and Ned sank into the metal frame of the chair.

"Oh dear," said Norman as Ned stared blankly up at him, daring him to laugh. "Can I give you a hand?" he said, smirking just a little. As it happened, Ned was reasonably gallant about the misfortune.

"What a ruddy bore," was all he said and even he was forced to laugh. "Give me a hand for God's sake.

"Norman grasped Ned's hands and, slowly, Ned managed to hoist himself upright.

"No bones broken?" enquired Norman as Ned replaced his hat.

"No," he said," but Birling beach will be forever embossed on my bottom." In fact the only bruises were to his dignity and he folded the chair up and laid the towels which Norman had packed down on the stones.

"No. I'm fine. You go off for your walk."

"Right-o," said Norman. "Use the other chair 'til I come back."

After he had taken off his socks, Ned lowered himself down onto the towels and sat with his arms around his knees and remarked to himself that old bones and old stones made an uncomfortable juxtaposition. He watched Norman moving tentatively over the pebbles to the sea. Where the pebbles stopped and the sand began, Norman removed his plimsolls and walked out onto the wet sand. Ned's attention wandered as a single girl, wearing a white T-shirt and black slacks with the ubiquitous running shoes, walked along the beach in front of him. The girl smiled, a sunny friendly smile that only certain women use. It spoke intelligence, confidence and respect and Ned approved of all those qualities. She's a pretty girl too, thought Ned and smiled in return. A few yards to the right of Ned's camp, the girl stopped, unslung the travelling bag from her shoulder and from it removed a towel which she spread onto the stones. Ned watched her as she took a hairbrush from the bag and set about her hair with deliberation and concentration.

Ned had not brought sunglasses with him and he closed his eyes and redirected his face to the sun. The warmth was soothing and Ned lay back once again in his chair, folding his arms behind his head. His concentration drifted. Dulcie had always hated having long hair. Her natural impatience, and Ned's daring her, had brought forward the parentally prescribed age for being allowed short hair. One morning, whilst he'd been in the drawing room having his piano lesson with Miss Holland, Dulcie had hacked off her magnificent tresses with a pair of her Mama's nail scissors. Ned smiled as he remembered the scene and the hullaballoo which had ensued. Dulcie'd rushed to the end of the garden and shouted for Ned from their secret place and when he popped his head up over the wall and come face to face with the unevenly shorn Dulcie, he had been rendered, just for a moment, speechless.

"Crikey, Hogge," he had finally said. He always called her Hogge. "I never thought you'd actually do it."

"Well I have, so there," Dulcie had said.

"But what are you going to do?" Ned had said, quite factually. Dulcie was caught short. She hadn't actually thought past the moment of impulse. All she had wanted was to be like Ned and now, it seemed, Ned didn't want her to be like him at all.

"Don't you like it?" she asked.

"You can say I don't," he said. "Only boys have short hair, Hogge. Girls," he said somewhat scornfully, "have long hair."

"I can grow it again," she protested.

"Ha," he said in disdain, "that'll take a million years. I'll have met lots of other girls by then."

"No you won't," said Dulcie. "I shan't let you." She looked at him in a funny way, as though he had let her down. She was thirteen. He was fourteen. It was a painful time. "Then won't you help me stick it back on again," she suggested, pathetically. "We could do it with glue. Please, Ned."

"No fear," he said. "I'd be an accessory."

"What's that?" asked Dulcie, trying very hard not to cry, for her misdemeanour was rapidly turning to martyrdom.

"I don't quite know," said Ned, "but it's something that lots of guilty people are. You read about it in the papers."

There was a shout from the house, Dulcie's house.

"Dulcie!"

"I'm off," said Ned. "That's your mama." He disappeared. To do so meant climbing down from the apple box placed on his side of the wall which was lower than the Fairlea side.

"Dulcie Hogge! If you don't come here this minute, you'll make it all the worse for yourself!"

Ned re-appeared just as Dulcie had decided that suicide couldn't be such a terrible thing after all, surely easier than facing the wrath of the parents and infinitely easier than this rejection by her blood brother, for so they had pledged themselves.

"Hogge," he said, a mite more tenderly, "It's not that bad." Dulcie hung her head. "You're rather lucky you're a girl. My old man would beat me ragged for pulling something like that. You'll just get locked up with bread and water. Good luck! I'll try and visit but can't promise much."

And he was gone.

"Dulcie!" called her mother, "this is the third time. If I have to come and fetch you . . ." The remainder of the threat was undelivered as Mrs Hogge appeared at the corner of the greenhouse, a handful of hair in her right hand. From over the wall, Ned looked at Dulcie and imagined the sword of justice and the tortures in store and watched her as she began the long walk back across the croquet lawn. He sort of felt it was in a way his fault. Never had there been so black and bleak a day. Dulcie had been forbidden association with Ned for a fortnight. From his own drawing room Ned remembered hearing the lugubrious sound of Dulcie playing the 'Funeral March' next door . . .

Overhead, sixty years later, two seagulls set about each other, squawking loudly in a dispute over aerial territory.

Ned opened his eyes and realised that he had momentarily dropped off to sleep. The past merged with the present as Ned turned his face and watched as the girl on the beach next to him finished brushing her dark hair. She bent forward and shook it, a mane of strong, young, healthy hair of which she was obviously proud and Ned wondered if the girl had a Ned Cresswell in her life too. But, on the other hand, Ned thought, things happen so much earlier these days. Puberty used to be such a dark, uncharted land full of confusion and blank walls and now . . . Now! Ned was jerked from his romantic reflections as the girl, who had already removed her slacks, crossed her arms in front of her and whipped off the T-shirt to reveal herself in full, very post-pubescent maturity, obviously as proud of her bosom as she was of her hair. Good Lord above, Ned muttered as he found himself staring open-mouthed at the sun-kissed Olympienne not five yards away and wondering whether the other bits were also about to be revealed. Ned managed to close his mouth in time to be able to force a flustered smile as the girl lowered herself down onto her towel, turning as she did so to face Ned.

"Wonderful day, isn't it?" she said to Ned and Ned, unable to reply, raised his hand instead in a gesture which could have been interpreted as acquiescent. Well, thought Ned, I'll be jiggered, now I've seen it all and, he reminded himself, on Birling beach. He wondered if he ought not to have erected the windbreak on the other side of their spot.

Ned returned his attention to the wandering Norman, who seemed to be waving and Ned waved back. Norman was obviously enjoying himself.

"Ned," came the sound of Norman's voice over the sound of the gently lapping waves. "Ned, come here!"

Ned cupped his hands to his mouth and shouted back. He felt rather foolish bellowing in the middle of a beach with a semi-naked person so close by, but he bellowed all the same.

"What do you want?"

He couldn't hear Norman at first and what he did hear sounded like something about someone called John.

"Can't hear," Ned shouted and cupped his hands to his ears instead. "Louder!"

What Ned heard next, he knew he heard because the sunbather also heard it.

"I think I've found a bomb!" shouted Norman, thinking that he would make himself hoarse.

The sunbather sat up immediately and clasped the top half of her bikini to her naked bosom.

"Did he say bomb?" said the girl, turning to Ned and covering her exposure. Ned wondered why suddenly the wearing of the bikini top had become necessary but it wasn't the moment to even think of enquiring.

"I think he did," Ned said. "Better go and have a look." He got up from his towel and pulled on his boots. Norman was bending down and poking at something in the sand with a piece of driftwood.

"Leave it alone," shouted Ned. "I'm on the way."

"Can I come too," asked the girl. "Do you mind?"

"Not at all," said Ned, clumsily securing his bootlaces. "It's probably nothing at all, knowing my friend."

The girl pulled on her sneakers and she and Ned slid their way down the sloping pebbles to the sea, Ned proving that his hiking boots really were rather more relevant to the terrain than Norman gave credit for.

"Then what do you think it could be?" asked the girl. "I'm sure I heard him say bomb."

"My friend, dear girl, is capable of seeing things which ordinary mortals only see in their worst nightmares."

"You mean he has a vivid imagination," said the girl. "My name's Kim, by the way. It's further than you think, isn't it? Do you want to slow down?"

"Asking me to slow down, my dear, is much the same as asking Dracula to hang on to a crucifix. You can call me Ned by the way." They reached the sand and Kim stopped to take off her sneakers whilst Ned strode on.

"Those boots are a jolly good idea for the beach," she said, catching up with Ned. "But aren't they a bit hot?"

"Hot, yes," said Ned, "but necessary. Saves us old chaps falling over all the time. You'll find out when you get to my age." Norman was waiting for them by his discovery and urged them on.

"Come on," he shouted as Ned sailed on, his hat in his hand like the aft pennant on a galleon's poop.

"Alright, Norman, don't panic. Whatever it is isn't going to run away." Ned was quite breathless when they reached the spot where Norman was standing. next to something sticking up out of the sand. The ebbing eddies of the tide still swirled around the half-buried object. Ned squatted down and the seat of his shorts was instantly soaked. Three pairs of eyes examined the object whilst the seagulls soared overhead, calling raucously to each other in their persistent challenges.

"Well," said Norman after a moment. "What d'you think?"

"Bloody hell," said Ned.

"Ned!" remonstrated Norman gently for as yet he had not been introduced to Ned's companion although he did remark to himself how little the young person's swimming costume left to the imagination.

Norman's discovery certainly looked ominous. It was made of metal, which had greatly rusted from long immersion in the salt water and there were spikes on its surface.

"Spooky looking thing, whatever it is," said Kim. "What d'you think it is, Ned?"

"It's a bloody mine," announced Ned. "I'd bet my boots on it."

"So it's not a bomb," Norman concluded, disappointed.

"Same thing," said Kim. "Except they float in the water for ships to run into. Hello, I'm Kim." She held out her hand and Norman and Kim made their acquaintance over the casing of the mine.

"Mr Rhodes," said Norman. "Pleased to meet you. And, of course, I know perfectly well what a mine is. We had them in the war."

"Which is exactly where this one came from," said Ned. "We fished most of 'em out but the odd one or two got away."

"Like unexploded bombs people find on building sites," said Kim. "Someone found a whole aeroplane last year at the bottom of a lake."

"My God . . . Norman!" said Ned as he stood up, "did I see you poking this thing?"

"Ought I not to have?" asked Norman innocently. "Surely it's a dead one?."

"You never can tell," Ned said thoughtfully. "Now," he said, slapping his thigh with the all the elan of a principal boy, "I think we'd better clear the beach."

Norman looked doubtful. Kim looked bemused.

"Oh, Ned," Norman ventured, "do you think that's absolutely necessary. Wouldn't it be better to go and tell someone first. Like the coastguard?"

"Or the lifeboat people?" suggested Kim. "Bill Bray's on duty today and he was in the army. He'd know what to do."

"Bosh," said Ned. "I was as good as in the bloody army too, young lady and I'm perfectly aware of the proceedure."

"The proceedure for what?" asked Norman who couldn't remember any of the colourful incidents in Ned's life ever having been connected with bomb disposal.

"The proceedure, Norman! First, clear the area of all civilians."

"But we are civilians, Ned," said Norman, "and we're still here. Surely, if this mine thing has been here all these years and hasn't exploded yet, it's not likely to now, is it?"

"It might have drifted in only recently," said Kim, feeling that Ned could do with some assistance. "Caught one of its spikes on a rock and got buried in the sand."

"Well," said Norman huffily, "I've been poking at it for five minutes and nothing's happened."

"You're not a battleship, Norman. They weren't designed to go off being poked by old men with sticks."

"Thank you!" Norman retorted.

Kim intervened.

"Seriously, Mr Rhodes, I do think Ned is right. We've got to do something just to be on the safe side. I vote we go and tell Bill Bray. Yes?"

Ned looked at Norman and Norman looked at Ned and then they both looked at Kim. Kim's motion was silently adopted without a vote being formally taken and all three began the walk back to the lifeboat hut on top of the cliffs.

"Just a minute," said Ned. "Perhaps someone should stay here."

"What for?" said Norman.

"To mark it, silly. Look, we're not throwing in the towel and going off to tell a bunch of sceptics that we've found a possibly unexploded mine on the beach. They're going to come trooping back with us and a pair of old fools we'd look if we couldn't find it again."

"Right on, brother," said Kim raising her clenched fist.

"I beg your pardon?" said Ned.

"Strike a blow for gray rights," said Kim.

"Oh," said gray Ned. "Yes. Quite right-on, sister."

"Well I suppose I'm going to have to be the one who gets left behind," said Norman. "I always miss out on the real fun."

"No one has to stay," said Kim. "We can leave something to mark where it is. Here," she said, "I'll leave my . . ."

"No!" said Ned, thinking that the unshockable Miss Kim was going to whip off her bikini top as a marker and then march half-naked up the beach and into the lifeboat hut. "It's alright. I'll leave my towel. It's soaking wet as it is."

"Oh, alright," said Kim. "I was going to leave my sneakers."

ELEVEN

Bill Bray had been joined in the lifeboat hut by Jimmy Kennard and Tom Ball. Together, it could have been thought that they represented the cream of East Dean's machismo and judging by the number of girls who were to be found hanging around the lifeboat hut on summer afternoons, such a thought would have been reasonably well-founded.

As Ned, Norman and Kim made their way up the beach, the three men were standing on the edge of the cliff and although they were undoubtedly admiring a view, the view they were admiring was Kim Maxwell's cleavage.

"Cor," said Tom Ball, the youngest, the unmarried one and therefore the one most likely to voice the unspoken feelings of the other two. "Cop a load of that!"

"I see what 'ee means," said Jimmy Kennard. "Wish I 'ad 'er 'phone number."

"You'd 'ave to ring Tom Maxwell's house," advised Bill Bray. "That's 'is daughter. I seen 'er grow from but a little seedling." Bill always used gardening analogies. He found it got him into less trouble.

"And 'as she grown!" slobbered the the lusty young Mr Ball.

"Now, now," reprimanded Bill, "that sort's not for the likes of you, young man. At the university so I hear."

"Tasty, though," was all the response Tom Ball could manage.

"Let's hope she don't turn out like 'er batty old aunt," pointed out Jimmy Kennard. "She were clever too, so they say, an' she was as cracked as an old pot."

"She was a good sort, was Annie Wingfield," Bill contradicted. "Do anything for anyone. No side to 'er at all and that young Maxwell girl's from the same packet of seeds."

"An' who would that be with 'er?" asked Jimmy Kennard.

"Ah," replied Bill, "They come earlier in that clapped out old Mini over there . Penny 'opper reckons one of 'em's got a wooden leg, so 'er mother-in-law says."

"Seems to be managin' OK over them stones," observed Jimmy.

Tom Ball had brought some lagers and after reviewing the beach once again, the volunteers repaired to the hut and commenced drinking. The car park was filling up quickly as day trippers and holidaymakers seeking a change from the seafront at Eastbourne arrived either for lunch in the Thatched Bar or a picnic on the beach. The ice cream kiosk was already doing roaring business.

Windsurfers arrived in Volkswagen campers, their boards, masts and sails strapped onto racks on the rooves. Hikers and walkers appeared from paths leading off the Downs from all directions, converging for morning coffee, sitting outside the hotel comparing favourite walkways and bridlepaths.

Families spilled out of cars, popping out like corks after the confinement of the two hour drive from London, Indians from Southall, West Indians from Hackney and Tottenham, young professionals from Clapham and Battersea.

Doris and Phil Dawes, with Shane, Shawn and Sharon drove past the car park once and thought it not worth the bother of stopping. Doris couldn't see any beach and she was not really one for the joys of nature. They had breakfasted in the dining room of their boarding house in Eastbourne and whilst the children spent the morning and a great deal of money doing the machines on the pier, she and Phil had had a stroll in the shopping centre. It was safe territory for Doris.

Ned and Kim, closely followed by Norman, climbed the steps and approached the lifeboat hut. Tom Ball could hardly believe his luck although he was less impressed by Kim's companions.

"'Ello," he said, "'ere they come, Flotsam and Jetsam."

The men were used to talking to the public, many of whom came to look at the rubber commando dinghy with its outboard motor which had been paid for and equipped with voluntary contribution.

"Morning, Bill," said Kim. "Great day, isn't it?"

Tom Ball blundered in immediately, his ego craving massage.

"Come for a litle sit down? Lotsa room 'ere on this bench." He shifted his position about six inches from the end of the wooden form and leered at Kim.

"Are you in charge?" Ned asked Bill.

"You might say that," Bill replied. "What can we do for you?"

"It's not what you can do for me," replied Ned. "It's what you can do for the welfare of the public at large. There's a mine on the beach."

"This is Mr Cresswell," said Kim, "and Mr Rhodes. Mr Rhodes actually discovered it."

"My friend thinks it could be dangerous," said Norman, butting in. "But it didn't explode when I poked it."

"So I can see," replied Bill, "else we'd be pickin' bits of you out of the sea by now, wouldn't we?"

The others found Bill Bray's sense of humour hilarious and laughed heartily.

"It's nothing to laugh about," said Ned. "What do you intend to do about it."

"Not a lot we can do," replied Jimmy Kennard.

"Are you in touch with anyone here," asked Ned. The men looked at each other and shook their heads. Tom pointed with his lager tin in the direction of the car park.

"'Phone box up there at t'other end of the car park," he said.

Norman felt awkward. He knew they were being made fun of and he could feel Ned's temper tautening.

"You don't seem to be taking this very seriously," said Kim. "Do you know something we don't?"

"Bin there for years, that old mine," said Bill, at last. "Surprised you haven't seen it before, miss," he said to Kim, "all the summers you been comin' down here. Shifts about a bit, mind, from season to season, dependin' on the tides and where the sand gets laid after a storm."

"Well, I wish you'd said that in the first place," said Ned.

"And so it is safe?" Norman asked.

"Oh yes," said Jimmy. "Bin looked at by experts."

"Then why doesn't someone come and take it away?" asked Kim.

"I'll give you a hand to lug it up the steps if you like," said Tom to Kim and giggled. Ned looked down his nose at the young man and thought him very silly.

"If your arms are as strong as your mouth, young man, I'm sure you could manage it very well by yourself. Come on, Norman." Ned turned on his heel. "Good morning," he bade them.

"Thank you for your . . . help," Norman added and followed Ned in the direction of the steps.

"Wait for me," said Kim. "I'll come with you." She turned back to Bill and the boys. "That wasn't very nice," she said. "They're really very sweet and they were only trying to help. I think you're all very childish."

Three pairs of eyes followed her as she walked back to the steps and down to the beach although three libidinous devotees having been censured by their goddess had to compensate for their loss of virility somehow.

"Well," said Bill, that's tellin' us."

"What did we say to upset 'em?" said Jimmy.

"Got a mouth on 'er, an' all," remarked Tom Ball who was not used to be answered back by any of his usual harem. "Wouldn't fancy an earful of that morning, noon an' night." They returned to their lagers, cracking open another round of cans and allowed their talk to return to the cricket.

At the top of the steps, Kim made a suggestion.

"Would anyone like an ice cream?" she asked. "I'm parched after all the excitment."

"Oh," Norman said, "how thoughtful. Ned?"

"Marvellous. I'd love a wafer."

"This is very kind of you, Kim," said Norman who loved

to make friends with all and sundry but wasn't yet used to such immediate generosity from what was after all a complete stranger. "Could I have a Ninety-Nine."

"What's that," asked Ned, wondering why Norman wasn't having a wafer too. As far as Ned was concerned, ice cream eaten publicly didn't come in any other form except as a wafer.

"It's a cone, with squirty ice cream from a machine," explained Kim, "and then they stick a flaky bar of chocolate down the middle."

"Yuk," said Ned. "But we haven't any money."

"Oh, don't worry about that," said Kim. "I have."

Where, thought Ned and Norman simultaneously? Where on earth could she possibly conceal coins, bearing in mind that she was wearing no more in terms of square area of fabric than would have decently made two handkerchieves.

"In my shoe," said Kim. "It's a trick I picked up on the road." Norman looked puzzled. "Hitch-hiking. You never know, do you?" she concluded meaningfully.

Off went Kim to buy the ices. Norman and Ned waited for her by the steps.

"I suppose she's one of what they call the now generation," said Norman.

"As opposed to what?" said Ned, "the then generation like us?" Ned chuckled, his laugh coming from deep amusement at his recently acquired knowledge of the now generation. "You wait. You've seen nothing yet."

"I wouldn't imagine there's very much else to see," Norman said. "I mean, I'm sure she's a very nice girl and all that but honestly, Ned, that bikini's almost scandalous!"

Ned laughed again.

"Norman, I can remember when we were the now generation as you call it, our bathing costumes were just as scandalous. Scandal is very relative, you know."

"That's rather a sweeping statement," observed Norman. "Most unlike you. Jolly unfair too. Boys who took their trunks off on the beach would probably he arrested."

"One has to keep in touch, Norman," Ned said with

authority, "and I do take your point about the injustice." They delayed further discussion on this topic as Kim returned with the ice creams.

"Awfully sorry, Ned," she said, handing one of the Ninety-Nines to Norman and the other to Ned. "They don't do wafers anymore."

Ned took the cone with the whipped ice cream twirled on the top and looked at it curiously, not knowing whether to be cross or not.

"So," Ned said wearily, plumping for resignation and taking a tentative lick, "Yet another cultural extinction. What next?"

"Thank you, dear," Norman said to Kim. "Lovely."

"Shall we go, chaps?" suggested Kim and so they went, these chaps, one from now and two from then, back to their spot on the beach.

Really, thought Norman as he followed Ned and Kim down the steps, Ned is impossible. Norman could not help remembering the heavy emphasis which Ned had laid not half an hour ago on privacy when here was the paragon of privacy deep in conversation with a perfect stranger. Norman shook his head.

TWELVE

Having driven on halfway to Seaford and having found no beach, Doris ordered Phil to turn the car round. Dutifully and obediently, having long learned the secrets of achieving a quiet life, Phil obeyed. The children were all demanding something. Shane was hungry and Shawn and Sharon were thirsty and so back they drove to Birling Gap. Phil parked the car. It sat uneasily next to a sparkling new Rover on one side and an immaculate, if aged, Mini on the other which, had the Honda been equipped with a memory, it would have recognised from their previous encounter. After much wrangling as to who was to have what and where, Doris grudgingly allowed Shane to have a drink with her and Phil inside the Thatched Bar whilst Shawn and Sharon were to remain outside where Phil was to bring them fizzy drinks and crisps. Dominance and pecking order having been asserted, tongues having been poked out and faces pulled by the younger children as Shane accompanied his parents into the bar, all remained quiet in the visitors enclosure for the next half hour, quite a record.

"May I join you?" said Kim as they arrived back at Ned's beach camp. "Seems silly not to as we're friends now."

"Oh, please do," said Norman. "We'd be delighted, wouldn't we, Ned?"

Ned smiled as he arranged himself on his towels.

"Well I would be," he said but wondered if Norman would be as delighted when every dimple of their new-found friend was revealed in its full frontal glory. Kim collected her towel and bag and came and spread her towel at Ned's feet. It is odd, thought Norman, how they flock to him. Norman, although timid, was not shy of people whereas Ned, although this was not broadcast, was chronically shy. Yet, people were drawn to Ned, especially young people like Kim, who found him fascinating.

"Oh, bother," said Ned suddenly. "I've left my towel down on the mine." He started to get up to go and retrieve it.

"Don't get up," said the girl, "I'll fetch it. It won't take me long," and she was off, leaping down the beach, over the pebbles, with all the poise and assurance of a deer.

"Nice girl," said Norman settling onto her chair. "I wonder where she comes from. She seemed to know those men quite well."

"Perhaps she lives here," said Ned. "probably a student visiting her family."

"Perhaps," said Norman. "You know, she reminds me of someone, Ned."

"She reminds me of Dulcie," Ned said quite abruptly, pressing his shoulders with the tips of his fingers and thinking that perhaps he really ought to put on some of Norman's sun cream. The impression of his finger left little white patches, a tell tale sign. Norman read his mind and fumbled in the bag for the tube.

"Here," he said, handing the tube to Ned. "Not too much. You don't need a lot."

"It's the reflection, you know, Norman. One forgets. Sun's rays off the water and onto the cliffs. Like a magnifying glass."

"Just as you say," said Norman refusing to be drawn into justifying the obvious, which was that it really was very, very warm. The windsurfers had come down to the water's edge and were standing with their fingers in the air as sailors are supposed to do when looking for a breeze.

"They'll be lucky," said Ned. "There's more wind in a tin of baked beans."

"You are so crude," said Norman. "I live in fear and dread of what you'll say next sometimes."

Kim waved to them from the mine and they waved back.

"What makes you think she's like Dulce?" asked Norman.

"Just a feeling," said Ned.

"I would have thought that she'd be besieged by admirers. You can hardly ignore her ample qualifications. She obviously doesn't believe in hiding her light under a bushel."

"I think I detect a note of censure," Ned said. "And, if I might say, don't you think that the pot calls the kettle black?"

"Me?" said Norman, feigning surprise.

"Yes. You. You've always had admirers. Only last year in fact. You could have taken up with that old buzzard in California like a shot."

"Oh, him," said Norman and giggled. "I'd forgotten all about him. He didn't want a friend, Ned. He was only interested in me because Jessica told him what a wonderful nurse I'd been to Cyril."

"True," said Ned, remembering the devotion Norman had applied to caring for his friend. He also remembered Cyril's oft-quoted yet never completed remark - "Ned, let me tell you something, it doesn't matter how much money you have . . ." Cyril always made this pronouncement with feeling for Cyril had devoted his life to making money only to be forced by his merciless illness to leave his not inconsiderable wealth to someone who saved bottle tops and jam jars and who had no predilection for playing the merry widow.

"You two look awfully serious," said Kim, handing Ned back his wet towel. "You can't possibly be serious on Birling beach. There's a by-law against it." Norman took the towel from Ned and draped it to dry on the back of his chair. "I'm going to have my lunch," said Kim. "Not much to share out, I'm afraid. Two bananas and some yoghurt but you're welcome to try."

"We have our own, thank you," said Norman, "but sweet of you to ask. In fact," he said, checking the time, "We might as well have ours too. Would you like a sandwich? I think there's enough."

"There's masses," said Ned. "Where are you from, by the way?" he said to Kim.

"London," Kim replied, taking the bananas out of her bag and peeling one. "But I'm at university at the moment."

"Really?" said Norman. "Where?"

"Oxford," said Kim. "Do you know it?"

"Oh, yes," said Norman as growing intimacy loosened his tongue. "Ned often goes there to do research."

"How exciting, Ned. Research into what?"

Ned glared at Norman. Being friendly was one thing but being quizzed put him on guard.

"This and that," said Ned as nonchalantly as possible. "What are you reading and where?"

"Oh, I've got my degree," Kim said halfway down the banana, "I'm doing postgraduate work now at Balliol. But do tell. What brought you to Oxford?"

"I . . . er . . . I . . ." Ned stammered, not sure of what to say. Norman helped out as he had done on many occasions in the past.

"Ned used to do a lot of work for a publisher," Norman explained. "He's only part-time now. Does it more as a favour really. When the mood takes him." Norman smiled at Ned as if to say, There, got you out of that one, didn't I? "Ginger beer, dear?"

"How marvellous," enthused Kim. "Perhaps you'll introduce me. I'm going to need a publisher one day. I want to turn my thesis into a book although my dad says he doesn't think I stand much of a chance."

"Why?" asked Ned, taking his third sandwich. "What are you doing?"

"The ANZAC involvement in Gallipoli," said Kim, carefully putting the banana skins back into her bag.

"Oh," said Ned, "I think your father might be right. Still, you never know. I know there are publishers who specialise in military topics. What do you think you'll do then?"

"Probably emigrate," said Kim.

"The grass isn't always greener, you know," said Norman. "When all's said and done, 'There's no place like home,'" he quoted. He had forgotten to pack the plastic glasses. Ned seemed to be having no problem with the can of ginger beer although Norman was finding that the bubbles were going up his nose and a lot of it was dribbling down his chin.

And so they talked, Ned managing to maintain his disguise, Norman abandoning the can of ginger beer and Kim, happy to chatter and to forget the real reason why she had left Oxford that weekend which was, as Ned had previously guessed, her own particular Ned Cresswell.

Phil Dawes was on his second pint, deep into the racing pages of the *Daily Star* and Doris was contemplating a third gin and tonic when Shawn and Sharon appeared in the doorway of the Thatched Bar.

"Can we 'ave some more crisps, mum?" asked Shawn.

"No," said Doris. "You've 'ad two packs each and that's enough. Why doncha go down on the beach. Yer dad an' me'll be down shortly."

"Don't want to," said Sharon sulkily. "Can we go and see the lifeboat, mum?"

"If you want," said Doris, signalling the barmaid to give her a refill. "Go with 'em, Shane, there's a love and no larkin' about, hear me?" Shane got up, taking the hint. He knew she wanted to be shot of them for a while.

"Can we 'ave some money for ice cream, mum?" he asked.

As she handed over a five pound note to the barmaid for her G and T, Doris could hardly refuse him. She sorted out a couple of pound coins from her change.

"An' bring us the change," she said. "There's two quid there. Ices don't cost that."

"Right," said Shane and left the bar which was now full to bursting with trippers.

"Come on," he said to his younger siblings, "let's go up on the cliff an' sling some stones. Betcha I can get one in the sea."

"How much d'yer bet?" challenged Shawn.

"This two quid," replied his elder brother

."But I want my ice cream," moaned Sharon.

"Shut yer face," said Shane. "Who d'yer think got the two quid out of 'er in the first place?" Sharon looked as though she was going to cry. "An' stop that," threatened Shane, "or we'll chuck you over an' all. Come on."

The children wandered out of the courtyard outside the Thatched Bar and through the car park. They passed the lifeboat hut where Bill and Jimmy were talking to two of the windsurfers. Tom Ball was sunbathing, visibly preening himself and trying to attract the attention of two Dutch girls who had just parked their Deux Chevaux opposite him.

"Here," Shane said as they reached a spot out of sight of the lifeboat hut. They lay down on the grass and elbowed their way on their stomachs to a point where they could see over the edge of the cliff to the beach below.

"'Ere, look," said Shawn. "Down there. Them old farts from the caff yesterday."

"Where?" said Shane, pulling himself into a better position.

."Down there. You blind or what?"

"Ugh!" said Sharon, wriggling back from the cliff edge. "You seen what we're lyin' in?"

"What you on about, Sharon?" said Shane.

"She's right," said Shawn. "It's rabbits' muck. It's everywhere." The three withdrew from their vantage point and Shane had an idea.

"Hey," he said, "I got an idea. What if we chucked a few handfuls down onto those old codgers? Wotcha say to that?"

"I'm not pickin' up rabbits' muck," said Sharon.

"It'd scare 'em silly," Shane went on. "They'd think the cliff was comin' down on 'em."

"Yeh," said Shawn, allowing himself to be effortlessly led on by his elder brother.

And so, leaving the doubting Sharon behind some distance from the edge, Shane and Shawn, each armed with two handsful of rabbit droppings, crawled back to the cliff edge and, without aiming, hurled the nasty little pellets onto the beach.

Ned had encamped quite close to the base of the cliffs and was very much enjoying the sandwiches. Norman had cut the apples and was coring them on a napkin when their lunch was scattered with what he immediately thought was a shower of chalk from the cliff above.

All three looked up but there was nothing to see as the two culprits had withdrawn from the edge as soon as they had loosed their missiles.

"There," Norman said to Ned with some satisfaction. "I told you about being too close to the cliff. You never take any notice."

"Just a few loose bits," said Ned. "Nothing to worry about."

"The big chunks only ever come down during the winter," Kim said, backing Ned. "Freeze thaw action, they call it. I remember it from geography."

Norman seemed satisfied although he had that feeling that he had felt last night in his bedroom before discovering the cat, the feeling that there was someone else with them. Luckily, none of the pellets had stuck on anything edible.

On the cliff top, after waiting what they thought was a suitably appropriate length of time, Shane and Shawn returned to the edge, on their stomachs and looked over.

"Must 'ave missed first time round," said Shane.

"Let's get some more," said Shawn and they returned to Sharon to report and to collect more ammunition.

Doris and Phil, feeling suitably squiffy, came out of the Thatched Bar. Doris repaired her make-up while Phil visited the gentlemen's convenience.

"I'm for a bit of a kip," he said when he returned. "Where are them kids?"

"Don't worry about 'em, Phil," scolded his wife. "I keep tellin' you, they're big enough to take care of themselves now. Let's go down the beach."

"But we 'aven't got anything to sit on," Phil complained. "I'd do very well in the car for 'alf an hour."

"Phil, we come all this way lookin' for a beach and this one 'ere's the only one around and if you're worried what to sit on, use the bit that God gave you 'cos from where I'm standin', 'e gave you double!" Doris cackled at her own joke. She always cackled after three gins and, being on holiday, she'd treated herself to what she'd just accused the good Lord of handing out to her husband. Doubles.

"Come on, then," said Phil wearily. "Though 'ow you're gonna walk over them stones in them 'eels, I'll wait to see."

"No bother, love. Shan't be goin' far."

They walked to the steps and, after waiting for a stream of people to ascend, began to go down to the beach. At the bottom of the steps, there was by now very little room to choose a decent spot and so Doris started to walk to the right, her heels sinking into the pebbles and scoring the leather, just as Phil had predicted.

"'Ere," she said, turning to her husband, "makes me feel quite sea sick, this does." Doris, when tiddly, was in her way as loud as Ned, being unable to monitor the pitch of her voice. The volume of her treble screech oscillated as she swayed dangerously on a particularly unsettled patch of beach and the decibels riccocheted off the cliffs behind her.

Ned peered over the top of the windbreak.

"Drunks," he said. "Adults too," he continued disparagingly. "What can one expect of the children if they see grown-ups behaving like that. If I was Prime Minister, I'd pass a law against people like that ever having children."

"No you wouldn't," said Norman. "You're only saying that just to be provocative. You don't even know that they've got any children."

"I didn't necessarily imply that," said Ned wondering whether to finish the other two sandwiches before going on to the apples, "Applies to any children who see adults misbehaving."

"I do apologise for my friend, Kim," said Norman. "He finds the imperfections of the world very hard to live with."

"Don't we all," said Kim. She peeled off the top of one of her yoghurt pots. "There's a million things I'd like to change."

"Take my word for it," Norman advised her, "you'll be a very lucky girl if you get round to even scratching the surface of one of them."

"She'll never know if she doesn't try," Ned said. There was another shriek from Doris who had keeled over, ending up on her bottom, her legs splayed out in from of her. She obviously found the experience extraordinarily amusing as her howls of laughter proclaimed. By this time, she and Phil were not three yards away on the other side of Ned's windbreak.

"Drunks," Ned said, reaching out for the penultimate sandwich. "Hooligans. Is nowhere sacred anymore?"

Norman took his turn to look over the windbreak and immediately recognised Doris from the previous day's incident. His eyes widened and he engaged upon some rapid thinking, trying to work out whether he should tell Ned or leave him to find out on his own. For Norman, honesty had always been the best policy and, in this event, he had no alternative but to impart what he had seen for Ned would not be able to resist the temptation to unleash his tongue.

"Ned," he started to say, "you remember that dear little place we stopped at yesterday for lunch . . ." Norman did not have a chance to finish as they were once again showered with a hail of rabbit droppings. Once again, they looked up and, this time, Shane and Shawn were not fast enough in retreat.

"Did you see them," Kim said. "Up there?"

"I certainly did," Ned said crossly. "I thought it was odd when it happened first. Things fall downwards, not outwards."

Norman looked down again as he felt the apple quarters sliding off the napkin on his lap and corrected the position of his knees. He didn't have to look twice to recognise rabbit doo doos.

"Oh, how revolting!" he exclaimed. "Ugh! We could have eaten that."

"What?" said Ned.

"That," said Norman pointing at the napkin in front of

him. "These. Those people have been showering us with rabbits' pooh."

Kim too found a couple of the pellets in her yoghurt and fished them out with her spoon, a look of distaste on her face.

Doris, with or without anything to sit on, had collapsed backwards on the beach. She was lying as though one staked out for sacrifice but clutched still at her handbag. Phil had removed his jacket and was adjusting it as best as he could beneath his already amply padded backside.

"D'you think they saw us?" said Shane to Shawn.

"I wanna see," piped up Sharon.

"Thought you was scared," accused her elder brother.

"Well I'm not," Sharon said defiantly. "Just didn't wanna lay in all that muck."

"There isn't any muck now," taunted Shawn. "So, I dare you . . ."

Sharon crawled on her tummy towards the edge of the cliff.

"Can't see," she said over her shoulder.

"Then get further," said Shawn, "or go sideways."

"Keep hold of me 'ands, then," Sharon said and Shane, crawling after her as she positioned herself sideways at the cliff's edge, took hold of her hand.

"No," she said. "Both hands."

Sharon's weight dislodged a few loose pieces of chalk which rattled down the side of the cliff. Ned was waiting below for a re-appearance of the two heads and as soon as the skyline was broken by Sharon's silhouette, he was ready. Sharon was some forty feet above but the sound of Ned's reverberant bellow scared the daylights out of her.

As she kicked out and backwards, the thin earth covering the cliff edge crumbled under her legs and she felt empty space beneath her. The earth sprayed down on the beach below as the weight of her legs falling twisted her whole body round. She screamed as she came face to face with Shane. She saw the blood drain from his face and a look of sheer terror come into his eyes which compounded the terror in her own.

"I've gotcha, Shar. 'Ang on!"

Sharon, too terrified to speak, continued to scream.

Below, the apple quarters now dashed to the ground, Ned, Norman and Kim were aghast as the girl's legs scrabbled and fought to find a toe hold on the cliff.

"Oh dear God," wailed Norman. "Please don't let her . . . please . . ."

"Hold on," Kim yelled. "Just hold on!"

Although Ned was often very good at creating crises, when such events turned into emergencies, he was also very good at coping with them. Immediately, he realised that nothing could be done from below. Even without his boots, Ned began to run down the beach in the direction of the steps.

"Kim," he called. "Come with me! Norman, you keep telling them to hang on. Give them encouragement." Kim was at first not sure of what to do and hovered. "Kim!" Ned shouted. "I said, come with me!" Kim obeyed.

Sharon's screams, emanating as they did from just above where her father was lying, woke Phil from the deep sleep into which he had fallen given the heady mixture of three pints of beer and the hot mid-day sun. Doris too struggled up from her prone position.

"Wos goin' on?" she said slurring her words. "Wossa matter, Phil?"

They turned, as one, to the accompaniments of shouts of desperation and encouragement from Norman, who was standing not five yards away.

"Blimey," said Doris, screwing up her eyes and focusing on the flailing figure on the cliff face above. "Look at that Phil! Some poor kid's got itself trapped!"

Phil was faster in his reflexes. There must have been a hundred young people on the beach that day wearing blue jeans and t-shirts but his father's instinct was paramount.

"Doris! That's Sharon up there!" He spoke in a voice no louder than a whisper. What he saw he couldn't initially digest and his reaction at first was of horror. He stared open-mouthed and transfixed, unable to move. Doris was more active; she panicked and ran screaming to the bottom of the cliff.

"Sharon! Sharon. Hang on, love! For God's sake, hang on!"

The noise attracted other attention as one by one the families and groups sunning themselves on the beach, realised what was happening on the cliff and that, far from being a stunt, a real-life, front page headlines drama was being enacted before their eyes. The reactions amongst the sunbathers ranged from people turning away and averting their eyes, clasping children to their bosoms, to those who ran to the scene to see if they could be of any assistance. One man began shouting orders, quite sensible ones, about fetching towels, anything soft, to spread at the bottom of the cliff in case . . . in case of the unthinkable happening. Men ran hither and thither, collecting inflatable dinghies, childrens' water wings and blow-up air beds and, whilst Sharon kicked and screamed, holding on for dear life to Shane, there arose a multi-coloured, plastic cushion of beach paraphernalia on and around the spot where she would be likely to land, should she fall.

Shane, to give him credit, had felt himself being also pulled further and further towards the edge as Sharon's weight excercised its gravitational prerogative. He screamed to his brother who, like his father below, was paralysed with horror.

"Lie down, Shawn. Grab my feet!" Shane found himself being able to think more clearly as the urgency of the situation impressed itself. "Don't let go! Just hang on . . ." He had the foresight not to announce the fact that he knew that Sharon was slipping from his grasp as that would have panicked the screaming teenager even more, but his hands were sweating profusely, as were Sharon's and he could feel the palms sliding over each other, millimetre by millimetre, like two vast shelves of continental mass separating under the pressure of unimaginable forces.

By the time Ned and Kim had reached the top of the steps by the lifeboat hut, they heard a crescendo from the beach as a heartstopping gasp went up from the onlookers.

Oh, no!" said Kim. "Please don't let her fall . . . Please."

Unlike Kim, Ned didn't stop to run back to look. As it

was, Kim was too late to see that Sharon had indeed slipped out of Shane's hands. Shane had been unable to prevent it and his face was buried in the wiry grass of the clifftop as he felt Sharon slipping away.

She slipped only a foot at the very most, for where the cliff had crumbled away, it had left a ledge, some eight inches wide and she had slid, not at a vertical, but at a less lethal angle , more slowly than she would have done otherwise. She came to rest, flat against the cliff edge, her feet propped on the chalk ledge, just a foot from the top.

Ned raced to the lifeboat hut where word of the disaster had not yet penetrated. Tom Ball had managed to grease his way into the affections of both Dutch girls and was busy showing off. He raised his eyebrows as Ned trundled across the stony clifftop, his feet seeming not to feel the pain. He was completely out of breath.

"Don't tell me," he said insolently, "this time you've found a submarine." Ned ignored him and ran up to the door of the hut.

Both Bill and Jimmy were inside the boathouse, attending to a patch on the side of the lifeboat.

"There's been a fall," Ned gasped. "Got any rope?"

Without waiting for either of them to answer, he saw a coil of rope hanging on a nail, grabbed it and ran off in the direction of where Shane and Shawn lay prostrate on the clifftop, thinking that their sister had perished. They were both terrified and wept silently, too afraid to look over the edge.

Bill and Jimmy ran after Ned, joined by Kim who had run back from the top of the steps, still ignorant of the fact that there was still a life to save.

"Leave those bloody women alone, Tom and get yourself along this cliff," shouted Bill Bray as he and Jimmy, also shoeless, followed Ned.

"Get more rope," Kim shouted to Tom Ball. "A child's fallen over the cliff." She ran on. "And first aid, too!"

Tom was not so stupid as not to realise that he was part of a real emergency and reacted swiftly.

There was a low wall on the other side of the lifeboat hut, most of which had fallen down over the edge over a succession of winters. Ned was too intent to think about obstacles and scrambled over the wall, immune to the scratches and lacerations which the sharp flints made on his thighs. He scampered over the grass and was soon standing over the prone forms of the two children at the cliff edge. He threw himself down on his stomach.

"Shift yourselves!" he ordered and both of them rolled over and wriggled backwards, out of the way, as Bill and Jimmy arrived behind him. Kim was not far behind them.

Ned elbowed himself to the edge of the cliff and peered over. At first, because of the angle, all he could see was a crowd of people, with Norman at the forefront.

"Norman! What's happened? Has the child fallen?"

"Yes," Norman shouted back. "But she's on a ledge. Just come forward a little bit and you'll see her. Ned! Be careful!!"

Ned inched forward enough to be able to see Sharon's hands, still extended upwards just as they had been when they had lost her brother's grip. Though still out of breath, Ned was cool and collected as he spoke.

"Ah," he said soothingly, "there you are! Thought we'd lost you."

Sharon's tear-stained face looked up. Her slide over the edge had grazed her cheek and her forehead and a little line of blood was trickling down, as though a zip had been opened in a packet of tomato ketchup.

"Help me," she said in a very small, beseeching whimper.

"Now don't you fret, young lady. We'll have you up from there in a jiffy. But you must remain absolutely still. Got me? Don't even move a muscle."

"No," said Sharon, shaking her head.

Ned looked over his shoulder to where Bill, Jimmy Kennard and Kim were standing. Tom arrived with more rope and the first aid box.

"Make a noose in that rope, will you, there's a good chap," Ned said to Bill. "I'm going to stay here and talk to the child. Quick now." He waited a moment while Bill knotted the rope in the safest fashion and passed the free end of the rope through the loop he had made.

"Soon have you up, dear," said Ned over the edge to Sharon. "Hope you're keeping still like I asked you? Are you?"

"Yes," Sharon said. "But please hurry, will you?"

Bill Bray dropped to his knees and then wriggled forward so that he and Ned were lying side by side. He inched forward to a point where he too could see the frightened girl.

"Hello there, young lady," he said cheerily. "Bit of an odd place to do your sunbathin', isn't it?"

Sharon nodded.

"Now," said Ned to Sharon. "You just listen to what this nice gentleman is going to tell you."

"Who? Me?" Bill muttered to Ned. "Seems as though you were doing alright on your own, sir." Their eyes met and the look that passed between them told much.

"What's your name?" Ned said to Sharon encouragingly.

"Sharon," the girl replied. "Sharon Dawes, sir."

"Well," Ned began, "what we're going to do, Sharon, is to lower a loop of rope down to you. What we want you to do is this. When you see the rope, bring your arms slowly, and I mean slowly, together above your head. But keep close to the cliff. Is that clear so far?"

"Yes, sir."

"Right," Ned said. "Here we go then."

Bill lowered the loop whilst Jimmy Kennard and Tom held fast onto the other end. The loop inched down the cliff.

"Now," Ned said, "bring your hands together and just let the loop slide over your arms."

Sharon obeyed as Ned kept up the encouragement.

"That's it. Easy does it, Sharon. There. Now, what we have to do now is this."

Sharon interrupted him and Ned heaved a sigh of relief as it was apparent that the girl was not so shocked that she was going to be unable to help herself.

"I know, I think; I've got to get this rope round me waist and under me arms, right?"

"Exactly right, Sharon, You've got it. Clever girl."

"You're doin' fine," said Bill under his breath.

"There's no need to make any move, Sharon. Just stay stuck fast to that chalk but just relax a little so that the rope slips over your shoulder then pull your arms down flat against your sides. The gentleman here will tighten it for you. You'll be quite safe."

Bill stretched his arms out and over the edge of the cliff and very gently inched the loop of rope taut.

"Right, young lady. Now what we're going to do is this. My lads 'ere are going to take the strain of the rope and gently, ever so gently now, we're goin' to have you up on the top 'ere in no time."

"Give them some help, Sharon. Like in the films when James Bond is scaling the walls. Try and find some toe holds to help you."

Bill looked over his shoulder.

"OK, lads. Start pulling, but keep it slow . . . Feel your way with 'er."

Slowly, very slowly, Jimmy and Tom took the strain of Sharon's weight on the rope and gradually she began to rise up the cliff face."

Hold onto the rope, dear," Ned urged. "You're not going to fall. Never fear."

Down below, Norman was holding his face in his hands while Doris stood by the pile of inflatables, breathing deeply, her arms stretched up in a helpless gesture of being ready to catch the uncatchable, her handbag still hung from her arm.

As the watchers saw Sharon being finally hoisted to safety, there was a ripple of applause, followed by an animated buzz of conversation.

Ned and Bill had rolled over and away from the spot where Sharon now lay gasping on the grass. Jimmy and Tom dropped the rope as soon as Sharon was lying at a safe distance from the edge and Tom ran forward with the first aid box.

Ned wriggled back from the edge too and then pulled himself up to his knees and stayed there for a full minute, his head lowered. Kim dropped to her knees beside him.

"Are you alright, Ned? You were magnificent."

Ned did not answer for a while but held out his hand and Kim grasped it. Shane and Shawn who had been watching all this from a safe distance, came forward.

"Will she be OK?" Shane asked Tom who was turning Sharon over, gently feeling her limbs for breakages and smoothing back the hair from her brow to discover the extent of the cut. Sharon smiled bravely. "You alright, Sha?" She nodded.

Ned got up, accepting a hand from Bill. Once on his feet, he accepted his other hand in acknowlegement of their joint effort.

"Phew," he said. "I'm getting too old for this game." He turned his attention to Sharon. "And you, young lady, I hope it'll be a long time before you go anywhere near a cliff again."

"Yes, sir," said Sharon, "thank you sir."

Ned looked at her and then at her two brothers.

"Don't I know you from somewhere? he asked. The boys stared back blankly at him, speechless. "I don't know, but you seem very familiar to me. Especially you," he said to Shane, the eldest. "Throwing things over the edges of cliffs at people. Should be ashamed of yourselves. Where are your parents? Eh?" Neither answered but both looked shamefaced at the ground. "Oh well, all's well that ends well," said Ned. "This might have taught you all a good lesson. Come on, Kim. Let's get back and see about poor Norman. He'll be nothing but a mass of jelly."

Ned and Kim left the lifeboat men to take care of the rest. Kim noticed the scratches on Ned's legs.

"Ned, you're bleeding. Shall I get something from the first aid box?"

Ned looked down at his legs, licked his fingers and wiped his hand over the grazes.

"Just a scratch. Nothing to worry about." He winced as his foot fell on a particularly sharp stone. "Ooh! These stones are sharp!" Kim took his hand and helped him back over the stony patch, over the wall and back to the steps.

A stream of people were filing up the steps from the beach. None of them, of course, were aware that it had been

Ned who had been instrumental in the rescue as they could not distinguish faces from so far below. Several pushed past quite rudely, including Doris and Phil Dawes who were almost the first in the rush. Ned came face to face with his former foe but Doris showed no signs of recognition. Ned and Kim stepped out of the onrush until it was past.

"I know that face," Ned said, peering after Doris as the anxious mother was swept along by the crowd. "Can't place her, though." Ned shook his head and made his way back to where Norman was waiting by the windbreak. There were still quite a few people gathered at the scene of the incident, chattering amongst themselves and retrieving their inflatable belongings from the pile which had been assembled at the foot of the cliff.

Norman ran towards Ned, threw his arms around him and burst into tears.

"Oh dear, dear Ned! Are you alright?" Norman withdrew and looked his friend over for wounds. He gave a little cry when he saw the scratches on Ned's legs. "Why, you *are* hurt!"

"Now don't fuss, Norman. It's nothing. It'll all be healed up in a couple of days."

"Still needs antiseptic," said Norman and fumbled in the capacious beachbag which always contained basic remedies.

Some men were talking as they returned to their families and Kim overheard them.

"Bloody wonderful those lifeboat men, don't you think?" said one.

"Fantastic," said his friend. "Should all get medals for this."

Kim began to bridle and was just about to say something to them when Ned restrained her.

"Leave it, dear. Leave it. Let them think . . ." He winked at Kim. "Gray power, eh? Sister?"

Kim smiled. What a wonderful old thing you are, she thought as Ned let Norman take over and surrendered to the pamperings which, after all, are the due of heroes, especially gray heroes.

THIRTEEN

It was about two o'clock when it started to turn chilly. Little wisps and blurs of cloud coalesced and where there had been no breeze before, a definite wind from the south west began to lift the surface of the sea.

"Told you it was still only April," said Ned who, since the rescue had been supine on the one remaining usable chair as Norman had thought that it was only right that Ned should be the one to occupy it. Ned's past heroics, such as the incident when the plumber had fallen through the lath and plaster ceiling and had been left dangling between two joists, unable to move, his arms trapped above and his legs dangling into Norman's workroom, paled to insignificance beside this latest feat. Norman had been most impressed even though his initial reaction on Ned's return had been to scold him for being so reckless. Kim too, was lost in admiration as she had never met a character so colourful. As with so many of the young, her previous encounters with the over-sixties had been limited to aunts and grandmothers and although Annie, Tom's aunt, had been somewhat reclusive, perhaps slightly eccentric, Ned represented the more attractive aspect of gerontia, one that a twenty-two year old could seize upon as a decent perspective.

"Yes," said Norman. "I think we've had the best of the day." He stood up and peered in the direction, westwards, of Seaford Head, as though by standing, he would somehow be able to see what the weather was doing as far away as the Western Approaches. "But we can't complain. I think we've all caught a bit of sun. Ned's legs are quite pink and Kim's . . . er . . . Yes. Well, Kim is a very good colour already."

Kim had been so engrossed in a conversation with Ned reliving the moments of the rescue that she had put total sunbathing out of her mind and Norman had been spared the pain of having to adjust yet another definition of what nice girls are all about in the age which had been ushered in by the first burned bra.

"What d'you think, Ned?" Norman asked. "Had enough?"

Ned shaded his eyes and looked at the sky, assessing the possibilities for the remainder of the afternoon.

"I think you might be right, Norman. And," he added, "if I lie here in this chair one moment longer I think I shall seize up. I'm getting a little old for dashing about without suffering a few consequences. Here, Kim," Ned held out his hand, "help an old radical up, would you?"

Kim got up and took both Ned's hands and pulled him out of the chair.

"You're not really going, are you?" Kim said plaintively.

"I think I'd better soak Ned in a hot bath," Norman said, folding away the towels and packing them along with their rubbish into the canvas beach bag. "Ned's father was a great believer in hot baths."

"And whisky," said Ned. "But he believed in whisky more. Very sensible man."

"We'll see about that," said Norman. "I shall have to buy some. Now, Kim, dear, can we give you a lift anywhere?"

"Thank you but I think I'll stick around here just in case?" said Kim. "I'm a great optimist." She paused. "I must say it's been a great pleasure meeting you both. Are you here for long?"

"Until Monday," said Ned. "If it's good tomorrow we'll be here again." Ned bent to try and tie his laces but he couldn't quite make it. Kim came to his aid and tied the laces for him. "Right, Norman. All set. What can I carry?"

"Just the bag and the windbreak, dear. I'll manage the chairs. I'll have to look for a replacement cover for that broken one."

"We'll buy her another," Ned announced. "Righto. Goodbye, Kim. Jolly good meeting you."

They all shook hands and Ned, re-attired in his colourful beach garb, his satchel slung round his shoulders, led the way, limping a little now. Kim watched them, regretting that their acquaintance had been so short.

Ned waited for Norman to catch him up. Even as one of the walking wounded, Ned was taking the march over the pebbles like an assault course.

"It's the great thing about getting away for a bit," said Ned. "You meet new people."

"You can meet new people in Sainsbury's," Norman observed "Any day." They trudged on. "You don't usually want to."

"It's different at home," Ned continued. "If you meet someone new at home, I always think that they expect to be given tea or something. Like neighbours. All very well in their way but you never know when they're going to over-step the mark."

"I don't think many people listen at the walls with upturned tumblers now," said Norman. "And they're much more likely to if you don't talk to them. You just remain a mystery and that really makes people nosey."

"I like being a mystery," said Ned definitely.

"So I've noticed, dear," Norman said wistfully. "You'e been a mystery to me for years."

They reached the bottom of the steps and the steps looked suddenly taller than ever. It was the third time Ned had climbed them that day.

"Well," said Ned, wondering if he'd make the top, "I think it's very nice to meet someone like that Kim, have a chat and say cheerio. Makes a jolly pleasant little memory."

"Oh, I agree," Norman said, allowing Ned to go first, "it's just that I always prefer to see if things develop."

"What things?" asked Ned.

"Things," said Norman. "A friendship, perhaps."

"God," Ned said, beginning to puff a bit, "if we'd made friends with everyone we'd met even in the last year, we'd have no time to call our own. Can't make friends out of everybody, Norman. If you can count your friends on the fingers of one hand, you're lucky. And," he added as an afterthought, "if you made a friend out of everyone, you'd have to start writing your Christmas cards in January."

"I don't think one should ever stop trying to make

friends," Norman persisted. "There's going to come a time when they'll be in jolly short supply. All ours are beginning to die off. Just think about that."

They reached the top.

"Let's have a breather," Ned said, "and one last look. I doubt very much if we will be able to make it tomorrow, whatever the weather."

"Especially if you're planning to demolish that leg of lamb alone," said Norman.

"I'm not," said Ned. "I'm going to ask Tom over."

"Ah," Norman said, his face brightening visibly. "How nice. You took rather a shine to him, didn't you?"

"So did you," said Ned. "And, let's face it, that's much more to the point." Norman giggled.

"I am silly, aren't I?"

"Never!" said Ned. "You might be getting on a bit but there's still no harm in a chap paying a bit of attention, is there?" He looked along the beach. "Look at that. Nothing like a seaside. Like some painter's palette. Little blobs of colour, squeezed from all these tubes." He indicated the car park. "All waiting with their numbers on to be joined up into a picture. Then the sea comes up and washes it all away in time for a new picture tomorrow. I love it."

"Come on," said Norman who was innured to Ned's whimsies, "let's go and do a bit more shopping."

They walked across the car park, past the lengthy queue for ice creams at the kiosk and to their car.

The Dawes family were sitting on the grass next to their Honda which, as will be recalled, had been parked in the space next to Ned's Mini. Sharon had been suitably patched up after Tom Ball had confirmed that there were no bones broken although she was unusually quiet. The experience had had a similarly sobering effect on the whole family. Doris had thought she was going to have one of her turns although the effect of her tipples in the Thatched Bar had been dissipated by the terrible prospect she had faced of seeing her daughter falling to her death. When she had arrived at Sharon's side, Doris reacted in the time-honoured way in which many relieved parents behave:

instead of clasping the rescued child tearfully to her bosom, Doris had berated her, yelling at the child at the top of her voice until Tom Ball had been forced to stop working on Sharon and perform a little first aid on Mrs Dawes. Having satisfied herself that Sharon was in good hands and unharmed, Doris had turned her attention on her benighted sons. Shane and Shawn stood like doomed men in front of a firing squad as Doris went through a repertoire of threats and abuses until she felt that her message had been understood. "'An' I'll 'ave the change from that two quid, an all," she had said in conclusion and Shane handed his mother the unspent ice cream money. Phil Dawes, in contrast, had remained quiet, cradling Sharon's head in his lap as she lay on the grass while Tom Ball bathed her cuts in Dettol and helped her drink a cup of hot tea which had been brought from the cafe. When Doris had finished with the boys and had withdrawn to take breath, Phil had gone over to his sons and quietly admonished them himself. Usually, Phil Dawes was all fingers and thumbs when it came to overt shows of affection, but he hugged his two sons to him. Shawn began to cry, sobbing on his father's shoulder and whispering over and over again how sorry he was. Phil had said, "There, there, old son. All over now, 'ey?" and felt that he had never been closer to his family.

As Ned and Norman neared their car, the real reasons for the incident were being wormed out of the children by the relentless Doris.

"What were you doin' on the bloody cliff in the first place?" she probed.

"Dunno," said Shane sullenly.

"You told me you were goin' to look at the lifeboat," she accused. "It's all your fault, Shane. You're the eldest. You should know better. What were you really doin'?"

"Just messin' about," said Shane. "We all was, mum. Not just me. It's always me. I always get the blame."

Phil tried to interrupt.

"Leave it, Doris. They're all OK and that's the main thing. It'll 'ave taught them a lesson. Right, kids?"

"He was really nice, that old geezer," said Sharon. "Really great, he was."

"What old geezer," Doris demanded.

At that moment, Ned appeared between the Mini and the Honda with the bag and the windbreak. He put down the equipment and searched in his satchel for the car key. Turning, Ned saw the Dawes family. At first he only saw Sharon and the two boys.

"Ah," said Ned, "there you are. Found your parents, yet?" Ned unlocked the car. "Feeling alright, young lady?"

"Him," Sharon said, pointing at Ned whom neither Doris nor Phil could see. "I was just tellin' em, sir. Thanks again. Dunno wot I'd 'ave done without you."

Doris stood up and, in the calm of the aftermath, recognised Ned instantly.

"'im?" Doris spluttered incredulously. "Wot the 'ell are you talkin' about, Sharon?"

Oh, Lord, thought Norman. He knew he ought to have told Ned about the dreaded Doris being on the beach but in the wake of the drama, it had completely slipped his mind.

"I thought I recognised those children," Ned said, turning to Norman who, for safety's sake, remained behind the car. "And I thought I recognised her!"

"Sharon, tell me," urged Phil. "What's all this about."

"That bloke," Sharon said, "he rescued me. Talked to me all the time."

"Don't be daft, Sharon," said Doris. "She's touched, Phil. Got that concuction or whatever they call it. I told you we should 'ave got 'er to the 'ospital." Then, to Sharon. "An' it was them lifeboat men who got yer up, love. Didn't they, boys?" The boys looked at each other, then managed to catch Ned's eye. Their look implored him not to tell what they were doing.

"Sharon's right, mum. He was great. Real hero," said Shane.

"Yeh," agreed Shawn. "Thanks, mister."

Doris was completely floored. She looked at each of her brood in turn, not knowing who or what to believe. Phil was less flummoxed, in fact he was positively animated in his gratitude.

"Well," he said getting up from the grass, "seems we've got a lot to thank you for, Mr . . ."

"Cresswell," said Ned, polite but cool, his pulse rate having subsided somewhat. "It was nothing. Anyone would have done the same thing. Good afternoon."

He opened the car door, pulled the seat forward and stowed the bag and the windbreak in the back seat. Norman had already put the chairs into the boot and was waiting to get into the car. Ned reached across and unlocked the door and Norman opened it.

"We do hope the little girl will be alright," Norman said brightly. "I'm sure she'll never forget it."

"Please," said Phil, seeing that Ned was fully intending to drive away. "Isn't there anything we can do for you? We owe you so much."

"Please," Ned said, waving away the offer as graciously as he felt polite, "if there are three more children in the world this afternoon who will think the next time they're tempted to do something stupid or dangerous, that's all the thanks I need." He looked at the boys. "You do see what I mean, you chaps, don't you?" he added meaningfully. Shane and Shawn nodded.

"Yes, sir," they said in unison, obeying Ned as they would a headmaster.

"You wouldn't be from London, by any chance, wouldja?" asked Phil.

"As a matter of fact we are," Norman began until Ned caught his eye and coughed loudly.

"Whereabouts?" Phil insisted.

Ned looked at Norman and although Norman looked at Ned, Norman couldn't resist.

"Islington," said Norman. "Do you know it?"

"Do I know it?" said Phil beaming. "I should say so. Part of my round takes me up your way. Thursdays and Fridays."

"What does your . . . er . . . round involve?" asked Norman.

"I'm a window cleaner," said Phil. "I'd be very 'appy to give you a couple of cleans. Anytime. Free, like, just to say thanks, like." He waited, expectantly; Norman had been looking for another window cleaner for three months and the prospect of discovering a free one was too joyful.

"Well," he said uncertainly, eyeing Ned hard, "it's up to my friend, really." Norman paused and turned to Ned. "Well?"

Ned knew it would be churlish to refuse, despite the awful Doris. He also knew that if he refused, Norman would never allow it to be forgotten as it was Ned who always envisaged Norman falling off the ladder at the back of the house and who had been insisting Norman find a windowcleaner.

"I would think . . .," Ned began, looking at Norman. "Very well. That would be very kind of you, Mr . . . I'm sorry, I don't know your name."

"Dawes," said Phil. "Phil Dawes. Hang about, I gotta card in the car, 'ere." He opened his driver's door and from the dashboard pulled out a wad of business cards and he peeled one off. "There we are, Mr Cresswell. Give us a ring as soon as you'd like your first clean."

Ned took the card, looked at it cursorily and handed it over to Norman.

"Thank you, Mr Dawes. My colleague will be in touch. Most kind of you," he said graciously and felt like a duke. "Most welcome. Come on Norman."

Norman got into his side of the Mini and pulled the door shut. Doris, who had been resolutely squatting on the grass, staring into the far distance in the opposite direction, defrosted. Ned was just about to lower himself into the car.

"I am very sorry," Doris began, looking at the ground and not really knowing how she was going to say the words, "about the . . . well, about yesterday. You were quite right. The kids," she said and at that point thought that with the initial apology over she could face Ned, "are very excitable at times. You understand, I'm sure."

Even Ned realised how hard it had been for Doris to swallow her pride.

"I don't," said Ned, "but I accept your apology. Thank you. Good afternoon."

Sharon had by this time positively fallen in love with Ned and waved happily.

"'Bye, sir. Thanks again," she said.

"Goodbye," said Ned and got into the car. They buckled up and Ned started Min who seemed to have benefitted from the sea air and sprang to life at the first turn of the key without the customary coughing complaints.

They drove slowly out of the car park and back onto the coast road which took them back to the village.

Two very large and very hot bulls lay in a field, too large and too hot to move. Cow parsley was beginning to flower on the road verges and clumps of cowslip and oxlip nodded in the breeze which ruffled the grasses on the gentle, downlands slopes.

"Now that wasn't too awful, was it, Ned?" said Norman. "And we've found a window cleaner. The gods must be smiling on us today. I thought they were a dying breed."

"Gods or window cleaners?" Ned said.

"Both," Norman replied. "But it just goes to show, doesn't it?"

"What does?" said Ned. "Shows what?"

"Oh," said Norman, "I don't know. But it does. Did you remember the digestives?"

"Yes. Both sorts."

"Oh good," said Norman. "It's sort of tea time, I suppose."

"Forget the tea," said Ned. "I'm having a whisky. I'm bushed. I don't think I've ever had a more exhausting holiday in my life."

"Your whole life is exhausting," Norman said. "I'm amazed you've never noticed before."

FOURTEEN

When they arrived back at *Barthorpe*, Norman and Ned saw Tom Maxwell out in his garden, piling up a bonfire. Annie Wingfield had been ill for some time before her death and her last months were spent in an Eastbourne hospice. Annie had been a passionate, if eccentric gardener and her abscence was noticed amongst the vegetables very soon after she had been taken into the hospice. Although Tom had immediately engaged the same contract landscapers who cared for the grass and hedges at *Barthorpe*, a huge pile of undegradable twiggy matter had accumulated in the middle of the patch of ground on which Annie had laboured with her beans and leeks. Tom discovered on further enquiry into the reasons for the build-up of the pile, that the landscapers did not do bonfires. He forked the last of the previous year's thorn hedge clippings to the summit of the fire and stood back, checking that the structure was safe to leave. He saw the Mini drive up and waved as Norman and Ned walked to their front door. He stoked up the fire and came across the road.

"Lovely smell," said Ned, the key in the latch. "I adore fires. It's a scent that should be bottled."

"Whoever would buy it?" said Norman. "I wouldn't wear it. No one would ever come near you. Would you like some tea, Tom?"

"I'd love a cup," he said and followed them into the house.

Upstairs, Albert had also heard the Mini pull up and, deciding not to tempt providence, reluctantly vacated the middle of Norman's bed and secreted himself beneath it. He had decided that he liked *Barthorpe* and he knew he liked Norman even more, but there was one feline problem which required immediate consideration. He was beginning to feel hungry, although sorting out the solution when faced with so many alternatives was taking some time.

As Norman put the kettle on, Ned took out the bottle of whisky he had bought at the grocer's and poured himself a generous tot. Tom blinked.

"Only medicinal," said Ned, noticing Tom's expression, as he watched Ned and a glass in the other. "Join me in one?"

"Thanks, but no," he said, laughing. "It's still just a little too early, even for me!"

"It's alright, Tom," said Norman, feeling that he should explain. "He isn't a dipsomaniac. Why don't you go on up, Ned and have that bath. Would you like me to run it for you?"

"No, I'm fine." He downed the first tot in one gulp. "After that. I'll see you all later," he said, already on his way to the bathroom and left Norman to exlain the rather special circumstances which accounted for the premature tot of whisky."

Good heavens," said Tom as Norman came to the end of the story, "plucky old thing. I take my hat off to you both. I should be the one giving you tea."

"Nonsense," said Norman," and while I'm about it, you're also asked for lunch tomorrow."

"Proper lunch?" said Tom, hopefully. "Real roast potatoes?"

"As Ned would say, 'The Works'," Norman said. "I rather think he needs to know that there really is something cooking tomorrow so he has a proper excuse to leave Genevieve's sherry party sooner rather than later. Well, that's my theory and I'm sticking to it."

They heard the bath water running upstairs and the sound of Ned's heavy footsteps as he walked from bedroom to bathroom. Then Ned called.

"Norman!"

"Oh crumbs," said Norman, recognising the implication in Ned's voice through second nature. "That'll be Albert," he said to Tom.

"Who's Albert?" asked Tom, prepared for any one of ten possible answers even after such brief acquaintance with his temporary neighbours.

"The bloody cat's in again," shouted Ned. "It's under your bed."

"Mrs Hopper's cat," explained Norman with a sigh. "I'm afraid it's rather taken a fancy to me." He called up to Ned. "You have your bath and I'll take care of the cat. Promise." There was a humph from Ned and a slam of the bathroom door."

And you," surmised Tom, "have taken rather a fancy to Albert, I think?"

"I'd better go up and fetch her," said Norman. "It's a she you see, not a he. Poor thing. Will you make the tea, Tom? I shan't be a tick."

Up went Norman to retrieve the luckless Albert. He didn't even have to reach under the bed. As soon as he had entered his bedroom and knelt on the carpet, Albert emerged, slowly at first, from beneath the valance surrounding the bed.

"Oh you naughty, naughty pussy," Norman said in a mock scold which chastised the cat about as effectively as hitting an elephant with three long feathers. His words only served to encourage the cat who arched its back, stiffened its tail and began to purr magnificently. Norman swore that it was the loudest purr he had ever heard. "Norman will give you something to eat, darling and a little milky too, eh?" At least the cat agreed although Ned, by now reclining in the bath, read Norman's thoughts.

"And don't feed it, Norman. You'll only encourage it!"

"Yes, Ned," Norman replied. "Would you like some tea in the bath?"

"No. I'll come down. This bath seems to have got smaller."

Rather, thought Norman, you've got bigger. Norman took the cat in his arms and went downstairs.

"Oh, that Albert," said Tom as Norman entered the kitchen and shut the door, preventing the cat from being able to run back upstairs to the bedroom. He put the truant Albert down on the floor. "You must have met your neighbour by now. With her eagle eyes, she would have seen the cat come in."

"Yes," Norman said. "We've met. But it's a sad story." He went to the larder and from the leg of lamb, cut off two juicy portions which he proceeded to cut up into bite-sized chunks. "I wish animals had as much choice as humans," Norman enlarged. "This poor cat obviously doesn't want to live where it lives. I wish there was something I could do about it." He put the meat onto a saucer and, opening the back door placed the saucer on the ground outside. The cat followed him immediately. First things first, thought Albert. Fate had been kind to the cat; at least the next meal had been found. Norman shut the back door. "Perhaps there is something I can do about it," he said to Tom mysteriously and opened the packet of milk chocolate digestives. "Come on, let's have our tea."

Tom and Norman went through to the sitting room. Overhead, there was a lot of singing coming from the bathroom and much gurgling and splashing as Ned emptied the bath.

Norman had poured the tea when Ned arrived downstairs. His face was redder than usual because of the sun and his hair was wet and uncombed. He was dressed in an enormous white terry towelling bath robe.

"That wasn't a very long soak," Norman observed. "And you might have dressed."

"Proprieties, proprieties, to hell with the proprieties," said Ned and eyed the plate of digestives. "To the victor, the spoils," he said and pounced on a biscuit. "They're milk! Where are the plain ones? You've more than likely fed 'em to that cat!"

"No I haven't," said Norman, getting up from his chair. "Cats don't like digestive biscuits." He went to fetch the plain ones as Ned took his tea and descended onto the sofa.

"Saw the damndest thing today, Tom," he said. "Pretty girl came down onto the beach.."

"And a nice girl too," interrupted Norman. He handed the whole packet of digestives to Ned.

"I'm telling this story, Norman," Ned said taking a biscuit and talking thereafter with his mouth full. "Norman was off on the beach somewhere . . ."

"Mine detecting," Norman said, butting in. Tom was like a spectator at a tennis match, his head turning this way and then that.

"Norman! Don't interrupt!" Tom's attention reverted to Ned who was sitting in the chair which faced the french windows through which was visible the front gate and the road outside. "Girl comes along, sits down and zip!" Ned paused.

"Zip?" said Norman.

"Well, maybe not zip but rip, should I say. Off comes the top of the bathing costume and there she was, naked as nature intended! And on Birling beach. Can you believe that?" Ned had leant forward to lend emphasis to his point when through the window he saw Kim. "Look!" Ned said, "there she is, that's her!"

Tom stood up to look. From a look of wicked amusement, his expression changed to horror when the subject of the story manifested itself in the form of his own daughter.

"Kim!" he said and Ned and Norman looked at each other in amazement. "Would you excuse me a moment," he stammered. "I'm awfully sorry but she won't be able to get in, you see." And he was gone."

You never told me that," Norman said. "Heavens! On Birling beach. Whatever next!"

"This next," said Ned who was now burning with curiousity, craning his neck to see what might be seen through the window. "I'll be jiggered."

"Do you think she's his . . . his friend," said Norman, not quite being able to find the word he wanted for mistress. "She's very young, isn't she . . . I mean, for him."

Both men were now at the French window through which they saw their new friend Tom Maxwell in fond embrace with their other new friend, Kim.

"Well, I'll be . . ." murmured Ned. "Celia Enderby take note."

"Why?" Norman said, half horrified and not knowing how he was going to accomodate this latest turn of events. "Do you think that's what the private detective was after . . . Evidence?"

"Bit late for that," Ned reminded Norman. "They're almost divorced now."

"Then this was the trysting place," said Norman delicately. "It really is astonishing what goes on these days."

"Bosh," Ned dismissed. "Always has gone on. Just never happened to us." He paused and looked at Norman. "Did it?"

"Who?" said Norman. "Cyril? Never. I would have known."

"How?" said Ned.

"I just would have known, that's how," said Norman.

"Uh oh," said Ned, turning quickly away from the window, "We're just about to be introduced.

"They re-assumed their seats.

"Oh, Ned," Norman said in a small voice, "What are we going to do?"

"Just act naturally," said Ned.

"How?" said Norman, who had by now assumed that Tom Maxwell was safe territory and, more than that, a useful prospective bridge partner.

"Follow my lead," said Ned, as Tom and Kim came into the house.

"Do you mind if Kim comes in?" Tom called from the hall.

"Please," said Ned, "Norman will fetch another cup. Won't you, Norman?"

Norman glared at Ned as Tom and Kim came into the sitting room. They stood at the door, arms around each other and looking very, very happy.

"We meet again," said Kim. She hugged Tom again and gave him a smacking kiss on the cheek. "I'm so pleased you've met the old man," she said. "He is rather delicious, isn't he?"

Norman looked at Ned and Ned looked at Norman.

"Delicious," they chorused. Norman at that moment envied Ned more than ever for the ease with which he could adapt to the requisite levels of worldliness called for in situations like these.

"And you, young lady," Tom said to Kim, "deserve a rap on the knuckles for frightening respectable people on public beaches!"

Ned and Norman both reddened.

"Oh, gosh," said Kim. "I never thought. Awfully sorry, Ned. It never crossed my mind."

"Oh, that!" said Ned, pretending at first not to recognise Tom's reference, "no harm done. One must keep up, mustn't one?"

"And keeping up with children these days is no easy task, I assure you," Tom said. "However old they get!" He pinched Kim playfully on the bottom.

Well, really, Norman thought.

"Daddy, you are the limit!" cried Kim. "I'm twenty two for heaven's sake."

Daddy? Ned and Norman simultaneously pricked up their ears and leant forward in their chairs as though operated by the same master puppeteer. Ned coughed and cleared his throat.

"Did I hear that correctly?" he said. "Did you say daddy?"

It was the turn of Tom and Kim to exchange a look.

"Oh, Kim," Tom said despairingly. "How many times have I tried to make you promise?" He disengaged her arm from his waist. "Let's do this properly," he said, "because I think we have our wires crossed. Mr Cresswell, Mr Rhodes, may I introduce my daughter, Kim. Kim Maxwell. Kim, this is Ned Cresswell and Norman Rhodes.

"Kim had been rather puzzled up to this point but the penny finally dropped. She covered her mouth with her hand.

"Oh, no," she said, "you thought . . .!"

"Norman," Ned said, "please close your mouth and go and fetch another cup for Kim." Norman, in a dither of agitation, scurried out for the cup and saucer, not wanting to miss a moment of the denouement. "Kim, dear. Sit down. Have a biscuit. Have two!"

Tom laughed.

"What will this place think of us?" he said. "The mad Maxwells." Norman returned with the cup and saucer and poured Kim's tea. "I'm awfully sorry, Norman, Ned." He laughed again and they all laughed and talked and chattered and Ned's hair dried in a most alarming way which it always did when he forgot to comb it after a bath. Kim recounted the full details of the rescue once again for her father's benefit and together they ate all the digestive biscuits.

"And so what brings you down this way, young lady?" Tom asked. "I thought you were supposed to be interviewing old soldiers this weekend?"

"I'm amazed there are any left," said Ned. "They must be even older than I am. The First World War was a awfully long time ago.

"There are one or two," said Kim. "One particularly but his daughter had to cancel as he wasn't well enough to see me." She sighed. "I just wanted to come here," she said wistfully. "It's always such a happy place."

"Ah ha," said her father, "I sense cupid's arrow has something to do with all this."

"Let's not talk about it now," said Kim.

Oh, let's, thought Norman who was always ready for a little romance.

"Perhaps tomorrow," said Kim. "I'm going to go and change. I'm sure I'll see you later," she said to Ned and Norman. She cast a baleful look at Tom who recognised his cue for a pow-wow.

"I'll be with you in a moment," he said. "Gentlemen," he announced, "I have tickets tonight for a show in Eastbourne. Are you game?"

"What is it and who's in it?" asked Ned. "Must tell you I'm not much of a one for end-of-the-pier stuff."

"An Agatha Christie," he said, "With one of the stars of *Coronation Street* . . . Fish and Chips afterwards?" Norman nodded his head in agreement. "Kim?" he said.

"Sounds wonderful," said Kim. "Please, Ned. It would be such fun."

"Count me in," said Ned. "Especially the fish and chips."

"Good," said Tom and got up. "Thanks for tea. Pick you up about seven?"

"That's very kind," said Norman showing them to the door. "We'll see you later." As he closed the door, he noticed a little feline face peeking out from the middle of the tulip bed but before he could tempt himself with second thoughts, he quickly closed the door.

"Well, that's a relief," Norman said, looking in the teapot to see if there was enough for a last cup. "I thought she reminded me of someone when I first met her. I'm pleased it turned out like that."

"Wouldn't have mattered," said Ned. "People should get married again, I suppose. And," he added, "if I was Tom Maxwell's age with a bit of pep left in me, would I want to trundle down the aisle with someone of my own age if I could do it with someone young and pretty? Answer? Distinctively negative, I would say."

"But would you want to trundle down the aisle at all?" Norman pointed out, a little censoriously. "You could plump for what used to be called living in sin"

"Sin is where you find it," Ned opined, "and as you only find things when you look for them, I say that there are better things to look for. Anyway, sin's a bit like the cold; some feel it more than others."

"Marriage wouldn't have been invented if it could be done without so easily," Norman said. "I mean, look at poor Tom, You can't tell me he's happier now he's about to be divorced than he was before. A blind man could tell he's like a fish out of water."

"Norman, that has nothing to do with anything and you're tripping over your metaphors again. You always have sailed off at the slightest tangent. Tom would be miserable whichever side of the marriage certificate he found himself on. Life is just a pest at times. You've just got to get on with it."

Norman got up and began loading the tray.

"Well, I think it's all jolly sad," he said. "I mean," he said thoughtfully, yet another shadow having crossed his mind, "there's that poor Mrs Hopper next door."

Ned got up and went over to the window. The sun was still up there, somewhere, but there wasn't much evidence of it. The unexpected heat earlier in the day and created a lot of mist which, like the previous afternoon, was gathering out at sea.

"You shouldn't get so involved, Norman."

"Can't help it," said Norman, taking away the tea things. "I've always got involved."

"But it doesn't do anyone any good, does it. I mean," Ned said, running a hand through his unruly hair in front of the mirror over the hearth. "You couldn't possibly get through to someone like that Hopper woman. She's too far gone. You know the signs only too well, remember?"

Norman had moved out of earshot. He was used to this sort of lecture from Ned.

"Why don't you have a lie-down before tonight," Norman called from the kitchen. "It has been rather a day."

"I'm not particularly tired," said Ned, looking round for something else to occupy him.

"You will be by tonight. After five minutes of Agatha Christie you'll be nodding off and snoring in the quiet bits. Everyone will be turning round and telling you to shush. It's very embarrassing. Have a lie down."

"Hmm," said Ned. "Perhaps you're right. It's bound to be dreadful. Those things always are."

"That's just like you, pre-judging things before you've tried them. It can't be that bad. There's that woman from *Coronation Street*? You like her. What's her name?"

"Alright, alright. You win. Haven't been to the theatre for ages so I suppose it doesn't really matter," said Ned taking up his satchel. He took out the newspaper and his book. "I will go up for a read. Then if I drop off, I drop off. What are you going to do?"

Norman plumped up the cushions in the sitting room and primped the posy of flowers Genevieve Withers had left.

"I'm going for a little walk. Shan't be long." Norman slung his cardigan around his shoulders.

"Just as long as you're not chasing after that cat," said Ned.

"I have no need to chase after cats," said Norman sniffily. "Cats, if you haven't noticed, chase after me."

Norman went to the front door as Ned went upstairs. "See you later," Norman called out.

FIFTEEN

Norman decided to walk up the road to where he remembered a path which ran up to the edge of the Downs. As he walked, he could not deny himself the freedom to indulge in thoughts about Albert and Mrs Hopper and of how, sometimes, fate presented chances which begged, by the very nature of their occurrence, to be taken.

The little houses he passed each had its perfect garden. In his life with Cyril, they had often talked about one day buying a house in East Dean. The area suggested a life more manageable to Norman than life in London, more akin to his early life in Canterbury where he had lived in the house his father had had built for his mother. But Applegarth , as was its name, had been sold to furnish his mother with sufficient funds for her own widowhood. Norman's father had been a very generous man, possessed of a cavalier negligence concerning anything to do with money. Whatever Dorothy, his wife, had wanted, she had. Her expression of the merest whim had been enough to prompt the purchase. His children were similarly indulged and, by the time Norman had been born, Mr Rhodes' expansive pocket book knew no limits.

In his mind's eye, Norman saw his parents still; in every elderly face he found something to remind him of mama and father. A man pushing a lawn mower smiled as Norman walked by; just the way his father had nodded to people over the wall at *Applegarth* when he himself took charge of the lawn mower, leaving the gardener to fume and fret about the resulting lack of symmetry in the stripes. Just like father, Norman thought as he bade the man, "Good afternoon!".

But no, he thought as he walked, not now and certainly not for Ned at all, this cosy, tidy, regimented layout of life. Cyril would have liked it. Before he died, Norman and Cyril would come more often to East Dean than Ned who always seemed to have other things to do when Norman suggested a trip down. Ned only needed to come once a year and that was on his wedding anniversary to Dulcie, this very weekend. When Cyril died, Ned continued the tradition but always included Norman even though, as Norman knew full well, Ned would have much preferred to be here alone. Dear Cyril, he thought. How he'd loved order. It was a characteristic they shared and one which had probably been contributory to Norman's very happy, though otherwise unremarkable, relationship.

At first, Norman missed the turning off the road and onto the path he sought. The cupressus hedges of the two houses bordering the path had grown up to such an extent that the opening was difficult to see. Obviously, the path was not much used as Norman pushed through cow parsley almost waist high. Norman climbed with the path until it forked to the right, in accordance with the boundary of one of the gardens. At this point, the land became as he had remembered it first. They had called it The Shawl, a little copse set in a dip in the Downs, where tall ashes and oaks grew out of a carpet of bluebells. He was looking for one particular tree, an ash and he hoped that time had not caused it to disappear either for firewood or through its own age and infirmity. It had not disappeared, although to its trunk was now nailed the wire netting that marked another garden boundary.

It was cool under the trees, few of which, except the alders, were yet in full leaf. Norman looked for the place.The tree had obviously grown since that time long ago and far away when two couples had stayed a long weekend, all together, in Ba's house. Ned was with Dulcie and Norman with Cyril. Norman remembered that weekend very well. Never had he felt closer to Ned and never more confident in himself than in those days when he had first lived with Cyril and understood that you could, after all, be queer and happy. Now, of course, they called it gay; Norman smiled, wryly. It seemed then that Norman's dream of being himself and himself alone had finally been fulfilled, that no longer need he fit himself into anyone's life except his own. Whilst they'd been at art school, Ned had always come first. Ned was the leader and Norman, the follower. It happens, often, that pre-ordained order of things and Norman, sweet, compliant, kindly Norman had always accepted the position, uncomplainingly. Then, with Ned so happy, finally united with Dulcie, Norman felt free to begin his own life. Terrible things were happening in their world, tyrannies raged and humanity was writhing in the throes of some of the most gruesome suffering it had ever endured. Yet, in the little copse on the Downs, there had been peace, a timeless tranquillity which, as they had each silently acknowledged, had been all the more precious because of its essential fragility.

Norman's hands scrabbled over the bark of the ash tree and he felt he really should have brought his glasses. The creases in the bark looked for all the world like the incisions he sought. But Norman found the place and the memory of that longago day was suddenly as vivid as bright sunlight. Norman could almost see Ned taking out his pocket knife, not the same one that Ned had once swapped with Dulcie for that one had been locked away with Dulcie's letters; Norman watched as Ned carved; NC and DH, CB and NR. Norman spoke the initials aloud as he distinguished their outline with his fingertip. He allowed himself a moment when he held his breath. Really, he didn't want to cry. Time past was not for weeping, although his memories were as poignant as the salt tears which were brimming in his eyes were pungent and as the lump caught in his throat was painful. But those feelings passed, as quickly and as fleetingly as the intervening years. So many years, so many wonderful, unforgettable people . . . Where had they all gone, Norman wondered? So much had happened and yet, so little. He heard the sounds of laughter coming from a garden higher up the bank on the other side of The Shawl. Wood pigeons purred in the branches of the trees above. The rooks and crows called, their cries harsh and grating, as they came and went bringing food for their fledging young. Norman wondered which way to proceed. If he followed the path upwards, there were yet more houses and gardens and new lives being lived on ground he had known in its virgin state. He decided to return to *Barthorpe* he had found what he had wanted to find and it was still there. Perhaps it was possible, he reflected, to have a little bit of heaven on earth.

He turned and began to walk down the overgrown path.

"Albert . . . Albert . . ."

Norman knew he was not mistaken. It was Mrs Hopper's voice and it was Mrs Hopper, in her woolly hat and nylon housecoat, who appeared in front of him, down the path, parting the cow parsley, stinging nettles and brambles with an old stick in one hand and the collar and lead in the other.

"Come on now, Albert . . . You're hiding somewhere . . ."

Norman hurried down the path. When Mrs Hopper saw him, she was startled and became agitated for Norman had not yet encountered Mrs Hopper face to face.

"Oh," said Mrs Hopper, quickly and nervously. "You gave me a start! I'm lookin' for the cat. 'Ave you seen a little cat? Black and brown, mainly, with a little bit of white; sort of blotchy." She broke off for a moment to probe the depths of a thick clump of dock leaves and nettles growing into a Wayfarer bush. "Little beggar, 'e is. Always off; always wandering. Too many cats round 'ere, you know. Too many goin's on an' that for 'im to settle."

Norman realised that Mrs Hopper didn't recognise him. Poor soul, Norman thought.

"I'm afraid I haven't seen a cat," Norman said. "But cats do wander, you know. It's in their nature."

Mrs Hopper abandoned her search in that particular patch and altered her perspective to include the trees overhanging the path.

"She'll be that cross," said Mrs Hopper, a faraway look in her eyes. "I couldn't tell 'er, just couldn't bring myself to tell 'er I'd lost 'im. She's that partial to 'im."

"Who is?" Norman asked, a frown of concern springing from the instant sympathy he felt for the woman, who was younger than Norman by a good few years.

"Mum," said Mrs Hopper. "She won't believe me, I

know 'er. 'Out you go again', she'll say, 'an' don't come back without 'im'. Id'lises that cat, she does."

"Does your mother live with you?" Norman asked, almost fearing the reply.

"Oh, no," said Mrs Hopper, "we live separate but I go into 'er every day," she explained, "sometimes twice. Since she 'ad the attack, she can't, you know. Can't do nothing for 'erself. An' me alone, an' all. But it's 'er whole life, that cat. Worships it."

Norman was several steps further on from the inescapable acknowledgement that Ned's opinion of Mrs Hopper's condition was deadly accurate. Except that too far gone wasn't the right way of putting it. Mrs Hopper was ill.

"Perhaps," Norman said, "you'd be better looking for Albert closer to your own house. Shall I walk back with you? I know a little bit about cats and I really think that if you look for him closer to home, you'd find him."

At first, Mrs Hopper showed not even the slightest response to Norman's suggestion. Her hands hung limply at her sides, the collar and lead trailing onto the ground.

"They're money cats, you know," she then said to Norman brightly. "All them sort are. If you keep them, it means you'll 'ave money. Did you know that?"

"No," said Norman, dismissing as gently as he could the myth about tortoise shells. "That's just an old wives' tale. We don't believe in all that, do we?"

"I dunno about that," said Mrs Hopper gloomily. "Mum believed it. Always told me that. Even," she said, looking first up and then down the path, "put it in 'er will."

Norman realised that gentle persuasion would not advance the situation and so he tried another avenue, that of a nurse's firm but incontradictable coercion.

"Now," he began, "what we'll do is this. I'll walk back with you to your house and we'll look for Albert together and when we find him, we'll both sit down and work out the best way of getting him to stay." He paused. There was a flicker of reaction. "Come on. The sooner we start, the sooner we'll find him." Norman took a deep breath and very gently took Mrs Hopper's arm, steering her down the path. To Norman's relief there was no resistance and they moved off as one.

"But we must keep lookin' for him," said Mrs Hopper, now joining in Norman's scheme as willingly as any child. "'E's that quick. Little rascal 'e is. Here one minute and gone the next. You'd never believe it."

"Oh, I would," said Norman. "I most certainly would."

SIXTEEN

Ned had lain down on top of his bed but no sooner had he started the *Telegraph* crossword than there was a ring at the front door bell. Knowing that he was going out to the theatre, he had dampened his hair and had brushed it back from his face.

Damn, he thought, he's done it again. Norman often forgot his key.

"Coming!" Ned shouted from the bedroom as the bell rang insistently again. He felt with his feet beneath the bed for his slippers and put them on. So much for a lie-down, he thought as he hurried down the stairs. The bell rang again. "I said I'm coming, Norman!"

The front door of *Barthorp*e had been fitted with a small window in which was set four little leaded panes. Through this Ned looked and, instead of Norman, on the porch stood a complete stranger, a man. He was young, in his mid-twenties Ned calculated. In his hand he held a notebook and over his shoulder was slung a camera.

"Yes?" Ned said from behind the door. "Can I help you?"

"I hope so," said the young man. "Could I speak to you?"

"You are speaking to me," said Ned.

"I mean, could I come inside and speak to you?" he asked.

"Certainly not," said Ned. "I'm not dressed."

"I could wait," said the young man, smiling. "I'm not a burglar or anything. I'm quite harmless." He spoke with a jaunty ingenuousness which Ned found deeply suspicious.

"I've known several burglars in my time," said Ned. "They were all harmless. But," he said ominously, "there are worse things in this world than burglars."

"But I'm not any of those things," said the young man, reaching into his breast pocket. He pulled out a card. "I'm a reporter. From the *Eastbourne Herald*."

"Thought you might be," said Ned, decidedly unimpressed.

"So, you believe me," said the young man.

"Of course. Smelled you coming."

"How?"

"Never you mind, young man."

"So I can come in, then?"

"Certainly not," Ned said acidly. "Especially certainly not."

Ned, with his sixth sense, had intuitively guessed the young man's occupation. His experience over the years of avoiding interviews and invasive publicity of any sort had honed his sensitivity to the prescence of the press.

"My name is Adrian Cork," he said, rather annoyed that his usual charm had not insinuated him into this old person's affections rather more quickly.

"How nice for you," said Ned.

"Look," he said, thinking that perhaps he should be more businesslike, "I can't take a picture of you from behind the door, can I?"

"You could try," said Ned. "But I see your problem. Perhaps I don't want my picture taken and so perhaps you should come to the point?"

Well, thought Mr Cork, he doesn't look mad and he doesn't sound mad and he could hardly believe that this was the man whom he had been told had rescued young Sharon Dawes from the jaws of death earlier in the afternoon. When they'd telephoned from the lifeboat hut, Adrian Cork had sensed the kind of story which could make the nationals. He'd already got the photograph of young Sharon with Bill Bray and the others but the key to the story was the role of the old gentleman. That was what was going to sell his copy for him and Adrian Cork was nothing if not determined. But, he needed the photograph.

Ned, of course, knew exactly what Mr Cork was standing on Ba's porch for and he was equally determined to have nothing to do with it. However, he was having to think on his feet. He exercised his ploy. He'd done it before and it had worked. So, why not this time?

"I suppose you've come about my friend?" Ned said.

"Ah," said Mr Cork, light beginning to dawn. "Then you're not the one." He also began to think that he would be able to succeed with the right wrinkly where he was failing dismally with the wrong one. "You must be very proud of him," he said. "That was a very brave thing he did."

"I am," said Ned, "and it was. Anything else?"

"I'd very much like to speak to him," said Adrian. "May I?"

"No," said Ned.

"Why not? A bit of publicity never hurt anyone," he said.

"That's what you think," said Ned.

"Why can't I see him?" persisted the dogged young searcher-after-the-truth.

"None of your business," said Ned, rapidly running out of holding tactics. Blighters, he thought. Never take no for an answer.

"With respect, sir," said the young man, "it's also none of yours . . ." Mr Cork waited, relatively safe for the time being on the other side of the oak front door, from the riposte he thought bound to come. Ned narrowed his eyes and squinted as fiercely as he could though the little window. However, Adrian Cork remained stalwart and unflinching. Damn, thought Ned.

"Actually," said Ned, "he's not in. That's why you can't see him." This was true, of course, yet Ned, agnostic though he was, sent up a mighty prayer to the powers-that-might-be that Norman would not decide to return prematurely from his walk.

"Oh," said Mr Cork and Ned thought he detected for the first time, a wavering in his intent. "When will he be back, do you think?"

Wrong, thought Ned who had had friends outside whose houses the inkhounds, as he called them, had encamped for days. He decided to effect another device.

Ned smiled at the young man. He was taken somewehat

aback by this abrupt reversal in the climate of the negotiations.

"He," Ned began, "my colleague, that is, has gone to Eastbourne. He won't be back until very late tonight as he is going to the theatre with friends. The Agatha Christie. My friend is very fond of mysteries."

"How about tomorrow," said the journalist, knowing that the all-important photograph had to be secured as quickly as possible especially for the nationals to take any notice.

"Tomorrow," said Ned rather loftily, speaking as a rather pompous social secretary to a frightfully important personage, "my colleague is very busy all day and won't have time to talk to you."

"How about Monday?" said Mr Cork who knew that as long as he had his story in by lunchtime his editor would be satisfied.

"Monday would be fine," said Ned. "Why don't you come here at about eleven o'clock and then you can talk and even take your photograph if you like. I'm sure he won't mind."

Mr Cork seemed very satisfied with this and Ned was even more satisfied. He knew that they were planning to leave *Barthorpe* soon after ten o'clock on Monday morning. If Ned insisted that the departure be an hour earlier, they would be almost back in London by the time Mr Cork came to call.

"Thank you," he said, beaming. "Just one thing, what is your friend's name?" Adrian Cork invested the word friend with a wealth of innuendo and delivered it wrapped in an oily smirk.

"My friend's name," said Ned, returning the innuendo with interest, "is Rhodes. Norman Rhodes."

"Thank you," said Mr Cork. "Thank you very much." He jotted down the name on his notebook. "You would be . . .?" he ventured, his pencil poised over the page.

"His friend," Ned intoned with a camp twang.

"Would that be friend?" pursued Mr Cork glibly. "As in . . .?" He winked.

Ned bridled as the young man smirked but he restrained himself.

"It's friend as in best," Ned said didactically, reverting quickly to true character. "Friend as in oldest, as in most loyal, as in lifelong," he concluded. "But you're far too young to know what any of that possibly means and as long as you keep grubbing about for knowledge whilst looking in cesspools, you'll remain as ignorant and soiled as the filth you purvey! Good afternoon." Ned turned from his porthole position and hid behind the wall, his heart pounding and cross with himself for taking Adrian Cork's bait.

"You won't forget," called Mr Cork, first laughing and then peering in through the window in the door. "Monday morning!"

Ned remained hidden until he heard Adrian Cork's footsteps retreating from the porch and down the drive. He dropped to his knees and crawled along so that he was beneath the little window in the door and waited until he thought the journalist had really gone before peeping out of the window to confirm his departure. Good, he thought, that's got rid of him. He felt profoundly satisfied as he went back upstairs to finish the crossword.

"'Course," said Mrs Hopper confidentially to Norman as they emerged from the obscured entrace to the path and onto the road, "'e could have gone with the strangers."

"The strangers?" said Norman wondering to whom Mrs Hopper was referring. "No. I'm sure not. Albert is much too sensible for that."

"She used to tell 'im, you know," Mrs Hopper went on. "She warned him over and over but it was no use. "She paused and took Norman's arm. "I think they've got 'im."

"Who?" asked Norman.

"Them next door," imparted Mrs Hopper. "I watched 'im in their garden. One of 'em picked him up. So," she concluded, "they could 'have kept 'im prisoner." Mrs Hopper looked deep into Norman's eyes at this point and Norman could see nothing. There was a dark vacancy in the other woman's eyes, a blankness, a strange incomprehension which cut Norman to the quick. "And one of em's got a wooden leg," said Mrs Hopper. "He told me."

Norman felt awful. Mrs Hopper was in a far worse state than he had first thought and Norman felt the tortures of the damned when he remembered how selfish and stupid he had been to even toy with the affections of the cat, someone else's cat as Ned had so rightly insisted.

"Now don't you worry," Norman said. "When we get you home, I promise I'll go myself and make sure that no one is keeping Albert a prisoner." Norman was trying to remember whether or not he had shut the kitchen window as he had a horrible feeling that Albert could indeed at this moment have been either on or under his bed.

"I called my Trevor," Mrs Hopper explained, "and he came to investigate. But he's only a boy, what can you expect."

"I thought he was a policeman," said Norman. "I'm sure he's very capable. We'll give him a ring when we get back. After all," said Norman, "we're going to need his help aren't we . . . to look for Albert, I mean."

A look of alarm crossed Mrs Hopper's face. It was pathetic, Norman thought. So unnecessary. Norman's heart ached for this woman, almost his contemporary, a woman with a son and daughter-in-law, something that Norman had always longed to have but had never achieved. So much to live for and yet, here she was, reduced to this debilitated state.

"No," said Mrs Hopper quickly. "We mustn't. I've been told. She doesn't like it."

Norman immediately called to mind another of Ned's deductions, the one about Mrs Hopper junior, Trevor's wife. Obviously, the two Mrs Hoppers did not get on which explained why Mrs Hopper senior had not been taken into the police house. But, Norman thought, how cruel, to leave a woman in a state like this on her own to suffer alone. Surely they must know how bad she is?

They reached Mrs Hopper's garden. A white Ford drove away from the front of *Barthorpe* in what seemed to be a tearing hurry but Adrian Cork didn't see Norman and Mrs Hopper in his rear view mirror and even if he had, he would not have thought to distinguish Norman from any of the other retired residents of this sunset haven. No, Mr Cork had other things on his mind.

"Have you got your key?" said Norman. "You'll need it to get in, won't you?"

Mrs Hopper fumbled in the pocket of her housecoat and took out her latchkey and two others, big old-fashioned keys tied together with twine. Norman walked the woman up her path but instead of going to the front door, Mrs Hopper beckoned Norman to follow her along the path to the back of the bungalow. It was a plain little house, unadorned by even the simplest climbing rose and with only a few lonely daffodils in a regimented, though straggling, line alongside the concrete drive. As he waited next to Mrs Hopper who began the process of unlocking the door, Norman smelt the emptiness which the house exuded.

"You do have a telephone, don't you?" asked Norman. Mrs Hopper nodded. "Good. I really think we have to ask your son to come and help us, don't you?"

"But first we've got to find Albert," said Mrs Hopper, her hand on the third key. She looked at Norman strangely. "Who are you?" she said remotely.

"I'm your friend," said Norman, butterflies beginning to flutter in his tummy. "Don't you remember, we're looking for Albert?"

"You can't come in," said Mrs Hopper.

"But I'm your friend," said Norman. "We can have a nice cup of tea and wait for your son."

"No!", Mrs Hopper snapped. "He told me. He doesn't understand. I've got to tell mum, first."

"About Albert?" Norman asked, now totally unsure of how he should proceed.

"She won't listen, she never does. I'll have to go out again." Mrs Hopper unlocked the third lock. Norman remained outside as the woman opened her back door and went in.

"I'll keep looking," Norman said. "I'll come back if I find

him."

Mrs Hopper made no reply but shut her door quickly.

Norman waited for a moment before walking back to *Barthorpe*. "Don't be so involved", Ned had told him. But what, he asked himself, could he possibly do? He was involved, like it or not.

Norman had indeed forgotten the key to the front door but went in at the back. He was pleased to see that he had remembered to close the kitchen window. He picked up the empty saucer outside the back door and hoped that Ned had not seen it.

"Ned!" Norman called. "I'm back. Are you upstairs?" He heard footsteps hurrying from the bedroom. Ned called from the landing.

"Norman? You didn't meet anyone, did you?" Ned said urgently.

"Yes," said Norman. "That's what I need to talk to you about. I think she's about to crack, Ned."

"Who?"

"Mrs Hopper," said Norman. "Wait. I'll come up." Norman scampered up the stairs. Ned went back to his room.

"So you didn't meet any men?" Ned asked nervously.

"What are talking about, Ned? I'm far too old to go out looking for men, dear and anyway, I don't know any men here except Tom Maxwell."

"Oh," Ned said, much relieved. "That's alright then."

"But as I'm trying to tell you, I did meet Mrs Hopper," said Norman. "Please sit down, Ned and stop looking out of the window. This is important."

Ned had been peering through the curtains which he had drawn as soon as Adrian Cork had driven away. He sat down on the edge of the bed.

"Now, what's all this about Mrs Hopper?"

Norman sat down in the tub chair which was already draped with every garment Ned had brought with him.

"I was up in The Shawl, where our initials are and I saw Mrs Hopper looking for Albert along the path . . ."

Norman recounted the story and ultimately credited Ned with all the observations and advice Ned had offered earlier.

"She's ill, Ned. She needs help. What should I do?"
Ned sighed and thought.
"It's all very fishy," he said in the end. "Very fishy indeed. Makes me suspicious. There's a touch of woman's work in all this."
"Why?" said Norman.
"Young Mrs Hopper," Ned said, "whoever she may be. Just think about it. The old lady gets left some money with a dotty codicil about looking after the cat. The son feels that the mother should come and live with him, the daughter-in-law refuses as she knows the old lady is potty but doesn't want the old girl to lose the money. So, to keep an eye on her and secure the money, they persuade her to get her own house locally. All that has to happen is for the old girl to finally go ga-ga and young Mrs Hopper is quids in."
"But that's awful," said Norman, horrified. "It can't be true. Her son couldn't be that heartless."
"He probably doesn't know a thing about it," Ned said. "It's very hard to accept illnesses like dementia, especially for children. Mrs Hopper may have been getting gradually worse for years and he just likes to believe that's how she is."
Norman groaned.
"So what can we do?" said Norman. "Call a doctor?"
Ned looked at the floor. He sat on the edge of the bed, his hands clasped, twiddling his thumbs, rotating them clockwise, then stopping and reversing the direction. Ned was thinking, deeply thinking as Norman knew from years of seeing Ned at his desk in his study, the electric typewriter whirring unheard as some particular knotty problem was unravelled. Ned sighed and finally looked up at Norman.
"I honestly haven't the faintest idea," he said. "Apart from telephoning the son. And I don't think we'd get much of a reception there."
"Do you think I should go out and look for the cat?" Norman said. "At least if she had her Albert back she wouldn't need to go out looking for him constantly."
Ned shook his head.
"It's got nothing to do with the cat," he said. "And

suppose, anyway, she gets the cat back. It'll only be a day or so before it runs off again. Apart from keeping it in a cage, there's not a lot that's going to stop that cat from getting as far away as possible."

"It's too agonising for words," said Norman. "I feel so helpless."

"Dear old Norman," said Ned, getting up and going over to where Norman sat on the edge of the chair. He put his arm around Norman. "You are so kind and good and even after I've said all that, I can only agree with you. You're helpless. I'm helpless. It often happens." He gave Norman an extra long hug. "There," he said, "let's be thankful at least that it's not you wandering about wittering after Albert."

"Would you have me locked up," asked Norman, weakly. "Put away?"

"I could ask you the same question," said Ned. "Who knows. It hasn't happened, has it?" Ned knew he had to change gear, reverse both him and Norman out of what threatened to become a maudlin situation. "What's the time?"

Norman looked at his watch.

"Six," he said, still in that little voice.

"Right," said Ned and clapped his hands together. "Time to celebrate!"

"I'm not sure I've got a lot to celebrate," said Norman. "You might have." He paused. "Well," he said thoughtfully, "at least I wasn't blown up by that mine and at least you didn't hurt yourself on that clifftop . . ."

"And," Ned said, accelerating Norman's brightening mood, "we going to be driven off in splendid style with two very nice new friends . . ."

"To that dear little theatre . . ."

"And pig out on Eastbourne's finest fish and chips!" Ned finished exultantly. "Not exactly the end of the world, is it, old chap?"

Norman got up and straightened his tie.

"Gin and tonic, dear?" he said but Ned was already on his way to crack the ice.

SEVENTEEN

Tom waited for Kim to come down from her bedroom for a drink. She was his only child and as such he worshipped her. They had talked for an hour at least about her particular Ned Cresswell except that his name was James.

Tom hated to see his daughter so upset and felt as helpless as Norman in the face of circumstance. There was no one to blame. Tom had met James many times; he liked the young man and certainly could not blame him for wanting to further his career by taking up an offer from an American bank. Tom had tried every which way to understand Kim's refusal to accept James' offer of marriage but at each turn, he had been confronted with her stubborn assertion. "I'm not ready for marriage, daddy", she would say.

Under the shower, Tom had had to accept that a part of the reason for Kim's dilemma must lie with him, with both him and Jennifer. Kim was very much like her mother in many ways, restless, impatient and impetuous. James needed a wife in his career, Tom knew that. Kim would have made a wonderful wife.

She was sparkling, intelligent and funny and possessed of the valuable facility of being able to put people immediately at their ease. But Kim was her parents' daughter. All her life, Kim had seen Tom working harder and harder, staying later and later at the office, leaving Jennifer more and more to her own devices. Their's had been a classic case, a standard set of circumstances and Jennifer had reacted in quite the predictable way. She had met someone else. Kim was determined that she was not going to make the same mistake as her parents. The problem? She loved James. For years, since they had first met when she had been a young schoolgirl at Malvern Girl's and James was an acned youth at Malvern Boy's, they had been inseparable. Now, the only way they could remain together was for Kim to abandon the strange security provided by her independence.

God, it's a mess, thought Tom. He poured himself a weak whisky, topping it up with Malvern water. He looked at the bottle and wished that he and Jennifer had never made the decision to allow Kim to go away to school.

"Drink, darling?" he said, calling up to her.

"Are you having one?" she shouted down.

"Just a small one," he replied.

"Then I won't. I'll drive." She piled her hair up on top of her head and inserted one cleverly placed comb which miraculously maintained the towering coiffure. "My treat," she said, grabbing her bag and denim jacket. She skipped downstairs and appeared in the doorway looking ravishing. God, Tom thought, you are so lovely. Simple black T-shirt dress and flat, black pumps, she looked all the world like a fashion plate from a glossy magazine. What did I do, thought Tom, to produce that? I must have done something right. "You can keep Ned company at the bar," she said. "I rather fancy he likes a tipple."

Kim poured herself a mineral water and sat down, cross-legged in what Annie used to call the throne, an over stuffed, overlong armchair made for curling up in and in which Kim herself had spent many summer evenings with Annie, listening to radio plays as Annie made endless darns in her much darned woollen gloves.

"You bet," said Tom. "We polished off three bottles of St Michael red last night."

"Daddy," Kim scolded, "you are silly. You're as rich as Croesus now and you're still buying wine at M and S. You should join the Wine Society if you can't be bothered to go to a decent off licence. They deliver."

"You're right," agreed Tom. "You know me too well, young lady." He sighed. "I'm not awfully good on my own. Are you sure you wouldn't consider moving back in? Not permanently, of course."

She laughed, a knowing, comfortable but slightly wary laugh.

"And cramp your style?"

"What style?" he said, with a hint of self-deprecation with which she was not about to let him get away.

"Now stop it! I won't have you feeling sorry for yourself. You're far too nice and far too good-looking to stay as you are. You're quite a catch, you know."

"But I don't want to be a catch," he said. He hesitated. "I suppose we're a bit in the same boat at the moment, darling. Neither of us know what we really want."

Kim shook her head, a young head but set on very old shoulders.

"Wrong, pa. We both know what we want. Trouble is, we can't have it." She fixed him and asked a very direct question. "Do you still love mummy? Honestly."

Tom drained his glass.

"As you're driving, darling, I think I'll have another snort." He got up and refilled his glass from the tray of bottles set on the sofa table.

"Silences usually indicate the affirmative," said Kim. "Am I being too pushy?"

"Not at all, my sweet. In fact, I appreciate your concern. In answer to your first question, though, I wish I could tell you yes." He took a sip from his drink. "But as your question included honestly, I honestly don't know. I think the truth of it is that I miss not having a wife."

"Daddy!"

"No," he said quickly, "not in the way you're thinking. I can't really explain. It's not that I mind doing the laundry, although I do, I loathe it, or anything like that. It's just that I feel so incomplete." He paused and took another drink. "You can't possibly understand."

"Oh, I do. That much I do understand."

"You see, darling, at my age, most of life and living seems such a great bother."

"No one said life should always be convenient," observed Kim wryly. "But as long as you've got it, you might as well enjoy living it. It won't stand still and lie down just so that you can take out all the choky bits."

"I wish I understood more," said Tom.

"About mummy?"

"No. I understood what she did very well," Tom said glumly.

"I don't think you did," said Kim. "I think you accepted it but I don't think you ever understood."

"I certainly don't blame her, if that's what you mean," Tom said in his defence, although Kim was not attacking him. "Anyway, it's all a bit late now, isn't it."

Kim uncurled from the chair. Perhaps she had been too probing, she thought. Perhaps he's still not ready to talk?

"Let's talk about something else," she said. "Something more cheerful."

Tom sat down again. He remembered Annie using those very words. "Let's talk about something else", she would say when a subject was being explored which had no obvious conclusion. As a small boy, staying with Annie when his own parents had left him for whole summers whilst they toured the watering places of Europe after the war, he remembered how much he missed them, how frightened he used to become when his imaginings led him into convincing himself that his mother and father were never coming back. "Let's talk about something else", Annie would say and then she would invent a game or tell a story or take him off for a walk, anything which would distract him.

"Does she dislike me very much?" he asked.

"Who? Mummy?"

Tom nodded. After a spate of suspicion and jealousy some months previously which had goaded Jennifer into having Tom followed after an argument, Jennifer had had to admit that there was no other woman and that Tom's excuses for spending so much time away from home which he blamed on business and company pressures were entirely genuine. Jennifer was not a vicious woman in any way and their ultimate separation had been entirely without vindictiveness on either part.

"Of course not. She's very fond of you, always will be."

"But it is too late, isn't it?" he said rhetorically.

"If you mean to get back together again, then yes, it is." Kim hesitated before continuing. "Is it that you feel you've somehow failed? Is that what makes you feel so . . . so resigned?"

Tom thought for a moment. As a man, in the eyes of men, he was anything but a failure. His drive, inventiveness and endeavour had made Maxwell a profitable, secure company so much so that it had attracted a substantial bid from its new owners. In his life, he had been nothing if not highly successful. But, in the way that men do, he had lived his life not supremely for himself but for other reasons; for the company, for the shareholders, for his wife, his daughter, his family, his reputation, his status. Now, although not as rich as Croesus as Kim had joked, he had achieved everything that he had been supposed to achieve.

"You're probably right, darling. Thank you."

"For what?" she said. "Being beastly isn't exactly something one has to be thanked for."

The telephone rang. Kim went to answer it. She thought it could be . . . But it was Ned.

"It's seven and we're quite ready," boomed the voice down the line. Ned could never wait. Five minutes before taxis were due to arrive, he was on the telephone giving hell to the unfortunate receptionist at the other end of the line.

"Yes. We're ready too," said Kim. "See you outside, OK?"

Ned had already put the telephone down. It was an unusual habit but once Ned had said what he had to say, he saw no point in waiting for the niceties of superfluous goodbyes. Norman winced as he heard Kim being unceremoniously cut off.

"Stand by for orders!" Kim joked, saluting her father. "The General is ready!"

Tom drained his glass and got up. He hugged his beautiful daughter and felt very, very lucky.

Tom Maxwell walked down his drive to the gate whilst Kim manoeuvred the car into a position where Tom could help Norman and Ned to get in. When Ned saw that Kim was driving, he was consumed and made up his mind that at a convenient moment after lunch the next day he would ask Tom if he too could take the car for a spin.

While he was waiting, Norman looked anxiously around for any sign of Albert. On returning from Mrs Hopper's house earlier, he had known, without having to go and search, that the cat had not been in the house. Had it been, Ned would have found it.

From Norman's summary glance around the garden, there was no sign of Albert although not being able to see the cat did not mean that the cat wasn't there. Albert had returned to his vantage point under the laurel bush, still replete after enjoying his plate of lamb. He had decided that strategically he could do no better than bide his time and wait until the kitchen window was open again.

"I shall ask to go in the front," said Ned as Tom Maxwell walked across the road.

"Ned, you can't. It's rude," Norman whispered. "Sit where you're put."

Ned took no notice.

"Norman will sit in the back," he announced to Tom. "I can't. It makes me feel sick."

"Gentlemen, your limousine awaits," beamed Tom.

Norman glowed. Ned of course ignored the remark although Norman luxuriated in it. As far as he was concerned, compliments from attractive men were far too thin on the ground to be treated carelessly. Tom seated them and then walked around the car to seat himself next to Norman in the back.

"Buckle up," said Kim to Ned and helped him with the clasp of the seat belt. "All set? Eastbourne here we come.

"The car moved off into the evening; it was by now quite chilly and the predicted mist was rolling up the Greensward like dry ice onto the set of a romantic film.

"What's in here?" asked Ned immediately he had settled and opened the glove compartment. Norman noticed what he was doing and hoped that Tom would indulge him. "What's this button?"

"Opens the boot," said Kim.

"And this?" said Ned, his itchy fingers reaching out for a lever next to the ashtray.

"Don't know," said Kim.

"Makes the seat go up or down, forwards and backwards," said Tom, amused that Ned should be so interested in the car.

"Incredible," said Ned. "Makes you proud to be British."

"I expect cadillacs make Americans proud to be Americans," said Norman trying to excercise a degree of diplomacy.

"You know that the gear boxes for these cars come from America," said Tom.

"Impossible!" said Ned.

"It's true," said Tom. "I found out when the gear box on this one broke down."

"Broke down!" exclaimed Ned, aghast. "The gear box in a Rolls Royce broke down?"

"'Fraid so," said Tom.

"Unthinkable," said Ned. "But then," he added, "now we know it's a foreign gear box, hardly surprising is it?"

Kim smiled. She found Ned's patrician convictions rather touching. "Isn't there anything this country makes all by itself any more," said Ned. "Next you'll be telling me that Maxwell typewriters are made in the far east."

Uh uh, thought Kim. Tom chuckled and Norman knew what was coming.

"Well?" said Ned.

"I'm afraid they are," said Tom.

"Well," said Ned, "bloody hell!"

The road into Eastbourne, as it climbed over the Downs, was obscured by mist. Kim turned on the lights as the Rolls sailed on, past fields of burgeoning rape and grain.

"By the way," Tom said, "What was that chap doing on your doorstep this afternoon?"

"What man?" said Ned.

"He arrived in a white ford. Youngish chap."

"I was asleep," Ned lied. "Went spark out over the crossword. Did you see anyone, Norman?"

So, that's why he asked me if I'd met any men, thought Norman to himself and reminded himself to tackle Ned on this subject later.

"No, dear," was all he replied. "I was out for a walk, if you remember. And I do wish you'd think what you're saying at times!"

"Probably insurance," said Ned, ignoring the rebuke. "Or estate agents. They stoop to any lengths now."

"Ah," said Tom, "that probably accounted for the camera slung over his shoulder."

Ned said nothing although he could feel Norman's curiousity had been roused. They began the descent into the resort, from the junction by Beachy Head where there were always magpies, down the hill where primroses and dandelions dotted the roadside verge.

"By the way, what is it of Agatha's we're seeing tonight?" Ned asked.

"*When a Stranger Calls,*" Tom said.

"Oh good," said Norman, "I like that one."

"You've seen it before?" Tom asked.

"Hundreds of times," said Ned casually.

"Twice," corrected Norman. "Take no notice, Tom. He's the world's biggest exaggerator."

"I would love to write plays," said Kim. "You must have met lots of writers, Ned, working for a publisher," she asked innocently. In the back seat, Tom could hardly suppress a snigger and Norman patted his arm encouragingly.

"One or two," said Ned carelessly, looking out of the window and beginning to hum something.

"Anyone famous?" persisted Kim.

"Depends what you mean by famous," Ned said. "It's a very much over-used word these days. Shouldn't we turn off here? The theatre's down there to the left," instructed Ned and Kim did not even suspect that she was being skilfully deflected.

It was still too early in the season for the town to be full although even in the mist, there was the usual parade of evening strollers, faces healthy and glowing after the sunshine earlier in the day but who had now resorted to anoraks and mackintoshes in the cool of the evening. The municipal parks department had as always achieved the magnificent and the promenade from the Wish Tower to the Pier was ablaze with tightly studded beds of tulips and pansies of many varieties and in every colour of the rainbow. The strollers stopped every now and again and little knots of admirers formed where a particularly notable specimen or variety had been spotted by the experts.

Kim slowed the Rolls at several zebra crossings to allow the mainly elderly pedestrians to cross.

"Makes you feel like royalty, doesn't it, Norman?" said Ned, who had manipulated the height of his seat so that he peered out at the inquisitive passers-by from his own special throne.

"You'll be saying you want one next," said Norman.

"I want one," said Ned. "Always have. Wouldn't Ba be tickled?"

"She'd think you were mad," Norman said.

"She already does," said Ned.

EIGHTEEN

Outside the theatre, Kim found a convenient place to park. Tom opened doors dutifully and Norman had to admit that it was a beautiful car. Tom shepherded his flock through the front doors and into the foyer. The Devonshire Park Theatre, like many institutions and landmarks in Eastbourne, had been named after the Dukes of Devonshire, whose patronage of the resort had promoted it in the latter part of Victoria's reign. The foyer had been much altered and no longer was there a box office with fat books of tickets on sale but a computer which chattered like a demented budgerigar and spat out a stream of unidentifiable bits of paper, which Tom collected before buying a couple of programmes and returning to his charges. Kim had gone to the Ladies.

"This theatre brings back so many memories," said Norman. "I saw Vera Lynn here at the end of the war."

"I saw my first pantomime here," Tom rejoined. "Mother and Annie brought me. Annie was excited as I was. I can remember her shouting "Oh no you can't" and "oh yes we can" as loudly as anyone."

"I love pantos," Norman said.

"I love traditional pantos," Ned qualified. "Soon as I saw the way they were going with pop songs and smutty jokes, that did it for me and pantos."

Tom looked at his watch.

"Look," he said, "we're in plenty of time. Anyone for a drink?"

"Take me, show me, buy me," said Ned as they went up the stairs to the bar.

"What about Kim?" said Norman.

"She'll find us," said Tom. "Don't worry, she has a pretty good idea about the vices of the older generation."

Norman giggled.

"She must think we're all alcoholics," Norman said as

they entered the bar which had been mercifully spared the worst excesses of modernisation. Framed photographs, signed by a host of the visiting actors and actresses in favour of the Devonshire Park Theatre, lined the walls.

Kim joined them as Tom went to the bar to buy drinks.

"You'll never guess who I've just seen," said Kim to Ned. "The girl who fell over the cliff. Seems to be with her whole family."

"Oh! Save us," groaned Ned.

"Don't worry. She didn't recognise me," Kim said.

"I rather liked the father," said Norman. "But I wonder what they're all doing here?"

"I do hope they don't see us," said Ned. "I don't mind rescuing people but having to socialise with them afterwards is a bit much!"

Tom returned with the drinks and they toasted the promise of a jolly evening.

The five minute bell rang and a voice like a station-master's called over the public address for the audience to take their seats as though directing them to a platform and a waiting train.

On his way in to the auditorium, Norman bought some noiseless sweets, ones which weren't wrapped in crackly paper. He knew that Ned would have a bad case of nibbles before the interval and, from previous experience, wanted to pre-empt the barrage of 'sshhh' which usually accompanied Ned's attempts to unwrap the unwrappable.

A young man, red-haired, willowy and as etiolated as a stand of forced rhubarb showed them to their seats. Gone were the smartly dressed usherettes, bobbing like housemaids, who had been on hand in days of yore.

The theatre was packed, a testament due, sadly, not to 'dear Agatha' as Ned had referred to the playwright but to the power of the magic box. The star of *Coronation Street* who led the company in its interpretation of Miss Christie's play was the only reason for the theatre's red plush seats being so cost-effectively covered by the bottoms of eight hundred television addicts.

"The place is full of wrinklies," said Ned rather too

loudly as he waited for Norman to enter the row and take his seat.

"That's not very nice, Ned," remarked Norman as he smiled kindly at their neighbours, front and rear. "I don't like to think of myself as a wrinkly and I'm sure they don't either, dear."

"It's a term of familiarity not abuse," said Ned. "We are what we are." He took his seat. Yes, thought Norman, but you'd hate anyone else to tell you!

"Anyone like an ice cream?" asked Kim but as she did so, the house lights dimmed and there followed the customary decrescendo of the volume of chatter as the elderly playgoers settled to see their heroine appear.

The old play creaked along and the star of the small screen shimmered as brightly as the part could be stretched to allow. As Ned remarked loudly in the interval, "at least they don't bump into the furniture".

"But I adore her," said Kim, thoroughly enjoying a vanilla tub. "My friends and I wouldn't miss an episode."

Ned was intrigued."But you're at Oxford," he exclaimed. "I can't believe that Oxford is interested in soap opera."

"Dear Ned, " Kim said, discarding the empty tub into an ashtray, "Oxford is a soap opera."

The bell rang and once again they returned to the auditorium. None of them, for indeed, why should they even be looking, spotted Adrian Cork skulking in the foyer.

But the erstwhile Mr Cork recognised Ned and, therefore, concluded that the other gentleman in the party could be none other than the heroic Mr Norman Rhodes. Already, the byeline was formulating in Cork's mind; the caption beneath the front page photograph bubbled in his brain. He envisaged something like: GLAMOUROUS GRAMPS BATTLES WITH DEATH . . . Something suitably subtle, he fancied. Having established that Norman was still in the theatre, Adrian Cork implemented the last part of a swiftly concocted grand plan.

Ned slept through most of the second act although no one except Norman would have realised. Through many years of sitting through performances which had bored him rigid, Ned himself went rigid. His head did not flop forwards or sideways or loll about in any alarming way. His eyes simply glazed over, his eyelids slowly drooped and he remained perfectly still and upright. Miraculously, he always awoke just as the curtains closed and the first ripple of applause welled from the audience.

The current Queen of *Coronation Street* came forward to take her bow after the remainder of the cast had deferentially retired. She took the plaudits with an accustomed aplomb, graciously acknowledging the loyalty and adoration sweeping in from the auditorium as the devoted ladies, and few gentlemen who it seemed had been press-ganged into the occasion, basked for these short moments in the reflected glory of this shining institution. In accordance with her gentling gesture, rehearsed to calm the excesses of the swell of adulation, the acolytes obeyed their goddess to a woman. Eyes shining with anticipation, the undulating sweep of blue-rinses waited for her to speak and speak she did, in character not as created by Miss Christie but as she was known twice weekly on the television. There ensued a moving speech of thanks. After wishing them all a very pleasant holiday, La Divina announced that in the audience that evening, there were two very special people and proceeded to recount the incident on the clifftop at Birling Gap.

Ned visibly crumpled and wished that he had been sitting on the end of the row, but it was Norman who after the interval had found himself in that seat. A knot of terror formed in the pit of Ned's tummy. Sharon Dawes' name was announced from the stage and from a flurry of activity in the fourth row, Sharon emerged, a plaster covering the cut on her head but otherwise unharmed in her best jumper and skirt. She made her way to the steps at the front of the stage and mounted them to be greeted by an embrace from the much made-up star. The embrace was recorded for posterity by Adrian Cork who had been waiting in the wings with his flash camera. Mr Cork was feeling tremendously pleased with himself. His plan had gone from first to last without a hitch. La Divina had accepted his suggestion with alacrity, it being yet another opportunity for a photo call which, if run in the national press, would encourage the ratings of her programme. The editor of *The Herald* had been more than pleased to pay for a night out for the Dawes family at the newspaper's expense in return for such a scoop.

"But," announced the star, calming the rapturous applause once more, "not only do we have this very lucky young lady with us tonight, we have also a very brave old soldier who played a vital part in Sharon's rescue. I will say no more about him but instead, ask him to stand up. Ladies and Gentlemen, Mr Norman Rhodes." More applause. "Norman, love, would you come up? Where are you Norman?"

The house lights had been switched on by this time and the audience, whilst still applauding, began to look round for the whereabouts of the heroic gentleman in question. The star shaded her eyes to better rake the stalls for Mr Rhodes.

Norman's face was a portrait of horror. Ned had hardly been able to believe his ears although had instantly recalled how the hero of the hour came to be Norman and not him. Norman was speechless. Kim and Tom, on Ned's right, leant forward with puzzled expressions on their faces.

"Come on, Norman, dear. Don't be shy!" encouraged the star from the stage. Adrian Cork, knowing full well where Ned was sitting, pointed out from her side.

"Tenth row, on the end," he said.

"Please, Norman," Ned implored. "Please do it!"

Norman was so flustered he didn't even hear Ned's plea but was impelled by the tide of the moment and rose to his feet. The ladies in the audience went wild as soon as they saw that the intrepid rescuer was, like the majority of them, past the first flush.

Mr Cork, a camera dangling from a strap round his neck, came down the stage steps and took Norman's arm. He led him forward, propelled him up the steps where Norman's hand was taken by the star and led to a position centre stage where Norman too was embraced and his arm held high in the air by the star in a symbolic attitude of victory much used by referees and boxers. The house went wild and Mr Cork snapped away from every angle at the hypnotised Norman. Sharon's look of utter puzzlement went un-noticed and she was too tongue-tied to offer any wise words either to Mr Cork or to the star, who launched into a eulogy of Norman's selfless courage and incandescent bravery which was an example to everyone. At the end of the speech, there was more applause and Sharon was led off by Mr Cork to the steps and then Norman to the steps on the other side of the stage.

Ned had long since vanished. He had made a very quick exit and was now trying to conceal himself in a cranny in the foyer. When Norman returned to his seat, the applause still thundering, Tom and Kim were waiting in the aisle and ushered him out of the auditorium as swiftly as they could. Bravos and Well Dones and Good For Yous echoed in Norman's ears.

In the corridor outside he regained a little of his reason.

"I will," he said, " I swear I will!"

"Will what, Norman?" asked Tom.

"Get my own back somehow!" Norman muttered through clenched teeth. Kim patted his arm comfortingly. "For years and years I've made excuses for him, indulged this silly nonsense of his but this time he's gone too far."

"But it might not have been Ned's fault," said Kim. "It could all be a huge mistake. You know what the newspapers are like. They always get things wrong."

"This," said Norman stopping for a moment to emphasise his feelings, "is Ned's doing, I can smell it."

"But where is he?" said Kim as they came to the foyer. "What's happened to him?"

Ned appeared from behind a doric column, sheepishly.

"You!" Norman said, feeling as though he would burst into tears. "I shall never speak to you again. Ever!"

Tom took charge.

"Now, boys . . . Not here." He shepherded them out of the double doors, across the drive outside and into the car.

Ned was silent. Tom settled them into the back of the car and he and Kim occupied the front seats.

"I can explain, old chap," Ned started to say. "I never thought, you see . . ." His explanation tailed off as he saw that this was not the right moment.

"I wish you would explain," said Kim. "It's a complete mystery to all of us."

Norman, who had been silent ever since his vow to send Ned to Coventry for eternity, spoke. He too had been putting a few things together. The audience had begun to spill out from the foyer and, seeing that the front runners had spotted the car with Ned and Norman in the back, Tom decided that retreat was the better part of valour. He started the car and they drove silently and regally away.

"Someone came to see you when I was out for my walk," said Norman. "Didn't they, Ned?" Ned, to his credit, felt very ashamed. "Didn't they, Ned?" Norman persisted. Ned nodded his head. "Was it that young man who was taking photographs?" Ned nodded again.

"In the white Ford," Tom interrupted. "I saw him."

"I'm lost," Kim said. "Will someone explain?"

"I think the person most qualified to do that would be my erstwhile colleague," said Norman imperiously. When roused, which was infrequently, Norman could be as implacable as Ned.

Ned took a deep breath and after it, took his medicine.

"Well, you see . . ." he began and whilst he explained the whole episode to Norman, Tom drove round and round Eastbourne. Kim didn't know whether to giggle or not.

". . . and I really am very, very sorry, Norman. I honestly never thought it would come to this and . . . and I'm sorry." Ned stared beseechingly at his companion and crossed his fingers and hoped. Norman tossed his head and pretended to look at something very interesting out of the window. Now he had had the full story, he knew he couldn't remain huffy for long. Ultimately he said nothing to Ned but reached out and found Ned's hand and gave it a squeeze.

"Now what about our fish and chips?" he said to Tom, who grinned and turned off from the circuitous route he had been following for ten minutes and drove in the direction of his favourite frying house.

Kim turned round in her seat. She had been looking to the back of the car whilst Ned had been putting his case and was relieved to see that at least Norman and Ned were not going to fall out forever.

"I'm afraid I'm still completely in the dark," she said. "Couldn't someone elucidate?"

Tom looked in his mirror and saw Ned look at Norman and Norman look at Ned. Norman shook his head, a kindly but very firm smile on his face.

"No, Ned," he said. "You do your own dirty work from now on."

And so Ned was forced to tell the story which he managed to make sound more like a confession. Kim turned round in her seat as Ned elucidated. Tom interrupted only once and, having taken orders and parked the car, left to collect their suppers; four cod and chips, Ned contritely asking if he could have a gherkin and a pickled onion with his.

"But it's nothing to be ashamed about," said Kim, reaching out and taking Ned's hands in hers. "You are a silly thing, honestly. You should be terribly proud of yourself. I'm proud of you."

"We all are," said Norman. "Can't you see that, Ned?"

Ned sighed and for the first time for a long time, Norman thought he sensed a little tear in his friend's eye.

"Yes," said Ned, "I know you are. But, you won't understand when I tell you that it's not me . . ." Norman and Kim looked blankly at him. "It's not me that writes, honestly. It's those other people. Ned Cresswell couldn't do it ... and Ned Cresswell doesn't. Those pseudonyms, they're not just names. They are people. I know them. I talk to them. I have conversations with them. I have to or else nothing would ever come out." Ned turned to Kim. "I've explained all this before to Norman and he doesn't understand but, surely, Kim, you do, don't you?" He paused. "Or am I really a senile old fool who ought to be put away?"

"Of course you aren't," said Kim. "And yes, I do understand. And I'm sure Norman does too."

"I've always understood," Norman said re-assuringly, "perhaps not in the way that Ned would like to hear. It's just that usually I'm the one who ends up with egg on his face because of it."

"Dear Norman," Ned said. "I am awful, aren't I? I don't know how you put up with me . . ." He sniffed and pulled out a handkerchief and blew his nose, a big snorting, trumpeting blow as Tom returned with four wrapped portions of cod and chips.

"God," he said, "that sounded like the *Queen Mary* docking at Southampton." He handed round the packets. "Ned, your's is the biggest one." The packets were unwrapped with great relish. "I think we'll drive up to the front and look at the sea while we eat."

As the others sampled first the crispy batter and then the chips, Tom drove. The mist had cleared and there was a big moon which was reflected on the water. For a while no one spoke as they ate. Tom suddenly laughed.

"What's amusing you?" said Kim.

"I was just thinking," he said, "if someone had told me after that day on Birling beach forty years ago that I'd one day be sitting in my own Rolls Royce eating fish and chips with my daughter and these two sainted personages in the back, I wouldn't have bothered to learn to swim."

"Why ever not?" asked Ned with his mouth full.

"Because life sort of works it all out for you," he said.

"But you have to give it a little help," said Norman. "In fact life needs all the help it can get." He smiled, rather pleased with his conclusion. "Would anyone like some of Ned's gherkin?" he asked as he noticed the giant green thing still intact in Ned's lap. "For once, he hasn't bitten off more than he can chew."

After a long, tiring day and the brief, exhilarating moment of fame, Sharon Dawes was feeling not a little confused as she stood in the foyer of the Devonshire Park Theatre with Shane and Shawn listening to their parents arguing. Sharon had already voiced the question that was on the family's lips as they were all at a loss to understand why it had been Norman and not Ned who had been called to the spotlight.

"I know," Doris snapped, "I know, Phil. But what can we do? Just leave it alone, will ya?" Doris had been counselling fast and furiously that they should say nothing and merely enjoy what else might materialise from Sharon's escapade. Doris was visualising breakfast television interviews and yet more treats from the the bottomless purses of the national newspapers.

"I can't just leave it," Phil countered. "I can't and I won't. It's wrong, Doris. It's not only wrong it's downright dishonest."

Doris pooh-poohed this moral interjection.

"An' who cares!" she said, determined that she was not going to be robbed of this brief moment of fame. "It's doin' no one no 'arm for Pete's sake! Those old buffers are no one's fools. They know what they're doin'."

Adrian Cork appeared on the steps leading from the auditorium with the manager of the theatre. He saw the Dawes family waiting in the foyer.

"Brilliant!" he said, walking over to them. "Thanks so much for your co-operation. I've got your address and I'll let you know what happens with this. There'll certainly be a big piece in *The Herald* but, who knows . . .? He leered. "There's bigger fish than that in the sea."

It was Sharon who settled the matter. It was she who had been rescued and it was she who was feeling the brunt of the mix-up.

"But it wasn't him!" she said urgently to Mr Cork who was just about to leave and develop his film. "It wasn't that man what rescued me. It was the other man."

At first, Mr Cork did not understand, as well he might not. Phil Dawes assisted his daughter.

"She's right, Mr Cork. You've been very kind, an' that and we're very grateful for the night out but it was the other chap, like. Sharon's right. Mr Cresswell was the one."

"So . . . so," began Mr Cork, gradually realising that he

had been robbed of the picture that would make his name, "you mean . . . Oh!" He was extremely cross. "The devious old bu . . . bu . . . buzzard!"

"Amen to that!" muttered Doris to herself. "But," she said to Mr Cork," you can still use what you've taken of Sharon, can't you?"

Adrian Cork ignored her. He was thinking. He looked at his watch. Too late, he thought, too late to drive over to East Dean tonight. Too late to get any sort of photo. Too late to get it up to London. Damn! he swore under his breath.

"You will, won't you?" Doris insisted, her urgent request disturbing his train of thought.

"We'll try, Mrs Dawes," he said encouragingly. "We'll most certainly try. I must go. Goodnight everyone and thanks again." He almost ran out of the theatre, his frustration tinged with a certain amount of relief. Had Sharon not spoken out, he reminded himself, his career could have been ruined, not made. But the apprentice inkhound remained undeterred; the truth had to be found.

"'Bye," called the Dawes family, all except Doris who was speechless with fury. She marched off, in what she thought was the direction of their guest house. She was half way down the road when they called to her.

"Wrong way, mum!"

NINETEEN

Ned had purposely left his curtains open and when he woke on Sunday morning, sunlight was streaming in through the east facing window. He opened one eye and glanced at his travelling alarm clock. It read eight o'clock. Ned closed his eyes again. Once awake, he never went back to sleep but he luxuriated in the hour's dreamtime he allowed himself before Norman came in with the tea.

Norman had been up quite some time. He had made himself a cup of tea and had sat in front of the french windows in his dressing gown, looking out at the beginning of another day. There was a heavy dew on the lawn and the grass was strewn thickly with the first flowering of daisies, sprinkled liberally amongst the green as though they had been set there by a shower of rain. As the sun rose over the brow of the Downs behind the house, so the daisies opened up. Quite delightful, Norman remarked to himself and thought of lines of cygnets at the ballet, rising up from recumbent passivity at the appearance and presence of the *premiere danseuse*. How nice, he thought, how nice it would have been if Biddy could have been here with them. It was so much more rewarding to share experiences and new friends and Norman remembered all the other times in the house, weekends often separated by years rather than months, when the three of them had done their catching up.

Norman was actually looking out at the garden in order to try and catch a glimpse of Albert. He had woken up with the greatest desire to restore the cat to Mrs Hopper. He had not forgotten that, if there was any way of achieving it, he would like to help the policeman's mother. Perhaps, he thought, I could have a word with the vicar or, better, perhaps even the kindly Genevieve Withers could be persuaded to involve herself.

Norman sighed. Neither of these alternatives would

probably materialise as he knew very well that neighbourliness was something of a fiction in the new England. But, he decided he would try. He looked at the clock. He was just about to make Ned's tea and think about the vegetables for lunch and whether there was enough young mint in the garden for the mint sauce, when the telephone rang.

Even Ned, drifting in and out of his dreamtime upstairs, heard it. Ba's telephone was one of the originals, a heavy bakelite one, now much sought after in antique shops by the cognescenti. It had a sharp, trilling ring, which echoed in the heavy casing. Perhaps it's Biddy, Norman thought as he hurried to the hall to answer the call.

"Hello," he said carefully. "East Dean 389."

"Well," gushed the voice at the other end rather loudly, "that would be Mr Cresswell, yes?"

"No," said Norman, carefully, instantly wary in case it was another ruse by the thwarted reporter, "it's not. This is Mr Rhodes. Can I help you?"

"Genevieve here," the voice battered on, "Withers. Hope I haven't got you out of bed. Just checking that you're still OK for sherry this morning. After church. Shall you be coming? Wonderful about your friend, I must say. Congratulations all round. Jolly good show." The voice tumbled out, babbling and rattling like a mountain torrent rushing over sharp granite. Norman was at a loss as to which question to answer first. He decided to ignore all of them and to merely reply to the most salient.

"How nice of you to call," he said, "Of course we're coming. How could we refuse?"

"Jolly good. About twelve-thirty? Ample parking behind me, by the way. Don't leave it in the lane. Trippers. See you later!"

Norman was about to ask whether he would see Genevieve in church, but before he had a chance, the telephone was replaced. She's a born organiser, Norman thought to himself. She's probably on every committee in the village; never an Indian, always a chief.

"Who was it?" Ned called from his bedroom.

Norman could hardly say "No one" and again he didn't want to say who it really was as he was by no means sure that Ned would ever get to the sherry party. He decided on a white lie.

"It was Tom," he called back. "I said I'd call him back after I'd made your tea."

"Aah," said Ned.

In the kitchen, after setting the tray, Norman opened a tin of tuna which Ned had bought in the hope of another day's picnic on the beach. He decanted half of it into a saucer and opened the back door. Albert, under the laurel bush, saw everything, although he sensed something in Norman's behaviour which didn't quite ring the bell.

Norman had yet to tackle Ned about the question of going to church which, he felt, had been implicit in Genevieve Withers' invitation. Getting Ned to church usually entailed a requisite birth, death or nuptials, all of which in present circumstances were conspiciously absent. Norman shook his head as the kettle whistled.

Ned, hearing Norman's footsteps on the stairs, disentangled himself from the bed.

"It is the most wonderful day," said Norman enthusiastically. "I've been up for hours. Why is it that here I never want to stay in bed and yet in London, I sometimes need an excuse to even open my eyes?" He put the tray down on the bed and sat on the edge.

"A wonderful, catless day, I trust," yawned Ned. "I presume it must be as we haven't had yesterday's early morning caller. As yet."

Ned stretched out his hand for the mug which Norman offered and winced.

"I take it that means you're feeling a bit stiff, dear," Norman remarked calmly, knowing full well that the wince was the first in a mounting and ever-worsening series of symptoms which Ned intended to use as an excuse for not going to Genevieve Withers' party. "Perhaps you ought to stay in bed today."

Ned knew that Norman was onto him.

"Perhaps I will," he said and sighed.

"What a pity it's such a lovely day," Norman continued. "After another hot soak, I'm sure you'd feel as right as rain and then you could enjoy the sunshine." He paused and sipped his tea. "But I quite understand if you'd prefer to recuperate up here. Such a shame I haven't got time to go and fetch the Sunday papers for you to read."

Ned was quiet for a moment. It was too early for his usually razor-sharp strategic instinct to exercise itself fully. Damn it, he thought. There was no other way out but to confess and face the music.

"I don't want to go," he said bluntly, sounding just like a naughty boy. "And I don't see why I should."

"I know you don't want to go," said Norman, comfortingly.

"So am I let off?" asked Ned eagerly, sensing a chink in Norman's armour.

"No, you are not," said Norman firmly. "As a matter of fact, I don't much want to go either but there are some occasions in life, Ned, which cannot be ignored and which will not just simply go away. This," said Norman conclusively, "is one of them."

Ned put in his teeth and gnashed them. He looked as black as thunder.

"Then . . .," he began, groping for a suitable threat and finding only one, "Then if I'm going to parade around in front of a houseful of complete strangers with a glass of sherry in my hand, I'm jiggered if I'm going to do it as a hypocrite."

"And just what does that mean?" said Norman peremptorily.

"It means that I'm not going to church," said Ned. Norman knew that this was the ultimate position of Ned's army and, as his was equally entrenched, a truce was going to be the outcome. Norman put down his cup and saucer and poured another cup. "So what have you got to say about that?" asked Ned.

"Should I have anything to say?" said Norman. Ned shook his head, puzzled.

"You gave in rather too easily," said Ned. "That's all."

"Dear, dear Ned. How suspicious you are! No, I'm quite content." Norman took more tea. "That this very small community should think you a rabid atheist is one thing, that they think you a rude, arrogant, crotchety old man is quite another and it is that I would have objected to." Norman finished. "I shall ring Tom and ask him if he will come with me to church." He got up and took his cup with him downstairs.

"But, I'm a hero!" said Ned indignantly.

"Not to me you aren't," said Norman at the door. "In fact," he said as he went down the stairs, "I believe that in the mind of the great British public, it is I who am the hero."

"Bah!" said Ned, almost spilling his tea. "My best friend! How ignoble!"

Norman looked at the time and although he felt that it was a little too early for telephoning on a Sunday morning, he called Tom nevertheless. He'd seen the curtains being pulled back in what he had deduced was Tom's bedroom.

Tom Maxwell was indeed not only awake but having toast and ginger marmalade in the kitchen, listening to Alastair Cooke on the wireless. He hadn't slept very well and neither had he come to any decisions. Since Annie's death and her bequest to him of the house, he had developed the habit of driving down to East Dean every weekend, although he had known that the routine was one which he had evolved to delay the inevitable decision he knew he had to make about his future.

This particular weekend, he had decided would be crunch time. Kim had been so accurate in their conversation the previous day. His lot should have been the envy of most men yet, although bells were still pealing out in celebration of his success, their knell rang slightly cracked. He had inherited Maxwell's from his father and grandfather before him and his thirty years of hard labour had been invested for many other reasons other than for his own satisfaction and fulfillment. Now he had the freedom he had always told himself he wanted and to compound the priviledge he had the time and money with which to enjoy it.

He put another slice of bread into the toaster and refilled his coffee mug. Upstairs he heard Kim going into the bathroom. He decided that freedom was a quality of mythical proportions and one which he was beginning to think was going to be more difficult to handle than he had thought.

He had concluded that his freedom necessitated the starting of a completely new life and a cutting of all the ties that bound him to a time which, by persistently revisiting it, made him feel empty and adrift. The toast popped out and triggered him into deciding that, after all, Annie's house would have to be sold.

The telephone rang and Kim called downstairs for him to answer it as it might be . . . But, watched telephones are like slow-boiling pots. He turned down the radio.

"Hello," he said and listened while Norman made his request. "I'd be glad to, Norman," he said. "I'll pick you up about ten to eleven?"

Kim came downstairs as Tom replaced the receiver. She looked at him disappointedly as he shook his head.

"Sorry, darling. It was Norman. Asked me to take him to church. Ned's not going. Coffee? Toast?"

"Just coffee, thanks," she said. "Men! I honestly thought that call might have been for me."

Tom made her coffee and they sat down at the table. Her hair was still wet and she had piled it under a towel tied like a turban.

"At the risk of sounding too much like a man," he said, "I rather fancy that you are supposed to call James, not the other way around."

"I know," she sighed. "It just seems stupid to me, though. Here we are, after all these years, we couldn't be any closer and yet suddenly there's this riduculous gulf between us just because he asked me a question."

"And when you've answered it," said Tom trying to be wise yet not clinical, "the gulf won't be there."

"Only if he gets the answer he wants to hear," said Kim.

"How do you know?" said Tom.

Kim reflected for a moment and then got up and cut

some bread. Of course, she thought, he does have a point. Kim waited by the toaster, rocking back and forth on her heels.

"This is the last of Annie's ginger marmalade," he said. "I'm glad you're here, darling."

"To share the last of the marmalade?" she said and laughed. "You are so sweet, pa."

"No," he said, laughing too. "Not only the marmalade although it is a bit of an omen." He wondered whether or not to tell her about his decision to sell. Why not, he decided, for his decision affected them both. "Kim, would you think it awful of me if I said that I was thinking of selling the house."

"That means you've already decided to sell," she said, taking the toast out and displaying no outward sign that she had been shocked or upset.

"Why?" he said. "Why do you say that?"

"It's one of your . . . little ways," she said, buttering the toast in a way and with an amount that always prompted Annie to ask if she liked toast with her butter. "Mummy and I used to look at each other and wink when you started off a conversation like that."

Tom groaned inwardly. "That was then," he said. "Old habits die hard, I suppose. I never wanted to upset anyone." Kim blew him a kiss across the table. "Thanks . . . It's just that there are so many memories everywhere. I want to . . . to . . ."

"Cut loose," Kim said, completing his thought for him. "I understand."

"Do you really?"

Kim paused and decided that she had to be honest.

"Actually, no. I don't understand but I accept your decision. It's hard, though. I suppose it means we aren't a family anymore, doesn't it?"

Tom felt panic. The last thing he had intended and certainly wanted was to alienate his daughter.

"Kim! Please . . . Of course I won't sell it if that's how you feel. Darling, I never wanted to hurt you; you, of all people!"

She put out her hand across the table and held his tightly."

Daddy, it's alright. Really. It's time." she smiled at him. "Time for all of us to . . . to put away childish things. Memories come into that category too. For each of us."

Tom felt as though he wanted to cry, not for her but for him. Perhaps, rather for them. He got up from the table, a lump of sentiment in his throat threatening to burst at any moment.

"I'm just going to check my bonfire," he said quickly and left Kim to finish the last of the ginger marmalade although the last thing she wanted was breakfast.

Under protest, Ned had again been persuaded into the shrinking bath tub. Norman had liberally poured in the last of the bath salts and had whisked up a tempting lather of bubbles.

As Norman prepared the potatoes and vegetables in the kitchen, he heard Ned singing quite happily in his bath and smiled to himself, satisfied that their compromise had not been too difficult for Ned to accept. Norman put the huge leg of lamb onto a wire tray in the roasting pan and was just going to cut some fresh rosemary from Ba's herb garden outside the back door when the front door bell rang.

He had already dressed for church and merely removed his apron before answering the door. As he opened it, he realised why front doors had little windows in them. Had he seen who was calling, he wouldn't have answered the door.

"Oh," he said, "Good morning."

Even though he had been nearly blinded by the popping glare of camera flash and the stage lights the previous evening, Adrian Cork's face was indelibly imprinted on Norman's memory.

Adrian was even more charming and smarmy than he had been the afternoon before as once again he found himself on well-trodden ground.

"Mr Rhodes," he said breathily, almost huskily,

imagining that such seductive sincerity would succeed with Norman where it had failed abysmally with Ned. "What a lovely day, don't you agree?"

"It was," said Norman frostily, thinking to himself that if Ned should catch a whiff of this young gentleman's prescence, the delicately negotiated order of business for the day would be instantly imperilled. "What can I do for you?"

"I was wondering if I might have a word with your . . . friend?" wormed Mr Cork. "Just a brief chat and perhaps . . .," he said as he patted his camera, ". . . a little snap?"

Norman smiled, very sweetly, perhaps a little coyly, and silently cursed Ned once again for making him invent yet another story.

"I'm afraid you're too late," he said. "He's gone, you see."

"Gone?" repeated Mr Cork, thinking first that perhaps the irritating Mr Cresswell might have passed over, so increasing the value of his story even more . . . The headline, he thought could then read: PLUCKY PENSIONER PERISHES SAVING TEENAGE GIRL.

"To the osteopath," said Norman quite credibly. "In London. You've only just missed him. He went by train . . . from Eastbourne. So sorry." Norman smiled again and began to close the door on Mr Cork. He even remembered feeling rather sorry for him. But Mr Cork was not to be outdone and his quest had now become a matter of pride. Was it not Adrian Cork who with carte blanche had never had a problem arranging interviews with or Ken Dodd or Winifred Attwell or any of the other stars who played summer seasons in Eastbourne?

Was it not Adrian Cork who had investigated the allegations of over-priced deck chairs on the promenade and who had been praised to the skies for his sensitive reporting of the recent conference on euthanasia? Indeed it was the very same Adrian Cork and he was absolutely determined . . .

"Will Mr Cresswell be returning to East Dean?" he ventured.

"Of course," said Norman, "next year. Oh!" he

exclaimed. "There's Albert!" The startled Mr Cork turned round and in doing so, inadvertently removed his foot from the door which Norman immediately slammed. The sight of a tortoiseshell cat stretching amongst a show of tulips was all that Mr Cork saw. Although a grown man, Adrian Cork felt like bursting into tears.

Ned was still singing in the bathroom closeted away in a cloud of steam. Mr Cork rapped again on the door but Norman ignored him. He ran to the sitting room and turned on the radio, full volume, hoping that Ned would not hear the persistent knocking on the front door. Secreting himself behind the curtains at the french windows, he watched as Mr Cork stepped back from the house and looked up at the bedroom windows. Scowling with an expression of undiluted exasperation, he returned to his white car. Norman watched him as he drove away. The radio was blaring so loudly that he did not hear Ned calling from the landing.

"Norman!"

Norman switched off the radio.

"What time are you making your peace with the Almighty?" Ned called down.

"I hope I already have," said Norman under his breath. "Ten-to-eleven," he called back.

TWENTY

Ned had driven down to the village to collect the newspapers. He was currently kneeling in the middle of the sitting room, as was his wont, surrounded by sheets of newsprint. He brandished a large pair of dress-making scissors and, as he turned the pages, would excise an article which particularly interested him. He kept the clippings in a big box file on his desk at home and at the end of each month he would sort through them, discarding the ones he had retained on impulse and filing those he deemed worthy with other source material in an old wooden filing cabinet. His filing system was entirely his own. It followed no recognisable logic either numerical, alphabetical or chronological. Indeed, it seemed to have been designed to elude logic.

At a quarter-to-eleven, Ned looked up from his surgery. Norman was quite ready for church and was waiting for Tom. He was leafing through one of the magazine sections of the newspaper and was wondering whether to send off for a complete set of saucepans which were being advertised as the bargain of the week.

"Is that what you're wearing?" asked Ned.

"God won't notice," said Norman. "Anyway, it's only the village church. I'm not going to the Vatican, dear."

"I'm not dressing up either," said Ned. "Not for Withers' sherry do."

"I never thought you would," said Norman who had decided against the saucepans.

"I've paid my dues," said Ned, his attention returning to the book reviews, "so people can take me as they find me. Agreed?"

"I rather think they haven't much option," said Norman. He saw Tom and Kim walking up the drive. "Oh, he's here. See you later."

Norman went to answer the door. Tom looked so

handsome in his charcoal striped suit. Kim, in her T-shirt and slacks was obviously not intending to accompany them to church.

"Thought I'd come over and chat to Ned," said Kim. "If he's not busy?"

"Absolutely," said Norman. "Ned," he called, "Kim's here to see you."

"Good," said Ned. "Come in Kim. I'm here, in the sitting room."

Norman and Tom called goodbye and left for church.

"Have a nice pray," Ned called back as Kim came in. "Hello, dear. Can I make you some coffee?"

"No thanks," said Kim. "Later maybe?" She sat down in an armchair as Ned heaved himself up from the floor and flopped onto the sofa. "Am I witnessing the tricks of the trade?" asked Kim indicating the pile of news clippings on the floor.

"Oh, those," said Ned and shook his head. "Not really. I can't really think why I do it except that I always have. Even as a child I kept mountains of clippings for scrap books. I look through them now and wonder what on earth it was of such significance that made me cut out them out in the first place."

"And you've still got them, these scrap books?"

"Trunks and trunks, dear girl. My childhood is thoroughly intact. Don't know what they'll think when I'm dead and gone and all that stuff gets turned out. People will think my life stopped at eighteen."

"But it didn't, did it?"

"I don't think childhood ever stops."

"I was thinking more about life," said Kim.

"Ah, life," said Ned in mock earnest. "Is that what we're going to talk about?"

"We could do," said Kim. "But perhaps you'd rather not?"

"Depends whose life we're going to talk about," said Ned. "Life in general's a bit of a bore to talk about as one never gets anywhere. More so as you get older, too."

"Does that mean life is supposed to go somewhere?"

said Kim.

Ned shook his head and replied with his usual candour.

"No. It implies that talking about life doesn't go anywhere. Only lives go somewhere and that's much more to the point. Where's your's going for instance, young lady?"

"I know where it's come from," said Kim rather miserably. "As to any other direction, I'm afraid I'm sort of stuck in reverse gear at the moment."

"Ah," said Ned clapping his hands. "Crossroads. I love crossroads, especially other people's and especially the ones that have no signposts."

"I can't bear being intelligent," said Kim. "Oh, I'm sorry, that sounded awful. I mean that I can't bear thinking . . . I'm forever thinking, weighing everything up in terms of pros and cons. I wish I could just do, just be and damn the consequences."

"Hardest thing in the world," said Ned, "being yourself. Virtual impossibility."

"You seem to manage it," said Kim defensively. "I don't think I've ever met anyone who's more definite."

Ned laughed. "Oh," he said wistfully," to see ourselves as others see us . . ." Ned paused. "What do you see?" he asked.

Kim hesitated, wondering if Ned would be annoyed.

"A strong person, very good at what he does, respected by everyone, perhaps a bit stubborn at times, kind, thoughtful, fulfilled . . ."

Ned waved his arms. "Dear girl, stop, for heaven's sake," Ned cried, laughing at Kim's definition, not to ridicule her but to immediately debunk what Ned saw as a myth. "Please don't misunderstand me but you really mustn't."

"Mustn't what?"

"Invest people with qualities you want them to have."

"But you have them, Ned."

"You see them. You create them. Doesn't mean they're there. You want to see them because you think you lack them yourself. I can tell," Ned said, wagging his finger.

"What was it . . . Strong? You couldn't be more wrong! Weak as a kitten, terrified, nervous, shy, that's more like it . . . What next, ah yes . . . Good at what I do? Was that it? Well, I don't think so. Just because I and a few other people have made a living out of my fantasies about myself doesn't make what I do good."

"Please don't," said Kim. "You're underestimating yourself."

"Not a chance," said Ned. "I know me too well to ever risk that. I know what I can do, what I can't do. It's up to other people to do the estimating."

"OK then," said Kim, shifting her position in the chair and curling her legs beneath her, "at least you're not afraid to know yourself. Perhaps that's what I mean by strong."

"My dear Kim," said Ned, becoming suddenly very serious, "I am an old man now . . . Once, I was a young man, not unlike you in character even though our sex is different. In between then and now an awful lot of very little has happened to me and what little has happened to me hasn't happened because I wanted it to happen. It just happened. Am I making any sense?"

Kim frowned."Perhaps," she said. "It just seems rather obvious."

"That's all there is to it. You can only see that things have happened after they've happened, not before."

"Ah, you mean you've got to let them happen."

"Too intellectual," said Ned. "Far too much use of the grey matter, my dear. Not enough heart."

"I think it's the heart I'm most afraid of," said Kim."I suppose I know I can depend on my head. All that heart stuff is a bit wobbly." She paused. "You were married once, weren't you?"Ned looked away from the young woman sitting opposite him. He looked at the walls, the mirror, the hearth, at the flickering memories which the question had revived."I'm sorry, Ned. That was rude. I'm awfully sorry." Kim sat forward in her chair, hoping she hadn't caused too much offence by her bluntness."I just felt that you might be able to . . . to help."

"As far as I'm concerned, I still am married, my dear,"

Ned said, his eyes still seeing something invisible and far away. "Even after all these years." He pulled back from the vastness of his contemplation. "So, tell me . . . What's your's like? Tell me about your young man?" Ned's hands assumed the familiar clasped position, his thumbs twiddling first one way, then the other, revolving quickly as though he was spinning a lengthening yarn.

Kim smiled. Ned had taken her by surprise. She'd never had to describe James to anyone before. James had always been James, to her, to her father and mother, her friends.

"Well," she began, ignorant of exactly where to begin, "he's . . . He's James." She laughed.

"Is that all?" Ned said, teasing her. "Not much substance there. Can't see why you're in such a whirl about him?"

"OK" said Kim. "This is James . . . He's not too tall, not too short, he's sort of good looking; well, I think he is. He's gentle but not weak or anything like that, he's good fun and laughs a lot, he's ambitious but not in a money way. He wants to do what he does to the best. I've known him since school. Forever, really." She stopped for a moment. "That's all."

"All?" said Ned. "You can do better than that."

"And he's going to take a job in America and . . . he's asked me to marry him . . ."

"And?" persisted Ned, determined to make Kim reach the end of the story.

"And he's asked me to marry him," she said finally.

"You haven't finished yet, dear girl," encouraged Ned. There was a moment's pause for thought as Kim's eyes closed for concentration.

"If I say yes, I'm scared it would fail, like their's," explained Kim. "Like pa and mummy. Yet, I can't imagine what my life would be like without him."

Kim was swallowing hard and knew that she was going to cry. Ned got up from the sofa and came and sat on the arm of the chair beside her. The embrace which ensued prompted the floodgates to open and Kim sobbed.

"Oh, what am I going to do, Ned. It's just so awful. I should be happy, I know I should but it's just the most miserable, damn awful feeling in the world. Tell me something good. Tell me anything."

Ned let her cry for a while. There weren't many tears but Ned knew that Kim had to cry.

"I can tell you one thing for certain, Kim" he said gently as Kim sniffed and withdrew from Ned's hug. "It's not even worth trying to imagine what life would be like without him. I shall say no more than that." Ned returned to the sofa but didn't sit down. He stood in front of the mirror over the hearth and looked at himself as he spoke. "I can't tell you what to do and I don't want to," he said. "You mentioned that you thought I could help. I can't. Only you can help and you'll always be the only one who can help. Does James know all about this confusion?"

Kim nodded and took a tissue from her pocket.

"Yes."

"And what does he say about it?" asked Ned, turning from the mirror.

"He thinks I'm creating problems unnecessarily."

"Damn him," said Ned.

"Why?"

"Because he's probably right," said Ned and reached out his hand to Kim. Their fingers touched and Kim knew that Ned was right too. "And I'll tell you another thing," Ned went on, "I only wish I had your problem!"

They laughed. Kim said nothing but her smile was her thanks. Ned clapped his hands, signifying that there was nothing left to say on that subject but also signifying that there was another subject he wished to raise.

"Kim, dear, would you do me a great favour?" asked Ned.

"Anything," said Kim.

Ned smiled wickedly.

"Come with me to this bloody sherry party?"

TWENTY ONE

"It's funny how everyone looks at you," said Norman to Tom, "when you're in a Rolls Royce. No one gives our Min a second glance."

"I rather think it has to do with small Sussex villages than cars," Tom replied.

"I wouldn't know about that," said Norman. "I've never lived in one. I came from Canterbury, you know, straight to London. That's all I've ever known."

Tom finally caught a break in the weekend traffic on the main road and pulled out. The sun had ensured a grand turn-out of Sunday drivers. He turned left along Upper Road towards the Green.

"That must be Genevieve's house," said Norman pointing at a large village house faced with plaster and flint. "So pretty, with the ramblers just starting to green up."

"That's the place," said Tom. "The hub of the universe." He grinned. "The local universe, anyway."

"I don't think I should like the country all the time," said Norman. "People say dreadful things about London but it's really very friendly. Would you ever consider moving down here permanently, Tom?"

"I think I'd seize up," laughed Tom. "Not a lot of scope really, is there?"

"Depends what you want your scope to encompass. But," he added, "though I don't know you at all, I would hazard a guess that you'd find things pretty dull."

"You hazard correctly, Norman. But I'm afraid at the moment, I'm the dullest thing around." Tom pulled up behind a long line of parked cars. "Something going on down here," he said. "And the pub isn't even open yet."

They passed the beginning of the old village green and there in front of *The Tyger*, on the green, watched by a fairly large crowd of onlookers were a troupe of Morris men, jigging up and down and twirling their be-ribboned staves.

"Look!" Norman squeaked excitedly. "Isn't that lovely. Americans would love that."

"Wouldn't they just," agreed Tom. "They think that anything English is the bee's knees in cuteness."

"Thank heavens they do. I like the Americans a lot, especially the men." He stopped himself. "Golly," he said, smirking, "that did sound fruity, didn't it, but you know what I mean. They're still very . . . very gentlemanly."

Tom once again had to wait to let a queue of cars out of a small side turning.

"Have you ever been?" he asked.

"To America? Oh, yes. Many times. Ned's been more than me. They rather like him there. He gives talks . . . to ladies. Luncheon thingummies."

"I would have thought he'd've hated that," remarked Tom. "Bearing in mind last night."

Norman shook his head.

"Not in America, funnily enough. That's about the only place where he'll let go. He says it's something to do with feeling anonymous. Have you ever been?"

Tom began to look for a place to park the car.

"Yes," he said, looking round to check whether one particular space was large enough to manoeuvre into. "But only ever on business. In fact," he added, "I'd rather like to have a crack at living there."

"And you think that would make you less dull?" observed Norman perspicaciusly. He winked at him. "Only teasing. You're not in the slightest bit dull and, I assure you, you don't have to go as far as America to find that out."

Norman unfastened his seat belt and Tom came round to open his door. Only a very few people seemed to be going to church.

"Well, something's calling me somewhere," he said as he held open the gate for Norman. "I feel a bit washed up here."

"Perhaps you'll both go," said Norman. "You and Kim. I have a feeling that she's not long for England."

Tom walked thoughtfully on Norman's right down the path which wound through the cemetery and up to the church door. It was a pretty church, small and flint-covered like many of the local houses, surrounded by its churchyard and a low wall. Forsythia bloomed in several places and everywhere there were daffodils.

"There isn't a cure for restlessness, you know," Norman said. "Except to keep moving. I know. Ned's always been restless. But," he added acutely, "he always comes home. We all do in the end."

"To the happy home," Tom said with a certain irony. "Wherever that might be."

They entered the church. The organ was playing a muted piece of Haydn and it was cold. Very few people were in the pews and there was no one who looked the slightest bit like Genevieve Withers. Tom and Norman took their seats towards the rear of the short nave and after a moment's prayer, sat upright and looked about them.

"It's ages since I was in church," Norman whispered. "I feel quite shamed. I think it was Christmas Eve the last time I went."

A couple came into the church behind them and as they passed, Norman glanced up. Neither was Genevieve Withers for they were both men. They nodded and smiled all the same at Norman and Tom.

Norman opened his hymn book to refer to the numbers advertised on the hymnboard. Someone tapped him on the shoulder and made him jump. He was aware of a perfumed and talcumed prescence behind him and the outer rim of a very large hat.

"Nice to see you!" hissed the voice none too softly. "I see you've met Mr Maxwell."

Norman turned round. This person must, could only be Genevieve.

"Good morning," Norman whispered. "We meet at last. Thank you so much for the milk by the way."

"Great pleasure, Mr Cresswell. Great pleasure." Miss Withers beamed and pulled the buttonless fronts of her silk coat together. It covered a silk dress of the same material and, as Norman had imagined, created a queenly, if not imperial, effect.

"I'm not Mr Cresswell," Norman whispered, smiling. "I'm the other one; I'm Norman Rhodes."

They shook hands and then Genevieve excused herself and reached across to shake Tom's hand.

"He is coming, isn't he," Genevieve said with a look of great concern. "Afterwards. So many people want to meet him, especially after yesterday. Such bravery!"

Norman barely had time to put Miss Withers out of her agony before a door opened by the altar.

"See you after," said Genevieve oozing charm. "So pleased to meet you. Heard bags about you!"

There was something very familiar about Genevieve Withers and all through the fairly tedious service, Norman was trying to place her. He was fairly sure that he hadn't met Genevieve before so why did he feel he knew her?

Tedious but thankfully short, thought Norman as the tiny congregation intoned the last Amen. Here we go, he thought as the worshippers rose to leave and Genevieve sailed down the aisle from her seat in the very front pew. Here we go.

The ritual now over, Genevieve obviously saw no point in lowering her voice and immediately began to organise.

"There now," she boomed, "all over for another week, what? Why don't you walk back with me, Mr Rhodes? I take it Mr Maxwell will collect our other guest? Couldn't help seeing the car, Mr Maxwell. I'd introduce you to Vicar but he's coming along later so you'll meet him with a glass in your hand. Much the best way to confront piety. Good morning, Mrs White," she said graciously to a woman who passed them on the aisle and who looked very curiously at Norman. "How's the toe today?" The woman opened her mouth to speak but ws silenced by another torrent from Genevieve. "That's grand. So pleased. Now, off we go. Sooner we get the corks out the better, what?"

And on she sailed, not even waiting for Norman who, followed by Tom, smiling to himself, had to almost run to keep up. Gosh, Norman thought to himself, Ned was pretty bombastic at times but this woman could run rings around him with both feet tied together.

Outside the church, Norman was pulled along in Genevieve's wake and turned rather helplessly with a shrug to Tom.

"Can you remind Ned that he's supposed to have put the meat in if he's forgotten," Norman called. "And can you explain?" Norman pointed at the vanguard surge which was Genevieve Withers under full canvas.

"Don't worry," said Tom and walked back to the car, around which an admiring group of men had gathered, discussing the finer points of carmanship.

"Lovely motor, squire," said one.

"Thanks," Tom replied.

"And British through and through," added another.

"Yes," said Tom and smiled as he closed the door, deciding that to enter into a conversation which would ultimately get round to the subject of the gear box and, yet worse, the origins of the gearbox, was not to be undertaken lightly.

He drove away, passing Genevieve and Norman on the way. Genevieve didn't even look round, she merely waved, a curious flourishing wave of acknowledgement.

"Charming man, don't you think," Genevieve said. Norman was slightly breathless. "Such a pity though. Always thought he and Jennifer a perfect couple. Still, these days . . ."

"Yes," Norman managed to say, again at a loss to know to which of her undoubtedly rhetorical questions Genevieve wanted an answer.

"Met the daughter? Hear she's down. Lovely child. Awfully brave about Mr Cresswell. Is that what he likes to be called? Supppose it must be. Odd lot, authors, for the most part. Be good to meet an ordinary one, don't you know? Arthur's one too. Probably have a lot in common."

"Probably," said Norman who by now didn't know whether he was on his head or his heels. He also wondered with trepidation what Genevieve's definition of ordinary was and how it could possibly apply to Ned. "We haven't met Arthur, have we?" he said, trying desperately to remember whether he ought to have known who Arthur was or not.

"My other half," said Genevieve. "Been together years. Came off the boards thinking he was going to make a quieter woman of me. Ha!" she boomed. "Still, bit late for all that now, isn't it. At our age. Not much point."

"No," said Norman, "I suppose there isn't," he added, wondering how to interpret Genevieve's intimation and thinking what a strange and odd place England was. People like Genevieve are bred only in England, he thought and Norman decided that he, if not Ned, was going to rather take to this Wagnerian woman.

The Morris men outside *The Tyger* had danced themselves out as Genevieve and Norman skirted the Green. With their audience, the dancers were enjoying pints of beer and their cigarettes, which Norman thought looked strangely out of keeping with their rustic costumes.

From the lane, a white-painted door set in an ivy-covered wall led into Genevieve's garden. The wall encircled the ground and concealed one of the most perfect gardens Norman had ever seen. Of course, the herbaceous borders set against two of the walls had not yet begun to show any sign of their potential. It was far too early. But the spring flowers were magnificent. Many different varieties of daffodils, narcissi and tulips had been planted in swathes of gradating colour around the flowering shrubs, forsythia, camelias and, because of the shelter provided by the high wall, early rhododendrons and azalea.

"Oooh," breathed Norman, lost in admiration, "This is lovely, Genevieve." It was by now a truly glorious day. The sun was hot and there wasn't a hint of a cloud to be seen. "The rhododendrons are magnificent. And so unusual for chalk."

"Thank you," replied Genevieve, beaming. "Tons of peat, that's the secret and lorry loads of leaf mould. Lots of work but we love it. Live for it. As soon as she had closed the gate, Genevieve removed the huge hat. "There!" she said with obvious relief. "Glad that's off. Arthur says it looks like a flying saucer." She shepherded Norman up the brick path, framed on either side with original Victorian plaited faience edging, the sight of which immediately made Norman jealous. In the lawn grew violets, scattered amongst the daisies which together gave the appearance of the contents of a button box, spilled out onto a green baize table. "Arthur!" Genevieve called to her spouse rather musically, beginning on a high note and placing the final syllable of his name lower in the scale. "We're ba - ck!" She seemed to sing energy and Norman could not imagine this powerhouse ever waning.

"I've got it!" Norman exclaimed for indeed he had. He had placed Genevieve at last. The inability to do so had been driving him mad with irritation throughout the sermon but now he had made the connection. Genevieve stopped and turned, a look of some astonishment on her face. "*The Silent Years*! At the Queens. My friend and I thought you were magnificent."

Genevieve beamed.

"Well, well," she said, obviously heartened considerably, "how wonderful of you to remember. That was donkeys years ago."

"I always wondered what happened to you," said Norman who was tremendously excited. Genevieve Gale had been his and Cyril's favourite actress, famous for her outspokeness, daring fashions and social connections.

"So, now you know," said Genevieve. "This poor old decrepit thing before you is an object lesson in what happens to racy young actresses."

Through the windows of what was Genevieve's sitting room, a white-haired man with a distinguished face appeared. The man smiled and waved, indicating the sherry bottle and picking up a glass.

"That's Arthur," said Genevieve proudly. She turned to Norman, her head on one side and gave a little smile. "I know what you're thinking, Norman. So, that's what she gave it all up for, eh? Well, come on in and meet him."

Arthur was indeed as nice as Norman had thought him

to be on first sight. Probably a couple of years older than Genevieve, thought Norman but he immediately felt comfortable with him as he stood in the low doorway of the beamed sitting room. He looked comfortable too, dressed in a baggy arran cardigan and brown cordueroy trousers.

"So, we meet at last," he said, shaking Norman's hand. "Elizabeth has told us so much about you over the years it's a scandal we've never met before. Welcome! Sweet or Dry?"

"Dry, please," said Norman. "It is funny," he said, "I call her Biddy, Ned calls her Ba and you call her Elizabeth." He hesitated. "We are talking about the same person, aren't we? Mrs Croker-Symes?"

"That's the girl," said Arthur. "Many a pint of Barthorpe's best has washed down this old throat over the years."

"And she's still at it," added Genevieve. "Ah, more people!" she cried and left Norman alone with Arthur to welcome her other guests.

"Damn good thing she is too," said Arthur. "We've got shares in Barthorpes." He poured Norman's sherry and handed him the glass.

Norman glanced out of the window and saw Ned with Tom and Kim coming into the garden through another door in the far wall.

"I've just placed your wife," Norman said as he and Arthur raised their glasses to each other. "Has she given up acting completely?"

"Genevieve? Never!" laughed Arthur. "Except that now we only allow her to do it once a year in the village hall."

"So what happened," said Norman, intrigued, "apart from marrying you, I mean?"

"Well, I must admit that I did have something to do with it," said Arthur jauntily. "At least, I hope I did!" Norman sipped at his sherry. "She was offered a part she thought she could never play and she just couldn't resist the challenge." Norman looked puzzled and Arthur laughed again. "Motherhood, Norman," he said in a stage whisper. Norman cottoned on.

"Oh, I see," he said.

"We had six in the end," he said proudly. "You'll meet one of them. Sally, the baby. She'll be here soon."

There was a ripple of conversation in the hall and Arthur excused himself to welcome Ned and the others. Norman sipped his sherry and looked around the room. There were photographs everywhere, in silver frames, brass frames, papier mache frames, photographs on every conceivable surface and all of children. Over the inglenook fireplace there hung an oil painting of Genevieve as Norman remembered her, of Genevieve the actress, standing by a window in a new look creation, shoulderless, strapless and held up by both will power and Genevieve's redoubtable bosom which the years had done nothing to diminish. Other than the painting, there was nothing theatrical about the room at all. A log fire burned on firedogs in the inglenook and a very old black labrador was stretched out on a charred Turkey rug. Norman noticed that the dog was wide awake, luxuriating in his dotage.

Norman waved to Ned across the room and was relieved to see that Ned looked relieved. He also looked relatively smart in plain green slacks and a shetland jumper.

"Hello, hello," said Arthur, going to greet them. "Mr Cresswell, what a pleasure!" They shook hands. "And the mighty Maxwells too." Kim kissed Arthur on the cheek.

"Children!" he said, "how you do grow up but you must be tired of hearing that!"

Arthur accompanied them to the tray of sherry.

"Obviously no need to introduce you lot," he said, pouring three glasses. "Sweet, I think you said, Mr Cresswell?"

"Thanks," said Ned taking the profferred glass and looking at it appreciatively. "What a wonderfully big glass," he said to Arthur. "I've been in swimming pools smaller than this. Cheers!"

Arthur laughed and handed glasses to Tom and Kim.

"See," Norman whispered to Ned. "They're awfully nice. Things aren't always as bad as you think."

"We'll see," muttered Ned although he had to privately

admit that he might have been too quick in his judgements.

Norman was so confident that there were going to be no sticky patches ahead that he launched into conversation with Arthur.

"Genevieve tells me that you're a writer too," Norman said. Ned glared at him.

"Oh, she did, did she?" said Arthur, pretending to be cross. "What have you been telling these good people, dear?" he chided as Genevieve approached with a tray of snacks and nuts.

"Well, you are," said his wife. "Sort of . . . Oh, there's Vicar with Horace and Enid." She started for the door and then turned and handed the tray to Kim. "Be an angel, Kim, would you?" and left Kim to pass around the tray."

I thought you were a boffin," said Tom Maxwell. "Something to do with cars, wasn't it?"

"I like to think of myself as an engineer," said Arthur. "Not a very glamourous profession, I'm afraid."

"So where does the author bit come in?" asked Kim.

"Engineering text books," he said, to a respectful response. "See, I told you. Not very exciting at all. You've heard the story of how I met Genevieve, Tom, surely?"

"I must say I haven't," said Tom, smiling.

"Oh, do tell," said Norman eagerly.

Genevieve had ushered the vicar and his wife in from the hall and motioned to Arthur for another two sherries. She crossed the room and took Ned's arm.

"Mr Cresswell, do come and meet the vicar – John and Louise. They're dying to meet you!"

Ned froze but Kim took his arm.

"I'll come with you, Ned," she said, "with my tray. I'm right behind you."

As Arthur told the story of his meeting with Genevieve, which, briefly, came about because Genevieve's car had broken down on the way back to the theatre from a weekend party she had been to in Warwickshire and along came Arthur on a very powerful motorbicycle and, unable to repair the car for her, had taken her all the way to London on the pillion.

"And you fell in love?" said Norman at the end.

"She was the only girl I'd ever met whose voice was louder than the motorbike. I've been listening ever since."

"Mr Cresswell, so pleased to meet you," said John Case, the vicar. "May I present my wife, Louise?" Ned shook their hands.

"Glorious day," Ned said and looked imploringly at Kim.

"Nuts, Mr Case?" offered Kim and John and Louise each picked one as Arthur brought their sherry.

"Take a handful," he said to the vicar. "Go on Louise, don't be shy. One nut doesn't feed a sparrow."

Ned smiled weakly and took another large gulp of sherry.

"No ill effects from yesterday, I trust?" said the vicar to Ned. "Bill Bray told us all about it in *The Tyger* last night."

"Oh, that," said Ned, dismissively. "Bit stiff, you know. Nothing serious."

"That's good news," said Louise, a tall, neat woman in a knitted woollen suit which Ned thought she had obviously made herself. "Your ears must have been burning. The public bar was ringing with your praises."

Odd, Ned thought; they both seem to spend as much time in the pub as they do in church."

I said to Louise we probably wouldn't be seeing you in church," said Mr Case. "But then we don't see many people in church at all these days."

"John seems to do more of his parish work in *The Tyger*," added Louise. "Suits him down to the ground!"

"The church still has its place," he said, "even though it's not in church anymore!" He laughed a little at his own joke. "Have you known this area long, Mr Cresswell?" asked the vicar.

"Best part of fifty years," said Ned. "My friend and I both spent our honeymoons here," he said, "in a manner of speaking, that is." He looked over his shoulder to catch Norman's eye. Ned gestured with a nod of his head for Norman to join them. "You must meet my friend Norman," said Ned and introduced Norman. "Now he is a one for churches. Would you excuse me?" said Ned. "I've been promised a tour of the garden."

As Ned detached himself from the ecclesiastical party, motioning Kim to come with him, Genevieve appeared in the doorway. Two other guests were behind her. Ned always made either for the garden or the smallest room in the house when he felt cornered at parties but Mrs Withers had other ideas. Ned and Kim were collared by the irrepressibly effervescent Geraldine and Norman was left with the Vicar and Louise.

"Mr Cresswell, you must meet my brother and his wife, Horace and Enid." said Geraldine. She stood aside and as she did so, Ned saw that Horace and Enid were in fact Major and Mrs Mace. "Enid, Horace, dears . . . this is the famous Mr Cresswell you've heard so much about from Elizabeth!"

The Major's face was a picture and, not a pretty one either. On seeing Ned, his jaw dropped and the veins on his neck, emanating from beneath a collar which was obviously too tight, seemed to bulge and pulsate with the rhythm of a war drum as his face became redder and redder. After Ned had registered his initial recognition of his former adversary, manifested by wide-eyed astonishment, his mouth set into the straight, vice-like line which indicated the rousing of his bull-dog belligerence. Had Norman been in the group, he would have noticed and understood the change in Ned immediately. Kim, ignorant of Friday's altercation at the bottom of the Major's drive, did not notice, although she sensed the change in Ned's composure and looked at him queerly.

Privately, hoping his cover belied his nervousness, Ned was experiencing the fluttering of a lifetime of butterflies in his tummy. Oh Lord, he said to himself, remembering Norman's ill-founded optimism and knowing that it had tempted providence to breaking point, what to do? Should he brazen it out and pretend he'd never met the Major? Should he retreat, he wondered, called conveniently by nature or should he stand and face the music? Oh, so difficult and all to be decided in a split second.

"Ah, Horace you devil, come and meet Tom Maxwell," Arthur called from across the room. The Major bolted and Ned was saved.

"The men, the men," Genevieve said sweepingly, "how they will stick together. Sweet or dry, Enid, dear?"

"Dry for me, Genevieve," said Enid, regarding Ned with dewy eyes and a bright, slight smile playing on her lips, unsure of how to begin a conversation with a hero. As Ned's eyes were firmly fixed on a point somewhere midway between the Major's shoulder blades as he retreated, he did not pay the slightest attention to Enid. However, as his hackles fell, he relaxed sufficiently to notice Enid's adoring, upturned face and flashed her a curt smile.

"Would you like a nibble?" asked Kim, stepping into the breach as she was stuck with the tray of edibles. "I'm Kim Maxwell, by the way. That's my father over there. He's Tom." Three faces turned in the direction of the fireplace where Tom was standing just in time to see the tweedy Major take his final step up to Tom and Arthur. His nervousness made him incautious and he omitted to spot the black Labrador stretched on the rug in front of the fire. The Major's brogue-booted toe landed squarely on the tip of the old dog's tail and there was a yelp and a snarl from the dog who, with surprising vim, sprang round and snapped his teeth shut around a fold of the Major's cavalry twills.

"Oh, dear," said Enid. Ned wanted to laugh but coughed instead. "Still," Enid observed, "perhaps it'll teach him to look where he's going." She took a handful of peanuts and returned her attention to Ned. "I'm Enid Mace, Mr Cresswell."

"I know," said Ned, valiantly seeking the strength to be interested.

"I can't tell you what a very great pleasure this is! You must find these occasions awfully trying but I just had to meet you." Genevieve swept in with the sherry and swept off again just as quickly. "Genevieve's a bit bossy on the outside," she said confidentially, "but she's a dear soul for all that."

"Haven't really had a chance to talk to her," said Ned. "So I really can't comment I'm afraid."

"First things first," said Enid, "and then we'll forget all the flattery. I just had to tell you how much your work has meant to me over the years. You've been a rock, I mean, your books have. Whenever I feel a bit low, which is pretty often just between ourselves you understand, I pick up one of your books and I'm in another world. Thank you, Mr Cresswell." She looked at Kim. "There, I'm finished."

"You see, Ned," said Kim. "Another fan."

"Well," said Ned gruffly, "thank you. It's always nice to hear. Do you have any favourites?"

"I must admit that your murders are frightfully good, absolutely convincing too. How do you dream up those grisly circumstances?"

Ned looked over his shoulder as the major looked over his and their eyes met, for an instant. It was enough. Each turned away.

"I think of people I don't like," said Ned. "Then it all comes quite easily. You'd be surprised."

"I don't think I would," said Enid. "I think it pays to have a vivid sense of imagination. Saves you from some awfully dangerous possibilities."

"Oh," said Kim, putting down the tray of snacks, "there's Sally." A pretty woman in her late thirties entered the room. Kim greeted her. Ned looked up. She had a sad, sweet face, a little pale but with wonderfully bright eyes that looked to Ned as though they were used to tears.

"That's Sally," Enid explained to Ned. "Genevieve's youngest. "The only one to follow in her mother's footsteps."

"And where did they lead," said Ned.

"Onto the stage," said Enid. "Didn't you know?" Enid sighed. "Poor girl," she said, "she's just been widowed. He was an actor too. William Cooke. Such a dear and so unassuming. They lived at Brighton. Genevieve says she needs to get back to work again. Something to occupy her mind."

Ned had in fact heard of William Cooke and had indeed

read about his tragic death in *The Telegraph* and now that Enid had mentioned it, there was something vaguely familiar about Genevieve.

"Such a handsome man," Enid said, turning away from that tragedy and looking across the room at another one.

"Which one," asked Ned, realising that Enid was waving to Arthur's group and assuming the woman was referring to her husband.

"Tom Maxwell," said Enid, coyly. Her eyes alighted on her husband and the charm slipped from her face. "I do hope Horace isn't boring him to death. He can be impossible at times."

"You don't say," said Ned distantly. "But I'm sure you've found the right way to deal with him. Looks pretty harmless to me." He paused. "He doesn't seem to get on with dogs very well, does he?" he added, noticing that the labrador was still eyeing the major's foot threateningly. Tom caught Ned's eye and winked.

"Horace doesn't get on with anything very well," sighed Enid. "Marriage is rather a battlefield, isn't it? But," she added more cheerily, "one has survived," whereupon, Ned surmised that Enid's insinuation was that she had basically given up the unequal struggle against Horace's various unspecified impossibilities.

Genevieve left Norman and the vicar to embrace her youngest daughter.

"Darling, I'm so glad you came. Excuse me, Enid. I want Sally to meet Mr Cresswell . . ."

And so Genevieve formed another little group, integrating every component part of her gathering with the effortlessness of an expert cake-maker, picking ingredients and mixing them without ever having to think of weight or measure. Ned watched her at work and envied her.

Norman listened attentively to the vicar, waiting for the right moment to bring up the subject of Mrs Hopper.

"Such a shame," he said, concluding his customary obituary on the demise of popular churchgoing, "people think they don't need God anymore." He shook his head. "They're so wrong."

"Poor John," abetted Louise, "he gets so despondent sometimes. He spends more time being a social worker than a man of God."

"Now I'm glad you mentioned that," said Norman, "because there is something I'd like to discuss with you . . ." Norman described the events of the past two days as far as he felt that they were an explanation of the current state of Mrs Hopper's mind.

"You mean Trevor's mother," said Louise, interrupting.

"Yes," said Norman, "certainly not his wife. We haven't met her," and he continued his story of his experience with Mrs Hopper the previous evening.

Genevieve did the rounds with the tray and set about trying to arrrange a better mix of the sexes in the little groups which had formed.

"Arthur, dear, more sherry!" she barked.

"Where?" said the jolly Arthur.

Everywhere!" commanded his wife. "Take the bottles round and mingle, dear!" Genevieve was becoming more theatrical by the glassful. "Mingling, dear Mr Cresswell," she boomed, "how dull it all would be without a bit of mingling!" She swept away once again, her hands fluttering as she directed her cast.

"I think I'd better go and see about Horace," Enid said and excused herself as she saw her husband's glass being re-filled for what she knew to be at least the second time. The major's face was beginning to redden and Enid knew that presaged a potential loosening of the tongue which could lead to trouble.

Kim saw that her father was standing alone by the fireplace and that he had decided his best occupation would be to pet the old labrador over whose prostate body people had been carefully stepping.

After exchanging a few preliminary pleasantries about the weather and the joys of the countryside in spring, Ned was quite content to listen to Kim and Sally chattering. Ned sensed a reticence about the young widow and felt very warmly towards her, remembering privately how he had felt in the first months, even years, after Dulcie had failed to come home."

Ned, would you excuse us a moment, I see dad's all by himself," Kim said. "We don't want him feeling lonely, do we?"

"By all means, my dear. And," Ned added, "why not take this sweet girl with you. I have to talk to Norman."

Ned had been trying to attract Norman's attention for ages. After securing a promise from the vicar that he would call on both Mrs Hopper and her Trevor in the course of the following week, Norman excused himself and joined Ned.

"At last," said Ned. "The sermon can't have been that interesting."

"We weren't talking about religion," Norman countered, "I was telling him about poor Mrs Hopper to see if there was anything he could do." Ned opened his mouth to comment but Norman cut him short. "And I know all about interfering in things that don't concern me, Ned. I'm not in the market for a lecture."

"I wasn't going to. Don't snap, Norman. I was merely going to suggest that he talks to the local doctor first."

"Well, that's up to him," said Norman. "But at least I've tried."

Enid had managed to drag Horace into her conversation with the vicar. Emboldened by the Withers' extremely hospitable sherries, Enid was recounting the Major's experience of the previous Friday at the bottom of his drive. Norman's ears pricked up as he reacted instantly to what he overheard.

"Oh, dear," he said in consternation. "Am I hearing what I'm hearing?" he whispered. Ned nodded and finished off his schooner in one belt. "Is that really him?" Ned nodded grimly. "I didn't recognise him."

"I did," said Ned.

"Has he recognised you?" asked a very worried Norman.

"He has," replied Ned. "I must say it's rather interesting to hear his side of it. Hearing oneself described as a common barrowboy isn't exactly flattering."

"Oh, Ned," Norman said anxiously. "Just pretend. Pretend you never heard it."

"Can I top you up?" said Arthur who appeared with the sherry. Norman covered his half-empty glass with his hand.

"Not for me," said Norman and then changed his mind. Arthur filled their glasses.

"Thank you," said Ned. "Lovely girl, your daughter."

"Oh, where is she?" said Norman. "I haven't met her yet."

"Chatting to Maxwell, I think," said Arthur. "Over there, patting our death-defying old dog."

And doing rather better that the unspeakable Horace, Ned fancied smugly to himself.

Genevieve joined them.

"We should be as lucky," she said, "they say it's a dog's life but as far as I'm concerned, it's one I rather envy."

"I don't think I'd like to be a dog," said Norman, "Far too energetic. I wouldn't have minded being a cat, though."

"Not as dependable," said Genevieve. "Never there when you want them."

"And always there when you don't," added Ned, looking meaningfully at Norman.

"Just like children," said Arthur.

"How beastly, Arthur," chided Genevieve. "How could you say that. Do you have children, Mr Cresswell?"

Ned shook his head.

"No. Lots of long-suffering nephews, though," he said. "I don't think I was quite cut out for being a parent. Other people's children are so much more convenient."

"His books are his children, really," said Norman. "Just like my cats were mine."

"Don't know what I would have done without my children," said Genevieve. "Dread to think how I would have ended up."

"But surely," said Norman, "you were set for such great things!"

"Brittle, my dear. Brittle and fraught. Just like a metal

spring; could've snapped at any time." Genevieve pecked her husband's cheek. "Got the mechanic here to thank for saving me from all that."

"I remember you!" Ned cried suddenly. "You were Genevieve Gale!"

"Still am, Mr Cresswell. After a lot of tempora and mores, Genevieve Gale is alive and well I'm glad to report. But now she lives in Sussex as plain old Mrs Withers."

"I would never have called you plain," said Arthur, "old perhaps, my darling, but never plain." Genevieve fluttered in the waft of his back-handed compliment.

"I'll be jiggered," said Ned. "Norman! Why didn't you tell me? Why didn't Ba tell me?" He beamed. "Why does no one tell me anything!"

"That was all a very long time ago," said Genevieve. "Not a lot of people left to remember."

Ned relaxed and became very comfortable after his third sherry and fell into a vortex of nostalgia, swapping names with Genevieve, whist Norman found out all about the how's and why's and when's from Arthur Withers about their life in Sussex.

Kim had been inveigled by the vicar into telling him all about her postgraduate work whilst Enid Mace, much to the Major's acute embarrassment, persisted in her relating of the tale of the invasion of their grounds by London picknickers which Horace had so valiantly resisted.

"I say, old thing," mumbled the Major as Enid's voice became louder and shriller. "It really wasn't as bad as all that." Enid looked uncomprehendingly at her husband.

"Well," she said, "you've changed your tune since last Friday." She turned to John Case. "Honestly, Vicar, from the way he told me, you'd have thought the Vandals and the Visigoths were sweeping through southern England!"

Tom found himself alone with Sally Cooke.

"I don't know how the dog stands it," said Tom, running a finger around his shirt collar. "He must be roasted. This room is like a furnace."

Sally laughed. It was the first time for ages that she realised that she was laughing. It was the first time since

William had died that she had allowed herself out in any sort of company other than her immediate family.

"I think I might pop out for a breath of air," said Tom. "Do you mind?"

"Not at all," replied Sally. "If you don't mind, I think I'll join you. It's such a lovely day, after all."

"Make the most of it," said Tom as they wove their way through the chatting groups, "though I really don't need to tell you that."

Sally smiled and followed Tom into the garden. Although cool in the shade, they made their way to a south facing seat in the sun, set under a big apple tree on whose twigs the tight pink and white buds were beginning to open. Tom laughed.

"What's so funny?" Sally said.

"Here. This seat." Tom smiled. "About nine hundred years ago, your father caught me and my best friend Antony Bennett scrumping apples. We were made to sit here until Annie came down to collect us."

"Ouch," said Sally.

"You can say that again," said Tom. "Annie's silver backed hairbrush! I can feel it now."

"I don't remember you at all," said Sally. "Funny how children feel age differences so much more than grown ups."

"I remember your brothers," said Tom. "But they never wanted to play with us. We were foreigners. They had the home gang. Bet you were spoiled rotten, being the youngest."

"I hated being the youngest. I suppose that's why I grew up closer to mum than any of the others. She knew I was the last and she was determined to make the most of it." Sally drained her glass.

"Awfully sorry, Sally . . . about William," Tom said gently.

Sally breathed in deeply, looking around the garden.

"Thanks," she said. "It's not so bad lately." She paused. "I never thought he'd ever go away. But he's gone now." She smiled and sighed. "I think I've at last been able to let him go."

"Awfully hard, letting go," Tom said. "I could do with a few lessons myself." Sally laughed.

"Isn't it pathetic," she said. "Look at us. Feeling so sorry for ourselves."

"At least you've got your family," Tom said. "Your mother must have been a rock."

"Well, that's one way of describing her," Sally said. "But rocks can become anchors too and it's awfully tempting when you've found a comfy little port not to sail away ever again."

"We must be a very impermanent generation, I think," Tom mused. "Always searching, always looking. But then we're the first generation that has lived most of its life without a war. We've always taken permanance for granted I suppose, reacted against it in a way, but always knowing that the safety line is still attached." He sighed. "Not easy, being adrift." Tom closed his eyes and turned his face to the mid-day sun. "Sometimes the future terrifies me," he said, lulled by the moment and then caught by another thought. "Or is it loneliness?"

"You're talking to a fellow sufferer, remember?" Sally said. Somehow, she didn't want to dwell in the gloom anymore and she felt a surge, an imperceptible pressure gently lifting her over the level of what had become a familiar and contemptuous horizon, one that she had contemplated too long.

"So what are your plans, Tom? What next for you?"

Tom opened his eyes. The strong light had created patterns which were superimposed over his vision. He blinked.

"I haven't the foggiest idea, Sally. All I know is that I'm bored stiff, in a rut, feeling useless and could do with a giant kick in the bum to get me going again." He laughed. "But I don't need two guesses to know what you'll be doing. Back to the stage for you, Miss Worthington."

Sally laughed.

"Easier said than done," she said. "The telephone hasn't been exactly red-hot. Death is pretty contagious, you know. I'd swear people think it's catching."

"Not unlike being an ex-managing director," added Tom. "They all think because you don't need to work that you don't want to."

Inside, Kim came over to Ned and Norman, seeing that Genevieve had left them to fetch the Case family's coats. Ned glanced out of the window.

"Those two seem to be getting on awfully well," he said.

"Don't they," said Kim. "Just what the old man needs."

"Probably the same for her," said Norman.

"Can we go?" implored Ned. "Please, Norman. I'm as drunk as a lord and starving hungry. I can smell that lamb from here." Ned noticed a little Tunbridgeware box on a chiffonier and his hand reached out to open it. Norman managed to catch him in time.

"Ned!"

Ned sniffed.

"Just looking," he said.

"I'll go and fetch dad," said Kim and went to the door to beckon her father.

"Are you ever in London?" Tom said as he and Sally walked back over the lawn.

"If anyone ever asks me to come up," she replied. "Why? Are you asking?"

"I'm asking," he said and grinned, feeling silly and seventeen again.

"Then I accept," Sally replied. "Brighton may be very healthy and all that but I do miss the odd lungful of exhaust fumes. Comes from having an engineer for a father."

The Vicar and his wife made their farewells. As Norman too made the rounds of the room, Ned found himself momentarily alone. He walked over to the window which looked out over the Downs in the direction of Beachy Head and as he turned to make his exit from the room, he was suddenly faced with the Major. He drew himself erect. Well, he thought, it's now or never and looked the Major straight in the eye. He coughed, averted his eyes and Ned knew that the hour was to be his.

"Um . . . er," mumbled the Major, as embarrassed as any

humiliated bully. "I'm . . . er . . . um . . .," he said, shuffling from one foot to the other and making little nervous coughs, clearing his throat after each utterance. "Most awfully sorry about the other day. Didn't realise, y'know ... Apologies and all that. Be very grateful if nothing is said." The Major nervously and repeatedly glanced over his shoulder and his words were whispered in a highly confidential tone.

"Accepted," Ned intoned grandly, wishing he could physically prostrate him and be photographed with his heel on Horace's head, a burning spear in his hand. Ned's sense of satisfaction was undiminished by the time he had to wait for his victory. In fact, he felt as though the delay, if anything, heightened the sensation.

"Assure you, dear chap," Horace spluttered, "it'll never happen again."

"Not if I can help it," said Ned.

"Er . . . um . . .," growled Horace tamely, ". . . Good show then . . . Must be going now."

"Yes," said Ned. "I suppose you must. I wish I could say it has been a pleasure but, frankly, sir, it hasn't. Please pass my commiserations to your wife. Such a nice woman."

"Commiserations?" queried the Major, puzzled and wishing that he was anywhere on the planet other than where he found himself. "I don't understand."

"No," said Ned. "That doesn't surprise me in the least!" Ned stood his ground and with a toss of his head indicated that Major Mace was at last off the hook.

Off galloped the Major, bolting for cover and as squiffy as a pig, Ned thought to himself. Enid collected him in the hall and waved to Ned and Norman as Tom, Sally and Kim came in from the garden. Ned joined the party in the hall.

"Thank you so much for asking us," Norman said, embracing Genevieve. "We have enjoyed meeting you, haven't we Ned?"

Ned nodded for in fact he had rather enjoyed it.

"Absolutely," Ned said. "In fact, you'll never know what a treat it's been." He shook hands with Sally. "And nice meeting you Sally. Good Luck."

"Anytime, chaps," said Arthur merrily, "Anytime you feel like a day in the country, don't forget us. We're always here."

And so the occasion came to an end as Tom and Kim led the lunch party back through the garden.

"She's awfully nice, pa, isn't she?" said Kim, taking her father's arm as they fell in behind Norman and Ned. "Why don't you give her a ring after lunch ask her up for a drink this evening?"

Tom smiled. He knew his daughter too well.

"Gently Bentley," he chided. "You take care of your own telephoning first and then . . ." He laughed. "We'll see," he said, "we'll see."

But they all noticed a spring in Tom Maxwell's step that April afternoon.

"There," said Norman confidently, "wasn't that nice?" He started to sing . . . "Oh what a beautiful morning, Oh what a beautiful . . ."

"You're drunk!" interrupted Ned.

"On two glasses of sherry!" exclaimed Norman.

"Three at least," Ned corrected. "One alone would have anaesthetised a horse!"

"So what," said Norman happily. "I haven't disgraced myself, have I?"

"Not at all," said Ned, smiling to himself. "In fact I think we both acquitted ourselves rather well."

Tom loaded his flock into the car and pulled out into Upper Road. At the junction with the Brighton road, there was a flashing light. It was the police car, parked on the verge. On the other side of the road, PC Hopper was leaning over the low slung coachwork of a shiny Jaguar. In his hand, he held what looked like a plastic bag.

"Oh no," said Tom, "some poor blighter's being breathalysed."

As he assumed the fixed look of one who is pretending that not a drop has touched his lips, Tom steered round the obstacle. PC Hopper ignored the passing of the Rolls.

"It's Major Mace!" exclaimed Kim. "Did you see?"

"Oh, poor Enid," said Norman, turning round in the

back seat to see the Major stepping out of the car and his wife's tormented face in the grip of the shame of it. "I rather liked her, didn't you, Ned?"

"Liked her," said Ned. "Didn't care for him much. I can't tell you how I envied that dog!"

"Ned!" said Norman, "don't gloat."

TWENTY TWO

Trevor Hopper was late for his lunch. Although he was rather pleased that Major Mace had successfully made the crystals in the bag turn the appropriate colour, he was hot and bothered. He knew that Penny would be in a very bad mood. However hard he had encouraged her over the years never to expect him at the time he had said he would be back for his meals, she persisted in timing the meals to the expected hour and paid no heed to the unforeseen course that the law often had to take.

As Penny had never been taught any respect for vegetables and had acquired even less for the process of roasting a chicken, Trevor's lunch was not a treat. The spring greens which Bill Bray had given him the day before fresh from the garden, had been reduced to the texture of seaweed and even the frozen peas had lost their plumpness and fell onto the plate from the spoon in the way that green gravel would fall from the tailgate of a gritting machine.

"So what was it this time?" said Penny wearily. She gleaned little satisfaction from being a policeman's wife, especially one stuck in the furrows of rural life.

"Bloke in a Jag," said Trevor taking up his knife and fork. "Blotto."

"Another one bites the dust," Penny said, remembering the words from a pop record she had been fond of some years before. "It's not something that's going to get you promoted any quicker, is it?"

"Suits me," replied Trevor, chewing on the chicken and remembering how different it both looked and tasted to how the televisiion advertisements would lead one to believe. "Any beer?"

"Hark at you," said Penny who had already eaten her lunch and had not even bothered to join her husband at the kitchen table. She was reapplying her mascara in front of a propped up mirror on the washing machine. "Nicks some poor blighter for 'avin' a drop too much and then turns round and swills away 'imself. Some example you are!"

Trevor got up, still chewing and took a can of lager from the fridge. He was stoic in his reaction to Penny's taunts. He was used to them, innured and numbed and had long denied the need to either talk back or talk to his wife.

"Where are you off to?" he asked.

"Up Rosie Ball's," she replied. "She's got the car today." More mascara was applied as the brush stabbed into the container with the staccato rattle of a machine gun. "Thought we'd go for a drive."

Trevor grunted.

"I'd better go up and see mother," he said. "Told 'er I'd do a bit of gardening."

"Should pay some attention to your own," said Penny, finishing off with her finger tip what she couldn't achieve with the brush. She packed up her make-up and made a 'moue' in the mirror. "That lot out there's a mess."

"I've only got one pair of hands," said her husband, "and only so much time. If we'd 'ad mum here in the first place, I wouldn't be run so ragged."

"You should 'ave thought of that in the first place," said Penny. "You were quite 'appy when we discussed it and you agreed, remember? No pets, no mother-in-laws and no kids 'til we could properly afford them." She put on her heels and smoothed down the denim skirt she wore with the brightly patterned cotton sweater.

"I hardly dare ask when that might be," Trevor said quietly, for no one's ears in particular although Penny heard it.

Penny swept her handbag off the fridge and leant on the kitchen table. She spoke very quietly but very firmly.

"When?" she said, snapping at the word like a terrier clamping onto a chicken bone, almost snapping the word in two. "You know bloody well when, Trevor Hopper. When we get that money of your gran's what should 'ave come to us." She stood up and having made her point was out of the room. Trevor heard her stiletto heels clacking on the parquet floor of the hall way. "Don't know when I'll be back," she called and before he could reply, he heard the front door slam.

He sighed, pushed what remained of the ruined lunch to one side on his plate and drank down the remainder of the lager. Trevor had had such high hopes but what had once looked such a bright future had melted into a mass of problems which he found himself incapable of sorting out.

Trevor glanced out of the window. It was rare weather, too good to spend sweating in his mother's garden, having her follow him round with the the cat on its collar and lead. With lawbreakers and with keeping the peace for other people, Trevor could cope but in confronting and dealing with his own problems, he was impotent.

He did, however, take pleasure in his friends, especially those he had made after coming to East Dean and he decided to drive down to the lifeboat hut and sun himself with Bill and Jimmy and young Tom Ball. Trevor smiled – Tom Ball, what a live wire he was, fancy free, not a care in the world. What I'd give to be Tom Ball, thought Trevor to himself as he put his jacket on and looked round for where he had put his hat. What would a bloke do, thought Trevor, without his good mates.

He was just about to leave the house when he saw through the frosted glass in his front door, the shadow of a figure approaching the house. He opened the door and there was John Case.

"'ello vicar," he said, noticing that the curate was in his shirt sleeves, "Not a bad day for April, eh?"

"Wonderful," agreed the vicar. "I haven't interrupted anything have I? I've just passed Penny down the lane so I thought you must have finished your lunch."

"That's alright, vicar. What can I do for you?"

"Well," began the vicar, "it's . . . er . . . Could I come in for a moment, Trevor?"

Trevor opened the door and stood back, ushering the vicar into the hall. John Case handed over his hat.

"We'll go in 'ere," said Trevor, indicating the sitting room which he hoped Penny had managed to tidy. "Just go through, vicar."

Trevor removed his hat and motioned the vicar to take a seat. The Hoppers' sitting room was not a testament to taste or personality but it was functional; modern warehouse furniture, assembled by Trevor was pushed against the walls, the positioning of the sofa and chairs being angled to the focal point of the television set and the video unit, with its attendant hi-fi sytem and speakers.

John Case took out his handkerchief and mopped his brow. He and Louise had discussed Norman's concern for Mrs Hopper throughout their own lunch and Louise had encouraged her husband to strike while the iron was hot.

"Well," said the policeman to the vicar. "What's so important?"

Explaining first of all that he hoped Trevor would not take offence, John Case gently set out the circumstances that Norman had reported to him.

"Now I've only met your mother once," said the vicar, "when she first moved in. I always try to get around all the new arrivals in the parish." He paused for a moment. These moments of emotional incision always un-nerved him. "But," he continued, "as she didn't turn out to be a churchgoer and as she was your mother, I've never felt the necessity to call again."

Trevor sighed. Hearing the situation explored by a third party had brought the implications of his mother's wanderings sharply into focus.

"But what do I do, vicar?" he said helplessly. "I try and pop in as often as I can but . . . I am a busy man."

"And Penny?" asked the Vicar. "What does she feel?"

"Forget Penny," said Trevor with some bitterness. "They don't get on. Never 'ave done."

"That is a shame," observed the vicar. "But something has to be done. Your mother's lonely, Trevor. She's spending too much time on her own. Things will get worse, not better. From what I understand, your mother has no one to look after now. She feels lost. Useless."

Trevor got up and went to the window. Cars full of families and children with happy, laughing faces were streaming past on their way to Birling beach or Beachy Head He thought about his wife and wondered whether she would have been any different, any happier, had she too had children to attend to although he had to admit that his conjecture was improbable.

"What a bloody mess, eh, vicar?" Trevor's thoughts tumbled out. "Not the sort of work that comes easy to a man," he said. "Mum's always been difficult. We've never been a . . . how can I call it . . . a lovey dovey sort of family."

"No," said the vicar, "I can see that. But," he added leaning forward in his chair, "there comes a time when you need a bit of lovey dovey as you call it. Everyone does. We all do. It's just that at the moment, it's your mother who needs it most."

John Case had made his point and he knew that there was nothing further he could do. That he had prompted a conscience and eased forward a situation which would have otherwise remained politely ignored, satisfied him. There would have been some in his position who would have added spiritual words of grace and benediction, talked at length of the love of God and the meaning of The Word Made Flesh but John Case knew that the first step in the reintroduction of humanity to loving God was to get humanity to love itself. But why, dear Lord, he wondered as he sensed the policeman's fears, why do people find it so damned difficult?

Trevor was silent for quite a while. The vicar stood uneasily in the loveless sitting room. Eventually he coughed.

"I'll be going now, Trevor," he said, putting a hand on the policeman's shoulder. "I'm sorry, but I had to let you know."

Trevor pulled himself together to shake the vicar's hand.

"Thank you, vicar," he said. "I am grateful. Thinking about it, of course, I should have realised. But," he said regretfully, "I didn't. I've a lot to thank you for."

"Don't thank me," said the vicar, "thank Mr Rhodes."

"Mr Rhodes?" replied PC Hopper, puzzling as he tried

to put a face to the name. "Who might he be?"

"He and his friend Mr Cresswell are staying at Mrs Croker-Symes' house, next door to your mother's," explained the vicar. "Such good people. You must have heard from Bill and the boys? It was Mr Cresswell who helped rescue that young girl yesterday."

"Oh!" said Trevor, "so that's his name. Oh, yes," he said, smiling, "I know very well who they are."

Trevor showed the vicar into the hall. John Case turned to make a final point.

"If everyone in this world was as concerned as those two," John said at the door, "and prepared to do something about their concern, there'd be a lot less for you and I to do and our lives would be a lot easier." The vicar replaced his straw panama which he had left in the hall by the telephone. "Well, goodbye, Trevor. And remember, now, if Louise and I can be of any help, please let us know. You know where we are. Church services will be held in *The Tyger* most nights as usual." They shook hands and even though he laughed at what he thought was the vicar's little joke, Trevor felt more than a small twinge of guilt.

TWENTY THREE

After having had lunch with Norman and Ned, Tom and Kim returned to their own house. Ned announced that he was going to have a lie down. He didn't so much announce it but collapsed on the sofa with the Review section of the Sunday newspaper over his face and began to snore. Norman removed the newspaper and quietly cleared the dessert dishes and wine glasses from the table.

The leg of lamb had certainly been big enough but it seemed that Tom's carving had hardly dented it at all. Norman cut off a sizeable hunk and chopped it into small pieces.

As soon as he returned from the sherry party, Norman had immediately, although surreptitiously, checked whether Albert had found the saucer of tuna an acceptable offering, although he could not of course be sure that Albert had been the recipient of the fish. Rooks, crows and the ubiquitous magpies were just as likely to have benefitted. However, the saucer was not only empty, but clean, which caused Norman to believe that Albert's tongue had at some point at least licked the plate. Norman refilled the saucer with the chopped lamb and opened the back door.

He put the saucer on the path. He crouched down and almost immediately saw a little face looking out from beneath the laurel bush.

"Now you're a naughty pussy," he said firmly, glancing over his shoulder to ensure he was being neither overheard or overlooked. "You shouldn't be here, darling, should you?" Norman preened and waited not so much for a reply but for the slightest sign that Albert might be lured out. He could tell that the cat was having the greatest difficulty holding back but at the same time he could tell that a cat knew a plot when faced with one better than any human. Albert blinked, acknowledging Norman but indicating that in no way was he, rather she, going to be drawn. "Norman's going back inside now, Albert. He's going to do the washing up." Norman stood up and wagged his finger at the laurel bush. "You're naughty, yes you are! A naughty, naughty pussy cat!"

But, thought Norman, you are so, so pretty.

He sighed and closed the back door. A raggle taggle tribe of rooks cawed and cackled their way into the branches of a chestnut tree in Mrs Hopper's garden and Norman knocked loudly on the kitchen window although they took no notice.

He continued with the washing up, thinking what a pretty girl Sally Cooke was and what an attractive couple she made with Tom Maxwell. Such a nice, nice man, he thought. And Kim too, so young and with so much to look forward to.

Washing up was never a chore to Norman. It was like darning or weeding or pruning, solitary occupations perhaps but to Norman they were never lonely ones. He couldn't help thinking too of Genevieve Gale and her much publicised romances with brilliant and dazzling men, of a life lived as fully in the spotlight as it was now being lived in the twilight. No, he thought, perhaps it's not such a bad thing to grow old.

He looked around the kitchen through which all his own nearest and dearest had passed at some time over the last fifty years. The room was still almost has it had been after that first summer holiday when as carefree, bohemian art students he and Ned and Dulcie had helped Biddy Barthorpe to move in. Everything was still in its place, the blue and white meat platters above the wooden pelmet, even the gingham curtains, the pine dresser with the green Berylware china, the now old-fashioned red-tiled floor, the cobwebs around the bellboard above the door. Norman felt curiously comfortable and at peace, even with the dead; with mama and father, with dear Mumfie, with Cyril whom he had loved through all those unremarkable but very happy years, with Dulcie, who, of all of them, had never had to know what growing old was like. Maybe, he thought, maybe there is a sense in it all.

"Norman!"

The dream broke.

"Norman!" Ned called, "that wretched policeman's coming up the drive!"

"What does he want?" Norman called back, wiping his hands on his apron and fiddling with the knot in the strings as he took it off."

How on earth would I know?" said Ned.

"Surely he's not going to breathalyse you?" Norman said. "He can't, can he?" Norman went into the hall to join Ned.

"Never heard of anyone being drunk in charge of a sofa," said Ned curtly. They stood peering through the leaded light in the door as PC Hopper strode up onto the porch. He saw them looking at him and smiled.

Ned looked at Norman and Norman looked at Ned. PC Hopper withdrew a piece of paper from his breast pocket and, still smiling, waved it.

"The man's an idiot," Ned whispered.

"Oh, Ned!" wailed Norman. "What are we going to do?"

Ned tutted, shook his head and opened the door.

"Mr Cresswell," said the policeman, "Lovely day, isn't it?"

It's true, thought Ned, the English are obsessed about the weather.

"Good afternoon, constable," said Ned. "If you've come to remind me about my documents, I haven't forgotten."

"Not exactly, sir," he said. "I just wondered if you could dispose of some litter for me?"

Ned frowned.

"Is this some kind of a joke?" he asked. Norman put his hand on Ned's arm to restrain any possible contretemps.

Looking Ned squarely in the eye and still smiling, PC Hopper tore up the piece of paper he had taken out of his pocket. Once, twice, three times he tore it and then crumpled the pieces into the palm of his hand.

"Thank you, both," he said. He stretched out his hand and Norman took from it the crumpled pieces of the ticket.

"But what . . . I'm afraid I don't understand," said Ned.
"No," added Norman. "Neither do I."
"That, Mr Cresswell, is your ticket. I have just torn it up. You won't have to produce your documents."
"Does this mean he isn't a criminal anymore?" said Norman who was still utterly confused.
"I never was a criminal, Norman," Ned said crossly. "But," he said to PC Hopper, "you'll still have to spell it out for me. Why?"
"In way of thanks, sir. Vicar told me about your concern for my mother." He took off his hat and scratched his head. "Very awkward," he said. "Very awkward but if you hadn't said anything to Vicar, I could have . . ." He paused. "Shall we say . . . Been remiss in my duty as a son."
"You didn't mind, did you?" said Norman. "I honestly spoke out for the best. If I hadn't thought your mother was ill, I would never have interfered." Norman glanced at Ned. "You see, I know about these things. I had to look after my own mother."
"We're awfully sorry," said Ned who, albeit unspokenly, had been mindful of the poignant reasons which had provoked Norman's concern for Mrs Hopper. "It's very painful, we know."
The police constable nodded.
"So what are you going to do?" asked Norman."She really should be looked after."
"Well," said Trevor Hopper, "there's a bit of sorting out I got to do at home for a start . . ."
The wife, Ned thought.
". . . and when I got that sorted, I'll be moving mother down to the police house."
"Oh I am pleased," said Norman. "But what about the cat? Has it come back?"
"That damn cat!" the policeman said. "As I've just told mother, she's to forget about it. Begging your pardon, gents, but it's been a bloody pest since the day it walked into my gran's back kitchen and that's twelve years that I can remember."
"Twelve?" said Norman. "So old." And, he quickly

calculated, it might be even older. Surely, he thought, surely now Ned couldn't refuse to look unkindly on a feline refugee and a gerontocat to boot.

Ned looked at his friend and narrowed his eyes. Norman might have been fluttering innocence in the eyes of the constable but he was a quiver of guile in Ned's.

"Mother doesn't even like cats," the constable continued. "And nor does my wife so, between the cat and the old lady, I know where my duty lies. Sorry to have to say it. You haven't seen it, have you?"

"No," said Norman quickly. "Have we Ned?"

"I can say in all honesty, constable," said Ned, eyeing Norman now with certainty rather than mere suspicion, "that I personally haven't seen the cat since yesterday."

"Well," said PC Hopper replacing his hat, "I hope to God we've seen the last of it."

"Indeed," said Norman solemnly. "But," he added, "the Lord does work in the most mysterious ways."

"Thank you again, gentlemen. Have a pleasant afternoon." PC Hopper touched his hat and went off back to his patrol car.

"Don't!" said Ned as soon as the door was shut, "Don't even think it, Norman!"

Ned went back into the sitting room.

Where are you going?" said Norman.

"I'm having the remaining thirty nine of my forty winks," said Ned.

"But you're awake now," said Norman. "You'll never drop off again."

"I can try," said Ned, "and if I do manage to, I can tell you I won't be dreaming about twelve year old homeless cats."

Oh, thought Norman. Right . . .

Tom Maxwell awoke from his nap to find Kim sitting on the floor beside his chair looking up at him. He smiled and stretched.

"Must have dozed off," he said. "What's the time?"

"Four thirty," she said. "Some nap! You've been out for

an hour."

"Good Lord," he said, "and I wanted to finish my bonfire." He started to get out of the chair.

"Wait, daddy," she said. "I've got something to tell you." Kim dropped her eyes to the floor, to the carpet. Tom had never replaced it as he had intended after Annie's death. It was still threadbare, worn in the very places where Annie herself had sat out her maiden days. "Actually, I've got something to ask and something to tell."

Tom reached down and raised Kim's chin up with his hand so that she was looking at him.

"Well," he said, "there's never been any harm in asking and never any point in not telling, so . . . ask and tell."

"Ghastly moment," she said and grinned. "The first decision I've ever had to make."

"Hardly," said her father. "No one can have lived twenty two years and not made a decision."

"Silly ones, yes. Unimportant ones. Shall I go for a swim or shall I sit by the pool, shall I go to this party or that party or shall I stay at home?" She paused. "But nothing absolutely major, nothing of vital significance."

"How about a cup of tea while you decide whether you're going to make this momentous decision," he said.

"Please," she said, "don't joke. I have made up my mind but please . . . Please listen."

Tom sensed that she needed him today possibly more than she had ever needed him. It was a realisation that went very deep, to the root of past, present and future. It was a glimpse of a truth he'd often sensed but never seen and he remembered, like a drowning man, the moment he had first held in his arms the tiny bundle of life that he had created, of how he had looked into the swimming blue eyes of the baby girl in wonder and incomprehension.

"You don't need the money, do you?" she asked, "from selling this house?"

"No. You know I don't. Why do you ask?"

"Then don't sell it, daddy. Never sell it. Promise?"

Tom felt very small and a little ashamed. How selfish he'd been, how thoughtless and extravagantly self-indulgent to have even thought of selling the house.

"Of course not, darling, not if you don't want me to. I thought . . ." He faltered.

"I know . . . I was trying to be terribly grown up when I said whatever it was about childish things. If you needed the money, it'd be different, of course, but we don't need it and so . . . I just want something, somewhere always to be the same. I know it never will be, but it will seem the same." Kim got up. She began to pace the room. "Of course, change the carpets, the curtains, throw out all the old furniture but leave the house standing. We haven't got a home anymore, not a proper one and as long as we can, let's keep this as home." She stopped in front of a painting which she had done one summer holiday when she was eleven, maybe twelve. It was of Birling beach and the Seven Sisters and Annie had loved it so much, Kim had given it to her aunt who had had it framed.

"Your wish is my command, princess. Your request is granted."

She turned and saw that he was smiling at her, a knowing, relieved smile.

"Well," he said, "get on with it. Kiss and tell." She crossed the room and kissed him. She too was grinning like a Cheshire cat.

"You already know," she said.

"Perhaps. But I still want you to tell me. I hope I'm the first to know?"

"You are," she said. "Although you're not, in a manner of speaking."

"I'm cut to the quick," he teased. "But then I suppose I've got to get used to taking second place, eh?"

She waited, savouring the moment, still unsure of how the words would sound on her lips, uncertain and ignorant of the ultimate significance of her decision.

"I've told him yes." She was trembling. "I rang him while you were asleep and said . . . yes!"

Tom jumped up and together they hugged and clung to each other, he laughing, she crying, whirling in a delirious rush of exhilaration. Eventually, they released each other.

"At bloody last!" said Tom. "What made you make up your mind?"

"Here," she said. "This place. You. Ned. Sally, Norman . . . Annie's ghost. I don't know. Everything was suddenly very clear."

"Marvellous," said Tom. "Absolutely bloody marvellous. Go and ring your mother. Go on."

Norman was in the garden, dead-heading some of the daffodils and, in truth, looking for Albert although the cat was nowhere to be seen. The spot in the tulips where the cat had obviously taken the afternoon sun was empty. Ned followed Norman with an old cardboard box into which Norman put the spent stems.

"I don't care what you say, Ned, I still think it's jolly sad," said Norman.

Ned tutted.

"You're just being petulent. You want your own way, that's the real problem," said Ned.

"I like that," said Norman indignantly. "You're hardly a paragon of selflessness."

"Oh, please don't let's argue," said Ned. "There's no point. The wretched cat's not here to argue about. It's obviously done another bunk. You heard what Hopper said. It arrived uninvited to his grandmother so it must have come from somewhere before that. It's probably had dozens of homes. Cats aren't like people, Norman. Some of them just don't need to belong anywhere. That's the joy of them. They're independent. Free spirits."

Norman snipped with the secateurs at a dead daffodil and wished that Ned would go away.

"That's rubbish, Ned and you know it. Everyone and everything on this earth needs someone, sometime. I can tell that cat needs a good home." Norman dropped the secateurs into a patch of honesty. "Oh, bother!"

"Would you like to go for a walk?" asked Ned.

"No," replied Norman.

"We could park Min up by Bel Toot and walk along the cliffs? Or we could leave her at Friston and walk down to

Crowlink. You like it down there."
It was Norman's turn to humph.
Over the hedge, Norman saw Tom and Kim coming out of Annie's house with their bags. Tom opened the boot of the Rolls and loaded the baggage.
"Look, Ned. They're leaving."
Ned too looked and saw the Maxwells walking down their drive towards the gate of *Barthorpe*.
"They'll be coming to say goodbye," Ned said. "How nice."
Tom and Kim walked into *Barthorpe*, arm in arm, just as they had yesterday.
"They look happy," said Norman. "I wonder . . ."
"We've come to say cheerio," said Tom. Kim kissed Norman and then hugged Ned.
"Thank you, Ned," Kim said. "You know what I mean."
Ned was quite taken aback and very flattered.
"What for?" he said. "What's being laid at my door this time?"
"It's your young man, isn't it?" Norman said, for the look on Kim's face was unmistakeable.
"Yes," said Kim. "We're getting married. Will you come? Please say you will!"
"Well done!" said Ned beaming, "and of course we shall. We'd love to. Hope your chequebook's ready for all this, Tom."
"It is. Ready and willing."
"So you're off then," said Ned.
The Maxwells nodded."Oh," Tom said, reaching into the pocket of his jacket. "Almost forgot. Here's my card. Just in case."
"We're in the business 'phone book," said Norman. "Gibson Square, N1 Under Cresswell Ltd."
"Why limited?" asked Kim.
"Anthony, our nephew, thought it would be best," said Norman. "So we wouldn't be bothered by odd 'phone calls," he explained confidentially.
"He means sex maniacs," said Ned. "As if at his age he'd be so lucky! So instead we get awful people asking

whether or not our pension plans are in order and trying to sell us office cleaning services."

"Well," said Tom, "'Bye for now. Hope it won't be too long."

Kim and her father walked away. Ned and Norman followed them to the gate and waited until the Maxwells had got into their car.

"'Byeee!" they sang out as the big car pulled away. They watched it, waving farewell, as Tom circled the Greensward, until the car turned into Hillside and out of sight.

"Oh, Ned," Norman said. "Isn't life grand."

"Yes," said Ned. "Walk. Please?"

"Come on then," said Norman. "Get your jumper."

TWENTY FOUR

On Monday morning, Ned had no problem persuading Norman to leave early. After breakfast, they tidied the house and changed the sheets. Ned left some money in an envelope on the laundry basket for the cleaning. He had already opened the front gates and as Norman finished packing the bags indoors, Ned took over and loaded them into the Mini. He left the car doors open as he returned inside for each load.

"I suppose we take the key back to Genevieve?" Ned called up to Norman.

"Suppose so. Hang on a minute. I've finished up here. Only one bag left."

"Can you manage?" shouted Ned.

Norman appeared with the final bag containing their washing things and the bathroom towels which Norman had brought with him.

"Ready?" he said."All ship-shape . . ."

". . . and Bristol fashion," Norman said, finishing off a saying Ned's father had always used.

"Goodbye, house," said Norman. "And thank you again. We've had a lovely time."

They pulled the front door shut and Ned carried the bag to the car, fitted it into the boot and closed the lid. Norman carried his bag and Ned's well-travelled satchel and walked down to close the gates.

Ned tried the engine. The car started on the second turn of the key and he reversed into the road.

Norman closed the gates, got into the car and buckled in. They turned to wave to the house as they always did.

"Until next year," said Ned and accelerated away down the Greensward.

There was no one in when Norman rang the Withers' door bell and so he posted the key in its manilla envelope and returned to the car.

"No one in," he said as he slammed the door. "I wonder who's coming next, after us?"

"God knows," said Ned, pulling out onto the main road. The little Mini crawled up the hill. "One day, we'll have to have arrange one last weekend with Ba, don't you think?"

"Don't say last, like that," said Norman. "Gives me the shivers."

"Alright, another weekend," said Ned. "Better?"

"Much," said Norman.

At the top of the hill where the road bends to the left for Seaford, Newhaven and Brighton, Ned indicated to turn right, to take the road across the Downs and back in the direction of Tunbridge Wells, London and home. As he waited for a break in the oncoming traffic, Ned was aware of an unexpected squeak.

"Never heard that noise before," he said. "Did you hear it Norman? Hope to God that Min's not going to crack up on us. That would be the final straw."

The squeak came again.

"We're not even moving," said Ned. "Listen, there it is again! It's coming from under your seat, Norman."

The traffic had passed and Ned accelerated over the junction as Norman looked round.

From beneath Norman's seat emerged a furry head. The eyes in the head looked up at Norman, almost apologetically.

"Albert!" said Norman in astonishment.

"What!" said Ned, "not that cat?" He pulled into a layby and pulled on the brake. "Must have got in while I was loading the car."

Albert deftly negotiated the leap from the back seat to Norman's lap and immediately curled himself into the folds of his jogging trousers.

"Oh," Norman said, captivated. "Look, Ned. Albert wants to come home with us." He stroked the cat's head and a very loud purring began.

"It's no good, Norman," Ned said falteringly, looking at the perfectly relaxed cat and his blissfully happy friend. "It's no good."

"What's no good, Ned?" mused Norman.

Ned sighed and then he smiled, threw the car into gear and set off.

"Bloody hell!" he said, "Why not? Let's just pretend we're going to live for ever."

Also available from Millivres Books

Summer Set

David Evans

When pop singer Ludo Morgan's elderly bulldog pursues animal portraitist Victor Burke - wearing womens' underwear beneath his leathers - to late night Hampstead Heath a whole sequence of events is set in train. Rescued by the scantily-clad and utterly delicious Nick Longingly, only son of his closest friend Kitty Llewellyn, Victor finds himself caught up in a web of emotional and physical intrigue which can only be resolved when the entire cast of this enormously diverting novel abandon London and head off for a weekend in Somerset.

ISBN 1 873741 02 2   £7.50

'Immensely entertaining . . .' Patrick Gale, *Gay Times*

Also available from Millivres Books

On the Edge

Sebastian Beaumont

In this auspicious debut novel set in the north of England, nineteen year old Peter Ellis is on the edge of discovery both about the artist father he never knew and whom his mother refuses to discuss and about the direction of his own life. Although he has heterosexual relationships with the teenaged Anna and the somewhat perverse art student Coll, it is with his life-long friend Martin, himself a painter of promise, that Peter seems happiest. On the Edge combines elements of a thriller - the mystery surrounding the life and sudden death of Peter's father - and passionate ambisextrous romance and provides an immensely readable narrative about late adolescence, sexuality and creativity.

ISBN 1 873741 00 6   £6.99

'Mr Beaumont writes with assurance and perception . . .'
Tom Wakefield *Gay Times*

Also available from Millivres Books

Heroes Are Hard to Find

Sebastian Beaumont

When his long-time lover returns to Greece to set up a new life for them both, Rick has to adjust to being on his own for the six months of their separation. He lives in Brighton and works as a model, meeting new friends, including the enigmatic Gary and the extraordinary Max, a hedonistic quadriplegic. Rick seems to be surviving the separation until he meets Oliver – a strangely charismatic young man with uninterpretable motives - and, in spite of a growing sense of community, he finds himself in a turmoil.

Heroes Are Hard to Find is a compelling, sometimes comic, sometimes unbearably moving novel about sexual infatuation, infidelity and deceit. It is also about disability, death and the joy of living.

ISBN 1 873741 08 1 £7.50

'I cheered, felt proud and cried aloud . . . I simply cannot recommend this book enough . . . A must . . .'
All Points North

Millivres Books can be ordered from any bookshop in the UK and from specialised bookshops overseas. If you prefer to order by mail, please send full retail price plus 80p (UK) or £2.00 (overseas) per title for postage and packing to:
Dept MBks
Millivres Ltd
Ground Floor
Worldwide House
116-134 Bayham Street
London NW1 0BA

A comprehensive catalogue is available on request.